"The strong romantic flavor...
in Ms. Ferrarella's
[The] Baby of the Month Club will win the hearts
of romance fans everywhere."
—*Romantic Times Magazine*

You didn't kiss one man while carrying another's child in your belly. What kind of woman did that make her?

A lonely one, Julie realized.

With all the people she knew, all the business that passed through her doors, she was lonely. Lonely for the right touch, the right caress. The right man.

The right man wasn't Gabe, she told herself.

But right now, all she wanted was this. This warmth, this heat, this passion, to singe her mouth, her soul.

Julie surrendered and felt as if she'd won. She'd never felt a need to outrun something, to take passion quickly. Never felt as if she would die if she didn't make love with a man before. This man. Here. Now.

Dear Reader,

Since I wrote *In the Family Way*, Gabriel Saldana has been on my mind. So much so that I broke one of my main rules for him. I try very hard not to reuse first names for my heroes and heroines. I had already used the name Gabriel for my hero in *Her Special Angel*, and when I originally created this Gabriel, he was meant to be a minor character, the hero's brother in *In the Family Way*. But Gabriel, with his gregarious nature and his sensitive heart, needed his own story.

So here he is, working undercover at an art gallery, the site of a potential drug-smuggling ring. The owner, Juliette St. Claire, is dealing with an unexpected pregnancy, a wayward mother on her doorstep and an art gallery in danger of going bankrupt. With such busy agendas, who has time for romance? Well, we all know there's always time for romance; otherwise, there'd never be any *Baby Talk*.

This book is also the latest in the BABY OF THE MONTH CLUB series. Our resident obstetrician, Sheila Pollack, is back to deliver yet another new bundle of love. If you haven't read the others yet, I hope this whets your appetite and you'll go back for second helpings.

As always, thank you for stopping by, for reading and for being you.

Love,

Marie Ferrarella

MARIE FERRARELLA

THE BABY OF THE MONTH CLUB:

BABY TALK

Silhouette Books

Published by Silhouette Books
America's Publisher of Contemporary Romance

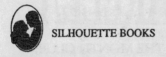 SILHOUETTE BOOKS

THE BABY OF THE MONTH CLUB: BABY TALK

Copyright © 1999 by Marie Rydzynski-Ferrarella

ISBN 0-373-48384-8

This edition published by arrangement with Harlequin Books S.A.

® and TM are trademarks of Harlequin Books S.A., used under
license. Trademarks indicated with ® are registered in the United States
Patent and Trademark Office, the Canadian Trade Marks Office and in
other countries

Look us up on-line at: http://www.romance.net

Printed in U.S.A.

Prologue

"**O**migod."

The three words ran into one and ricocheted around the small, shell-pink tiled bathroom like an echoing, mocking refrain from a song long best forgotten. Certainly the encounter that had gotten her to this pass in her life belonged in that realm.

Hardly aware of dragging wayward blond hair out of her eyes, Juliette St. Claire stared at the small beige indicator perched on the edge of her sink. The spoon portion was turning blue, clashing with her decor. Clashing with her life.

Numb, dazed, Julie moved like someone trapped in a nightmare as she reached for the box she'd tossed aside an eternity ago. Still in shock, she searched for the expiration date.

If the product was out of date, the results might be inaccurate, right?

It was a hope she clung to for the microsecond it took

to locate the date and discover that she had another eight months in which to confidently make use of the pregnancy test.

"Terrific."

Julie threw the useless box in the general vicinity of her wastebasket and lifted the indicator wand in appalled disbelief.

For a moment she entertained the idea of rushing out to the drugstore to buy another home pregnancy test. Maybe even two. Three. As many as it took to give her the answer she wanted.

Cloaked in denial, Julie fought the battle for a moment longer before she surrendered to the inevitable. To the knowledge that she was pregnant. She wouldn't have bought the test if she hadn't suspected.

Feared.

"Damn."

Disgusted, agitated and upset, Julie dropped the indicator back into the sink. Threw it into the sink was closer to the truth.

Hands braced against the edge of the counter, she took in a deep gulp of air. Julie felt moisture forming around her lashes as she tried to blink away the sudden onslaught of unhappiness.

It wasn't fair.

But "fair" was only a word that was found in weather forecasts. She'd learned a long time ago that the adjective didn't have very much to do with her life. From early on, she'd made her own luck, her own terms.

Even in this.

Her condition was a result of a temporary and uncharacteristic indulgence in self-pity. Because she'd felt lonely, she'd thrown a Christmas party for the artists she knew, the ones whose works hung on the walls of her Newport Beach art gallery, the ones who had moved on to greater things, and the ones who aspired to having work good enough to one day hang anywhere but exclusively on their own walls. The holidays always made her feel sad and this year, for some reason, the feeling had been worse than usual.

She'd tried to lose her mood amid the noise and the people and somewhere along the line, she'd had more to drink than she should have.

It had made her light-headed and impaired her judgment, which usually was so sound, so good. It had made her give in to Justin when she shouldn't have.

He had been the one to pursue her. She'd kept a safe barrier up between them, until that night she'd weakened. Justin had seen his advantage and he'd taken it. And now she was paying the price.

Her baby's father was a struggling artist she'd been foolish enough to take in. The apartment across from her own was reserved for artists who needed a place to stay so they could focus on nothing but the work that consumed them and gave them purpose. The light there was perfect for painting. It had once been her mother's large studio. Her father had boarded it up when Elizabeth St. Claire had run off with her lover over fifteen years ago.

But her father was gone now, too. By the time Julie had finally been able to buy back the gallery he'd lost to drink and depression, the owner at the time, Edmund Raitt, had converted the living quarters above it into two separate apartments. A life-long bachelor, he'd told her that he had no use for that much space and thought it a waste not to do something with it. Before he'd sold the gallery back to her, and while he employed her as an assistant buyer, Edmund had allowed her to live over the gallery in the smaller apartment. He'd taken up residence in the larger of the two, but now lived in a small town house overlooking Laguna Beach.

Justin Avery had been the last tenant to live there.

He had since moved on to parts unknown—at her terse suggestion. It had taken her a little bit, but she'd finally realized that Justin had thought of her as nothing more than a shortcut to success. Granted, he'd given the illusion of caring about her, and he'd been handsome, but not even shallow enough to qualify as a wading pool. He was focused only on his own potential, which, looking back, she realized would never be more than moderate.

This was what she got for being such a soft touch.

Again, Julie ran her hand through hopelessly tangled hair as she stared into the mirror.

"Not exactly a great gene pool to dip into," she murmured to the shadow of the tiny entity that had become a reality in her life this morning, thanks to a blue line on a pregnancy wand.

"Now what?"

For the moment Juliette St. Claire, owner of a much frequented art gallery, daughter of a once incredibly promising artist who'd been reverently heralded as the next Georgia O'Keeffe and the late Miles St. Claire, a brilliant art critic whose career had been diluted and dissolved at the bottom of a sea of alcohol, had absolutely no idea.

With no other course to follow, she resigned herself to putting one foot in front of the other until she could think more clearly.

Chapter 1

"**Y**ou've been quiet most of the evening. That's not like you." Dr. Rafe Saldana crossed his parents' living room and sat beside his brother on the sofa.

Sergeant Gabriel Saldana looked at the man who had once been his partner in childhood crime. The brother who, along with him, had helped turn his mother's hair gray thanks to the stunts they'd pulled off, or tried to pull off. He thought of confiding in Rafe, the way he'd done most of his life. But the words stuck in his throat. He wasn't ready to tell Rafe, wasn't ready to tell any of them. He knew they'd worry, even though they'd pretend not to. Even his solemn-faced brother.

He wanted to spare them as long as he could.

Gabe shrugged amiably. "Who could get a word in edgewise with these hellions of yours making such a ruckus? Between that and the two of you and Ma getting giddy because you're going to add a third hellion to the pack in seven months, I haven't had a chance to say anything."

But it wasn't the noise that was really bothering Gabe. It was that he was going to be without it very soon.

For now, though, the very windows seemed to rattle with it. It was always this way when Rafe, his wife Dana, and their kids, Mollie and Megan, were here. It occurred to Gabriel that he didn't get enough of this, didn't get enough of being the beloved uncle, the ringleader of the games that Mollie and little Megan loved to play so much.

As they squealed, trying to get him outside to indulge them on the swingset John Saldana had put up expressly for his granddaughters' use, Gabe realized that he was trying to absorb every sound, every scene and imprint it on his mind. On his heart.

He had no idea how long those impressions would have to last him. Technically, the assignment was only supposed to last three weeks. But who knew?

That was the downside of the road he'd chosen for himself, the one that now led him to the path he'd so unequivocally agreed to yesterday. He'd traded the warm, secure peripheral edges of his life for excitement, justice and danger—possibly a whole truckload of danger. Captain Nolan had been honest with him, saying the undercover assignment might take itself in completely unexpected directions, and then it would become open-ended.

It was this unpredictability that fascinated him—and yes, scared him a little—about his job. He'd made his peace with it. He just hadn't made his peace with not seeing his family for an indefinite length of time. That was harder.

Mollie raised her eyes to Rafe, the center of her universe. "What's ruc-us, Daddy?"

Standing, Gabe ruffled Mollie's fine blond hair and was rewarded with a beatific smile. A heartbreaker already, he caught himself thinking. And she was only this side of eight.

In reality, she was Dana's niece, her adopted daughter,

not her natural one. The little girl had adjusted remarkably well to being orphaned at five and then adopted less than a year after that. Her resilience never ceased to amaze Gabriel. He was in awe of her as much as he adored her.

"It means you and your sister are making too much noise," Rafe said, pushing up the drooping strap of her coveralls.

Carol Saldana entered the living room and set a tray of brownies on the coffee table. All around her, hands reached for the pile on the tray.

"No, they're not," she protested, the doting grandmother to the very end. She stepped back, out of the way, and looked at Rafe. "You think this is bad? You obviously don't remember yourselves as boys." She laughed, shaking her head. Not for the world would she admit that part of her fiercely wished to have those years back again. "Mollie and Megan are church mice compared to you two."

Gabe grinned. "Gee, Ma, you must be thinking of two other guys, not Rafe and me." He took a brownie. "We were perfect angels."

Carol looked at her younger son. There'd been an underlying pensiveness about him all evening. It wasn't anything he'd said, or refrained from saying, it was just a feeling she had. A feeling that something wasn't right. She gave her son a penetrating look. "What's up, Gabe?"

John Saldana looked at his son. On the force for thirty years, he could smell an assignment twenty feet away. It had to be dangerous if Gabe wasn't talking about it. "Leave the boy alone, Carol," he reprimanded gently.

The last of his brownie gone, Gabe slipped an arm around his mother's waist, hugging her from behind. More than a head taller, he towered over her.

"No, don't leave me alone, Ma." Gabe looked at Mollie and her little sister. "Make as much noise as you want. I'm just enjoying my family and my best girls, that's all."

Gabe's look encompassed his mother and his two nieces before he glanced toward Dana. Now that she'd settled in, a man couldn't ask for a better sister-in-law, he mused. Savvy, sharp, with a sense of humor, and very easy on the eye. Rafe had hit the jackpot, Gabe thought not for the first time.

Concern nibbled at Rafe, though his expression remained unchanged. This was definitely *not* like Gabe. Rafe exchanged glances with his father. "Some girl dump you?" he asked none too tactfully. Just because he was the more serious of the two didn't mean that he didn't enjoy teasing his brother once in a while.

Gabe laughed at the very idea. "No woman's ever dumped me."

Rafe sighed and looked over his daughters' heads toward his wife. "The sad part of it is, he's right. That's why his ego's so impossibly huge."

Gabe put up with the crack. He knew it was all in fun. Rafe didn't have a jealous bone in his body. Looking at all of them now, Gabe couldn't help thinking how much he loved these people. They were his anchor, his port. The beacon from the lighthouse, guiding him to shore through the fog. He knew they would all be here, clean and pure and good, waiting for him once this assignment was over.

He focused on that.

John caught his younger son's eye and nodded toward the kitchen.

Carol, handing Mollie a napkin for her sticky fingers, saw the exchange and became very quiet. She hadn't been a policeman's wife all these years without having developed a sixth sense that something out of the ordinary was up. She also knew it was fruitless to ask what. Gabe wouldn't tell her. Men liked to believe they were protecting their women, shielding them. She quickly wiped Megan's mouth, clearing away crumbs that had gathered in the folds of her skirt as the two-year-old sat, devouring her brownie. The truth of the matter was, all they were really doing with such secretiveness was adding to the anguish and prolonging it.

You'd think they would have figured it out by now, she thought, watching her husband and son disappear into the other room.

Walking into the kitchen ahead of Gabe, John opened the refrigerator and took out two bottles of beer. The dark kind he knew Gabe favored. He found the variety too bitter himself and had never developed a taste for it.

With a snap of his wrist, John removed the bottle cap, then handed the beer to Gabe before repeating the process with his own bottle. He took a long pull and let the liquid slide down before speaking. He eyed his son over the bottle.

"So, what's up?"

Gabe followed suit and drank deeply. He was far from quenched, far from satisfied. He figured beer wasn't going to do it tonight.

With a shrug, he looked away. "Nothing."

John huffed a short laugh. "Nothing my Aunt Fanny. I can smell an assignment a mile away." He narrowed his sharp green eyes, looking at Gabe intently. Yeah, he was right. No doubt about it. "They have you going undercover, don't they, boy?"

The protest rose and faded before it was voiced. Not saying anything was one thing. Lying was another. He didn't believe in lying to the people who mattered. Gabe raised his bottle and silently toasted his father with the easygoing grin that had seen him through many difficult moments.

"Damn, but you're good, Pop."

John accepted the words as his due. "Of course I am, I'm your old man." He took another pull, shorter this time, then looked thoughtfully at the bottle. There had to be something better in the back of the fridge. "Anything you can tell me about it?"

His father knew better than that. The question was one of support more than anything else.

"Just not to worry."

"Me, I never worry." John saw no point in telling the boy about sleepless nights spent doing exactly that. It would ruin his image. He set the bottle on the counter and opened the refrigerator again. "Your mother, however, she worries." He rummaged, going haphazardly from one shelf to the other. He spotted his quarry on the last shelf and felt as content as a hunter bagging dinner for his starving family. "She worries you don't eat right. That you won't meet a girl—" John glanced over his shoulder at Gabe. "That you'll meet too many." Gabe flashed a grin as he handed his father the bottle opener. John opened the cherished bottle of domestic. The discarded bottle cap clinked onto the counter. "That you'll be in the wrong place in the wrong time."

It was the throwaway line that they both knew was the crux of the matter. Gabe decided to keep it light. There was no point in dealing with it any other way.

"Not me. I'm always in the right place at the right time." Gabe raised a brow, remembering his grandfather's words. Gaetano Saldana had been the first to join the police force over his own mother's protests. He'd lived to the ripe old age of ninety-three and died in his sleep. "Saldana luck, remember?"

John sighed. It was one thing to believe in your own immortality. It was another to watch your kids buck the odds and run headlong into danger. He squelched the desire to surround his son with protective bubble wrap. They didn't make it that size, anyway. "Yeah, I remember. I'm the one who perpetuated that myth."

Gabe shook his head. "Not a myth, Pop. Fact." Part of him really did believe he had a charmed life. Several brushes with death, both on and off the job, only reinforced that belief.

John wanted to believe that it was fact. For all their sakes. He knew there was no use in hoping that his son would ask out of the assignment. Twenty years ago, in Gabe's place, he wouldn't have been dissuaded, either.

"So when are you leaving?"

Gabe turned in response to Rafe's question. His brother joined them at the counter, picking up the bottle that their father had rejected. Gabe eyed Rafe ruefully. Did everyone read him like a third-grade reader? "What, you, too?"

A smile creased Rafe's mouth. "Give me a little credit, Gabe. It's not all that hard to put together. You've spent almost an entire evening here and the telephone hasn't rung for you once, which means you didn't tell any of your legion of feminine admirers where you'd be for the night. You haven't even made noises about cutting out to see Debra, or Suzy, or Michelle—" Rafe ticked off the first three women who came to mind, not even sure if he was naming the current flames that flickered so brightly around his brother.

Gabe waved a hand at the names. With one final swig, he finished off his beer.

"Past history." He debated helping himself to another bottle, then decided to hold off for a while. He didn't want anything to cloud his memory of tonight.

Rafe grinned. "With all your philandering, it's a wonder some woman hasn't made *you* history."

The comment made Gabe laugh. He doubted very much if there was a woman out there he'd want to remain with for the rest of his life. He just wasn't cut of the same cloth as his father and his brother. He was far too restless to settle down, to be content with waking up to find the same woman beside him, morning after morning. Commitment to his family, to his job, was easy. Commitment to one woman scared the hell out of him.

"Never happen," he proclaimed. "I'm too light on my feet to be caught."

Rafe toasted his brother with the remainder of his beer. He wasn't thinking of Gabe's love life at the moment, but something far more serious. "See that you keep it that way, little brother."

"I intend to."

There was a time, Gabe mused silently, when he was much younger, that he had believed he would make a great actor. It wasn't that he hadn't liked his life—he liked it just fine. Nor had he felt a need to pretend to be someone else. Yet the very same restlessness that kept him from forging any permanent relationships with the women who came in and out of his life, made him want to escape, to pretend to be someone else, to be somewhere else for a finite space of time.

He was playing someone else's brainchild now, someone created only a week ago—created not for the purpose of entertainment but for a far more practical purpose. To gather evidence. The small-time pusher they had caught last week had been more than anxious to flip and give them a bigger fish, in exchange for a walk. He had said that word on the street was that there was going to be a big payload at the end of the month. Its source, he'd claimed, would be coming through the St. Claire's Art Gallery in Newport Beach. Cocaine, and possibly other drugs as well.

That gave them less than three weeks.

Taking the high road, Gabe knew, meant walking in with a search warrant, which might have gotten them a few ounces, maybe more. Maybe nothing. And probably no leads. It was best to handle it this way. Hang around and listen. And wait.

For all they knew, the tip might have been bogus, surrendered by a weasel trying to buy time and leeway. But the department wanted no rock unturned in their sweep to eradicate drugs out of the city.

Even if there hadn't been a detective shield waiting for him at the end of the assignment, he had no tolerance for people who dealt in the powdery substance responsible for terminating so many lives and ruining so many more. He wasn't naive enough, nor egotistical enough, to believe that he personally could eradicate crime, or even make a huge difference in the balance of things. But he knew he could make a dent. And if everyone who could did, who knew where that would eventually lead?

Gabe also knew that the main reason he had been chosen for this assignment was not so much for his detecting skills but the fact that he could put brush to canvas and actually come up with something other than a sick-looking stick figure.

The man he was pretending to be had only the sketchiest of backgrounds when Captain Nolan had pulled him off patrol and briefed him about the assignment. Gabe had spent the better part of two days giving struggling artist Gabriel Murietta a past, a life. A reason for being in this particular place at this particular time.

To keep things simple, he'd given his character the same outgoing, laissez-faire attitude that he himself possessed. With one very large difference. Gabriel Murietta was lax, unfettered by a sense of which side of the law he was on. Even as a child, Gabe Saldana hadn't pilfered so much as a candy bar. He'd been given a very strong sense of right and wrong and had always known on which side he belonged from the very start.

Gabe had studied the dossiers of all the people he would

find himself interfacing with. If the gallery was a front for a drug operation, he wasn't dumb enough to underestimate the people he was up against. Those who were had a very short life expectancy. For the present, he was as armed as he could possibly be.

Though he appeared to be devil-may-care to the others on the force, Gabe liked having all his *i*'s dotted and his *t*'s crossed. He wanted little margin for error to trip him up. It was an inherent trait. He had a greater chance of remaining alive that way.

He'd said his goodbyes last night, telling his mother and his sister-in-law that he would be out of town for a while. He knew they'd had questions, but they'd played the game.

And now he was the lead actor in a deadly one. He was on his own here, walking a tightrope without a net. Gabe knew he was either going to have to be very careful, or learn how to fly. Fast.

Parking the beat-up van he'd driven off the police lot only hours ago, Gabe shut off the headlights and scoured the area behind the large building. Rain lashed against the windshield. It had been raining all day, all week. The February sky was dark and forbidding. Not the best day to begin a new venture, he thought. Turning up his collar, he got out and hurried around to the front of the building.

Braced, psyched, he pulled open the heavy wooden door to the St. Claire's Art Gallery and stepped in out of the rain.

And into his destiny, he thought cryptically. Whatever that shaped up to be.

Chapter 2

The gust of wind and rain that came rushing unannounced into the gallery made Julie turn toward the front door. The weather was far too miserable for her to expect walk-by traffic to be drawn in by the paintings displayed in the front window. It was almost as miserable outside as she was inside.

Julie sighed even before she raised her eyes to greet the walk-in. Being friendly was normally not an effort for her. It was as natural as her smile. But today, her mood swaddled in a blanket of despair and fledgling panic, her smile approached as reluctantly as her friendly, trusting nature: with heavy feet.

Setting down the small-framed painting she'd been angling against the wall, Julie crossed over to the broad-shouldered, good-looking man in a dripping, all-weather poncho. His damp, black hair was on the long side and seemed pretty tangled, thanks to the wind. He had the smell of rain about him. And the scent of danger, as well.

She was also much too much the romantic, Julie upbraided herself silently. That, too, had always been a failing of hers. Raised in a world that abounded in deep, philosophical conversations, sumptuous art and very little logic, she'd struggled to develop skills to deal with reality. Learning how to cope with and pay the bills that would make a go of the gallery had been a plus on the good side of character-building. Romanticism, Julie had long ago decided, was a heavy slash on the negative side.

She turned her attention to the man who was standing, dripping, in the front of her gallery. The clothes she made out beneath the poncho placed him in the "middle price" range.

Was he shopping for himself, or looking for a gift? She wondered if there was any tea left, or if Jeff had managed to feed it all to his cold.

"May I help you?" she asked, forcing herself to smile.

Her voice was low and throaty, Gabe thought, like smooth brandy poured into cut glass that reflected the firelight. Sparkling and enticing. While he knew all about Juliette St. Claire, nowhere in her five-page dossier had it said her voice was the type to float to a man in the middle of a long night and leave him sleepless.

Though the dossier had given her height, weight, and coloring, it hadn't alluded to how well everything had been packaged, how exceptionally well it all came together. The summary hadn't mentioned she had curves that would jeopardize the strength of a man's knees or that her eyes weren't just blue, they were *blue*. So blue, in fact, that it was almost too difficult to look anywhere else but her eyes.

Although the effort to tear his eyes away to take further inventory was well rewarded.

"They tell me you take in strays."

She blinked. "Excuse me?"

His grin was quick, Julie thought, and surprisingly lethal, given her present frame of mind.

Behind her, she heard Jeff approaching. Or rather, sneezing. Julie turned toward her assistant. When she had bought the gallery over three years ago, she'd kept Jeff Connolly and Mike Evers on, having no reason to break up a team to start from scratch just because she could.

She smiled at Jeff sympathetically. Virile was not the first word that sprang to mind when she looked at Jeff. Or even the second or third. Medium height and thin enough to look undernourished, he was incredibly susceptible to almost anything in the air. Jeff brought out the mother in her, even when "mother" felt as stressed as she did now.

"Why don't you take the rest of the day off, Jeff? Go home and nurse that thing before it turns into a full-fledged attack. I doubt we'll see many customers. I can handle whatever comes in today." If the week so far was any indication of how the remainder was going to go, she'd be lucky to see two people all day.

"But I'm your assistant," he interjected halfheartedly.

"There's nothing to assist. Go home, Jeff. That's an order."

Snuffling, a wadded-up handkerchief pressed to his nose, Jeff nodded gratefully. "If you think it's okay." Doubt as well as a cough punctuated his statement, as he took down his raincoat from the coatrack. Sneezing again, he missed the sleeve he was aiming for.

With an affectionate shake of her head, Julie came up behind Jeff to help him on with the coat. More than anything, he reminded her of a hapless little brother even though he was older than she was by five years. "Yes, I think it's okay," she assured him firmly.

"I'll be back tomorrow," he promised, pulling open the front door.

Realizing that he was about to leave behind his umbrella,

Julie grabbed it and rushed to the door. "Don't forget this," she chided gently, pressing the umbrella into his hand.

"Thanks," he mumbled, embarrassed. Another sneeze, accompanied by a rain-filled gust of wind saw him out.

Julie stepped back and closed the door. Turning toward her customer, she wiped a few scattered raindrops from her face with the palm of her hand.

"I'm really sorry, you were saying?" He'd been very patient through all this, she thought, giving him her full attention.

"They were right about you."

So far, the man had uttered exactly two sentences, neither of which had made any sense to her despite their being spoken in her native tongue.

Catching her lower lip between her teeth, Julie cocked her head slightly. Light blond hair brushed against one shoulder. "I hate to sound like a one-phrase parrot, but, excuse me?"

Gabe had entertained himself by watching her. He learned a lot more by way of observation than by reading any report. His first thought was that the sexy voice was accompanied by a kind heart. Which could all be very clever camouflage. Gabe could understand a man giving her a few extra yards of play on the line. Pretty women got away with more, and this one was far more than just pretty.

"They said you were part guardian angel, part den mother—that you had a soft spot in your heart for struggling artists."

So much for his being a customer, Julie thought. That would explain the edgy sense of danger. A brooding would-be artist, probably with little more than a few dollars to his name. Had the jacket beneath the poncho been a gift, or was there a silent, indulging "patroness" in the wings somewhere?

Julie raised a brow. " 'They'?"

"The community." Gabe knew that the fewer names he used, the less likely he would be to trip himself up. "I don't want to drop any names or get anyone in trouble." He underlined his words with an engaging grin.

The phrase he'd inadvertently used leaped out at Julie.

In trouble.

In the family way...

Wasn't that what her condition used to be called back when embarrassment was hidden behind euphemisms? Now, it was just trouble, plain and simple.

Maybe not that simple, she amended. But definitely trouble.

She had to stop torturing herself and keep her mind focused on work.

"You won't get anyone into any trouble," she promised him. "Who told you I was quote, 'part guardian angel, part den mother'?" She had to admit the label appealed to whatever small measure of vanity she possessed. Not that she did what she did out of a desire for payback. She'd known first-hand what it was like to struggle to reach your dreams. In her case, it had been to buy back a piece of her childhood. And her father's life's work, if not his reputation. Everyone needed a helping hand now and then. And if she were in a position to offer it, so much the better.

But she wouldn't be used, she added silently, thinking of Justin.

Gabe offered the only name he knew could be safely bandied about. "Eric Cassidy told me you were a godsend in his leaner years." Currently backpacking through France, the rising artist would not be available to tell Julie that he'd never even heard of Gabriel Murietta.

Eric Cassidy's leaner years had occurred just after she'd graduated college and come to work for Edmund Raitt at the gallery. At the time, she'd been religiously saving every penny to buy the gallery back from Raitt.

But she had slipped Cassidy more than a few dollars on several occasions and, more importantly, gone to bat for him with Edmund, the man who'd bought the gallery from her father. Edmund had been her father's close friend and a man who had benevolently deferred to her judgment time and again, praising her eye and her natural ability to pick talent.

Cassidy had been one of the artists who had benefited from that deference.

Julie smiled now, thinking of Cassidy, an impassioned, somewhat ill-tempered artist whose gift for composition was enough to make a stone weep. At first evaluation, she couldn't see Cassidy and the man standing in her gallery sharing the same conversation. But then, she got along with Cassidy, although that meant nothing because according to something Edmund had once said, she was easygoing enough to get along with the devil himself.

"How's Eric doing?"

"Well." Gabe almost envied Eric's connection with Julie. He made certain he didn't make the mistake of avoiding her eyes. No sense in arousing her suspicions. "He's in France right now."

"Yes." She smiled. "I know."

She would, he thought. She was the type to remain on top of everything. Including, he wondered, taking advantage of certain opportunities that might turn up on her doorstep?

Well, that was his assignment, wasn't it? To find out the truth of that, one way or another.

Gabe took his first step on the taut tightrope. "He thought you might like my work."

"Direct." Julie inclined her head, amused. She liked direct, although not brash. He struck her as about two steps from brash. "Usually, struggling artists meeting me for the first time try to snow me a little longer."

Her smile widened invitingly. Gabe felt as if he'd passed the first small hurdle.

"What's your name?"

It took half a second for him to remember. His distraction bothered him. It wouldn't happen again. "Gabriel Murietta."

"Gabriel Murietta." Her tongue curled around the name. It fairly sang. "Very romantic. It'll look good on a show brochure someday." She could see him with a legion of women flocking to him. More, if he really was talented. "Tell me, Gabriel Murietta, do you have anything for me to look at?"

Other than the obvious, Julie tacked on silently. The longer she looked at him, the more amazingly good-looking he seemed, with finely chiseled features that stopped just short of being described as pretty. That, coupled with light green eyes heavily framed with long, velvet-black lashes, made him a definite heart-stopper.

She had no doubt that he knew it, too.

Thinking it over, he probably did have a patroness backing him. An older, well-to-do woman with an eye for paintings and an even better eye for well-toned muscles and taut, firm hips.

Gabe caught the smile playing across her lips and wondered what that was all about. "As a matter of fact, I've got a couple of paintings in the van."

That didn't surprise Julie. What did surprise her was that he'd brought only "a couple." She'd known artists who'd piled everything they'd ever worked on into a van, intent on a private showing the moment they managed to button-hole her.

It was dark enough outside the show window to be three o'clock in the morning instead of afternoon. She couldn't see very far. "Where did you park your van?"

He nodded his head toward the rear of the gallery. "Out back, in the lot."

"Well, bring them in."

God knew she didn't have anything else to do, and she welcomed the respite from her thoughts.

"Wait," she called after him as he started for the front door. "Do you need anything to wrap them in? I've got waterproof cloth right here."

He flashed her a grin that could be called nothing less than charming. "Already wrapped."

She nodded her approval. At least he had a spark of practicality. "Use the back entrance," she instructed. "It's shorter than having to come back around to the front. I'll meet you."

Gabe nodded and then went out. "Thanks." The word was partially blotted out by the wind.

Well, he came prepared, Julie thought. That was a good sign. She really disliked people who were completely and continually at loose ends. They were the bane of her existence, especially since she felt a moral obligation to take care of them.

As she had with her father, Julie thought with a slight wistful pang. The older she'd become, the younger her father had seemed. She missed him, even though theirs had never been a loving relationship, at least, not on her father's part.

Feeling suddenly cold, Julie rubbed her hands up and down her arms, knowing even as she did so that it wouldn't chase away the chill.

Julie made her way to the back of the gallery where a great many empty frames and several of the paintings that defied purchase were housed. Some belonged to people she'd floated loans to. The paintings were in lieu of payment, markers until such time as the artist was on his or her feet. A few of the paintings had been here since even before she'd bought the gallery.

Just as Gabe reached the back entrance, she unlocked the door and opened it. He was struggling with a 16 by 24 canvas in each hand. Both were wrapped in black oilcloth.

This time when he entered, Gabe was close to being completely drenched. Water pooled on the floor around his feet and slid off the oilcloth, as well. He was not unaware of the mess he was making. Years of hearing lectures from his mother echoed in his brain.

He noticed that he'd accidentally gotten Julie wet, as well.

"Sorry," he murmured.

Being wet should have been the worst of her problems, Julie thought. She laughed at his sheepish apology as she brushed the rain from her face and off her pullover sweater.

"Don't worry about it. Unlike the Wicked Witch of the West, water doesn't make me melt." She glanced at the fast-forming puddles on the floor. "And the floor can be mopped up." Curious now, Julie stepped back into a better light. "So, let's see what you have."

Not waiting for him, Julie knelt in front of the first painting, quickly undoing the ties around it. An eagerness came over her. It always did at the prospect of discovering a new find, a new talent. She dearly loved her work. Unable to paint a stroke, she had inherited as compensation her father's eye for composition and for talent.

Gabe left her a clear field, moving behind her as she unwrapped the first painting. For the first time he felt a little uneasy. Even though he painted, the works he'd brought to win her over and gain a toehold in her world weren't his. They were Rafe's.

Rafe had been the first to lift a brush and Gabe had been quick to emulate him. In those days, Gabe had secretly wanted nothing more than to be just like his big brother.

Gabe hadn't expected the pleasing rush he'd felt putting brush to canvas. That had been a plus, a spectacular plus. Even now, he would paint on occasion, just to unwind, to put the grittier side of his work behind him. And he had to admit, the finished product usually came close to approximating Rafe's work.

But even though their styles were similar, in Gabe's opinion Rafe had always been the better artist. The more gifted one. It was Rafe's work he had brought in now to pass off as his own. He figured it was safer that way.

Gabe had asked to borrow the paintings and Rafe had agreed, without asking questions. Rafe had understood he needed them for his work.

What if she didn't like what she saw, if she didn't think it was good enough to display? The whole plan hung by this slender thread.

Gabe watched as Julie pulled away the oilcloth as gently, as lovingly, as if she were undressing a lover. Most especially, he noticed her hands. Long, slender, delicate, they looked as if they belonged to an artist.

Fitting.

Having unwrapped the first painting, she turned her attention to the second. Finished, she placed them side by side within the crowded storeroom, leaning them against the wall.

She was quiet for a long time.

It made him nervous. Gabe didn't realize he was holding his breath until Julie turned toward him. Her eyes were sparkling. He told himself it was going to be all right.

"I'm impressed." Julie drew out the words, giving them emphasis. "They're very vivid. I can almost feel the water."

The strokes were bold, yet precise and unashamedly realistic. There was no pretentiousness in either of the two works. She liked that. Liked, too, that they moved her.

Spoke to her. There was an underlying sensitivity beneath the strokes. She realized that she was glad.

Studying the paintings a moment longer, she felt as if she'd been there herself. "The scene looks familiar."

It was the view from Rafe's window. He and Dana had a house not far from the gallery. "It should be. That's the beach about a mile or so from here."

Rising, Julie was surprised when Gabe took her hand to help her to her feet. Not too many courtly people around these days, she mused.

"Tell you what, Gabriel Murietta, let me hang them in the gallery for a while and see what kind of a reaction they attract."

The way she said the name he'd given her, as if she were teasing him, momentarily distracted Gabe.

"Both of them?" He reminded himself to sound properly excited.

Julie liked his enthusiasm, though it, too, surprised her. He didn't seem the type to become enthusiastic, or at least not the type to allow it to show.

"Both of them. I'll choose the frames," she promised. She could think of two that would do splendidly. Subdued, they wouldn't detract from the work. If she didn't miss her guess, she would have no trouble selling these. "Where can I reach you?"

"Ah, that's going to be a little hard right now," Gabe hedged. "I'm temporarily between places." The look he offered was properly contrite and embarrassed. A man down on his luck. He knew all about the apartment upstairs. And that it was currently empty. "Why don't I give you a call?"

His comment about her taking in strays replayed itself in Julie's head. So that was what he'd meant. It made sense now. The man was hinting, but not too heavy-handedly. "'Temporarily between places'?" she repeated.

He gave her a sheepish grin. "The building I was living in went co-op." He shrugged carelessly. "I couldn't afford to buy my way in. Right now, I'm storing my paintings at a friend's apartment, but there's no place for me."

"She can't let you sack out on the sofa?"

"He," Gabe corrected amiably without missing a beat. He figured it would go down better if the friend was male. He was playing every angle he could to get in. "And someone else already beat me to that prime location. His dog and three cats have dibs on the floor," he added before Julie could suggest that space to him.

In response, Julie couldn't help laughing. When Gabe looked at her quizzically, she raised her hand and waved away his unspoken question. "Sorry, I was just amusing myself."

"Do that often?" he asked, smiling.

As a matter of fact, she did, though she wasn't about to go as far as to admit that to a stranger.

"I like my own company," she conceded freely. She decided to let him in on it, since he'd been the one to inspire it. "It's just that I thought I heard the sound of violins in the background while you were filling me in on the details."

"Pretty pathetic state to be in at thirty," he agreed. "My parents figured I'd be a respectable businessman by now."

She knew the weight of parental expectations. Her father had been adamant that she "apply" herself and reach the potential having Elizabeth St. Claire as a mother automatically afforded her. He could never get himself to truly believe that she had no artistic talent whatsoever.

"And where are they now?"

"Gone."

Julie flushed, realizing she might have stirred up painful memories with her question. "Sorry. Mine, too."

At least, her father was, she thought. And for all she

knew, her mother was, too. She might as well have been. Fifteen years had gone by since her mother had last spoken a word to her. There'd been no communication from the time she'd run away, to her daughter or anyone.

Gabe tried not to look surprised. He knew Elizabeth Warren St. Claire was alive, though her whereabouts were unknown. Was Julie lying, or did she know something? And how did that fit in with the rumors, if at all?

Leaving that to explore later, Gabe initiated Phase Two of his plan. "Well, I've kept you long enough. I really appreciate this opportunity." He took her hand, shaking it.

The warmth traveled up Julie's arm. He had a strong, firm handshake. She liked that.

The windows rattled as the wind picked up another notch. Releasing her hand, Gabe glanced toward the front window. "I'd better go before some old man decides to start collecting two of everything and stuffing them into an ark."

He was right. The rain was coming down harder than she remembered in recent history. It wasn't the kind of weather a man with no place to stay should be out in. She thought of him spending the night in his van.

It looked as if it probably leaked.

As he began walking away from her, Julie made up her mind. A small, nagging voice inside her whispered that she'd probably regret it, but it didn't stop her from making the offer.

"If you really don't have anywhere to go," she called after him, "you can stay here."

Chapter 3

Yes! Gabe thought triumphantly. He banked down his enthusiasm to sound sufficiently surprised. "Here?"

The exodus he had never really intended on making was aborted. As a last resort, if she hadn't offered, Gabe was going to ask her if she knew of anywhere he could stay temporarily. He figured that would be enough to trigger the invitation. Living here would allow him the excuse he needed to nose around.

But for the sake of the situation, he pretended to look a little puzzled at her suggestion. "You mean, in the back room?"

Julie bit back a laugh. To do that, Gabe would have to learn how to sleep standing up. Aside from a small path to the back door, the room was a catch-all for everything, and utterly crowded.

She nodded toward the ceiling. "No, there're two apartments upstairs. I live in one and usually rent the other one out."

At least, that had been the original plan, but somehow she'd never actually gotten around to charging anyone who stayed in the other apartment. It always went to someone in need. Someone without cash in his or her pocket. She looked at Gabe. Like now.

"Oh." Pausing, he hesitated for what he figured an appropriate length of time.

Julie eased past the obvious embarrassment on his face as if she hadn't noticed its existence. "Tell you what, you do a few chores for me around here and pay me what you can for the apartment." And if he had no money at all, there was a way around that, as well. "We could even make it a contingency arrangement."

"Contingent on what?"

It was a way for him to save face. *Oh, Julie, will you never learn?* she mocked herself.

But she was who she was and there was no way of changing that. She tried to see the best in everyone, to make life easier for them.

"On the sale of one of your paintings."

She said the words as if the sale were already a foregone conclusion, Gabe thought.

"Whenever you sell one of them, you can pay me for the rent then."

It had to be an act. There had to be some sort of catch here he just wasn't aware of yet. No one was that generous. Not even someone who looked like some man's fantasy come to life.

But he nodded as if he bought into the act. "Sounds more than fair."

Julie felt herself responding to the light of appreciation in his eyes.

Once a sucker, always a sucker, she couldn't help thinking. But she couldn't very well turn her back and close her doors to him on a day like today. Not if he didn't have a place to stay. Her conscience would never let her hear the end of it.

"Well, now that we're agreed, how soon can you move in?"

He laughed. "How soon can you open the door up-stairs?" The fact that she didn't appear surprised at his response told him that the apartment had had occupants in similar situations before. "All my worldly goods are in the back of the van."

Her mouth curved in a half smile. "Handy for quick getaways."

For a moment the comment brought him up short. But then he realized that she was talking about something in her past, not any suspicions she might be harboring about him.

His eyes held hers for a moment as he tried to get a handle on what she might be referring to. "I don't operate that way."

Julie half inclined her head. "Nice to know that some people don't."

Had someone pulled a vanishing act on her? In Gabe's estimation, that didn't seem possible. What man in his right man would have walked away from such a class act as Juliette St. Claire? Unless, of course, this was only veneer he was dealing with and there was another, completely different Julie beneath.

He figured it was more than entirely possible. It dove-tailed perfectly with the rumor about the gallery and the purpose of his current assignment.

Pausing for just a moment, Julie glanced toward the front door. There was little doubt in her mind that this was not going to be one of the gallery's more stellar days as far as sales went. If possible, it had gotten even darker outside. On the off chance that someone did enter St. Claire's, there was a bell that would ring on the second floor, to let her know. There was no reason not to take her new resident artist to his quarters.

She gestured him away out of the back room. "C'mon, I'll show you where you'll be staying."

Crossing to the rear wall, she reached over to a small, cheery-looking board where several keys hung suspended from the tails of seven dogs and took one down. Julie opened the narrow door next to it, exposing a small foyer and a staircase beyond.

"This way," she said over her shoulder. Habit had her placing her hand on the banister. When it shook slightly, testifying to its growing unsteadiness, she merely sighed. She had to get that fixed someday.

The lights flickered, momentarily bowing before the storm. She hoped they wouldn't go out.

Gabe was treated to the view of a very shapely posterior leading the way up the stairs. The short, straight, navy-blue skirt made her legs seem that much longer. That much shapelier. The three-inch navy pumps didn't hurt, either.

Gabe found himself definitely warming to his assignment.

At the top of the stairs was another door, the top half comprised of frosted glass with roses etched along the sides. It was unlocked, and Julie pushed it open.

The gallery below seemed a world away.

Separated by a little more than eight feet of parquet flooring, two apartments stood opposite one another.

His, Julie pointed out, was the apartment on the right.

Inserting the key, Julie discovered that the door was unlocked. She'd forgotten about that. Justin had left quickly and loudly, slamming the door in his wake hard enough to make her think that he'd knocked it off its hinges.

She remembered testing it now. And leaving it unlocked. Not that there'd been anything in there to steal, unless you were partial to narrow beds and large bay windows.

The apartment was half the size of her own, but then, no one lived here for very long. There was a huge main room, with a cubby of a kitchen off to one side and an equally small bedroom just barely large enough for a single bed and a bureau—off to the other. What was exceptional about the living quarters was the main room. And the afternoon light that came spilling in.

Absently pocketing the key, Julie walked into the apartment. She switched on the light, and waited for his reaction.

Gabe's attention was immediately drawn to the bay window. "How good is the light in here?"

She liked the question. Little things like that were telling. It meant painting was his work, not his affectation.

"None better," she assured him. Julie gestured toward the window. "You'll feel like God is peeking in to review your work."

The comment was something she remembered her mother saying the first time Elizabeth had walked into the room. At the time it had been her father showing off the room with such pride that Julie had believed he was personally responsible for each and every sunrise. But she'd been eight at the time and incredibly impressionable, thinking her father responsible for everything monumental in the world.

Learning otherwise came soon after that.

The grin on Gabe's face was quick and she found it remarkably sensual, especially since they were virtual strangers. "Then I'd better make sure I give Him something worthwhile to review when I get started."

Gabe turned to take in the rest of the surroundings. It didn't take long. The large room was devoid of furnishings, except for one large wooden table slightly right of center. No chairs surrounded it. He wondered if the last occupant had eaten sitting on the floor.

Two of the walls were lined with rows of canvases. The

canvases in front were barren, but Gabe thought he could see a hint of color on a few of the ones in the rear.

He supposed, if painting were all he cared about, this would be the perfect place to be. It had a nice "flavor" to it.

"I feel like I've just died and gone to heaven." Gabe turned toward Julie and found that he was talking to himself. She had left the room. "Ms. St. Claire?"

"Keep talking…" Her disembodied voice floated to him from across the hall. "I'm just getting you a few essentials." Less than a minute later, she reentered, hugging linens to her chest. "And call me Juliette—or Julie, if it's easier. I haven't been 'Ms. St. Claire' since my last year in college." She deposited the armload on the table. Deep green mixed with light beige. "There. Soap, fresh sheets, fresh towels." Julie passed her hand over the bounty on the table. She stepped back. "Need anything else, just tell me."

"Something else" occurred to him with the unexpected immediacy of a sudden summer shower. The only warning he'd had was his very male response as he'd followed her up the stairs. Gabe had a strong hunch Juliette St. Claire wouldn't take kindly to hearing the request vocalized.

But he did have a very strong sense of curiosity as to the exact taste of her lips and whether or not her body was as soft and inviting as it looked.

Not the kind of thoughts an undercover police officer should be having about the subject of his investigation, he told himself, mildly amused at his own reaction. There had never been any question in his mind that he would compromise either himself or the investigation, but Gabe was somewhat surprised at the level of attraction he was experiencing.

Attracted or not, it wasn't anything he couldn't easily handle and keep a lid on.

He purposely looked at the floor. "This is much more than I have a right to expect."

To make it work, he would have had to attempt a half-hearted kick at imaginary dirt, Julie thought, suppressing a smile. "Humble doesn't quite suit you," she informed him glibly. "And it doesn't get any extra points around here."

"What does?" he asked, grinning.

She'd bet that Gabe got away with an awful lot because of that grin. She could feel its effects even fully armed and cognoscente. And pregnant, she reminded herself—as if she could forget.

"Honesty," she said simply. "Total and complete honesty at all times—even if I ask you if a dress makes me look fat," Julie tacked on after a beat just to prove she was serious.

Well, that certainly left him out of the game, Gabe thought. His purpose was to be a walking, talking, living lie the entire time he was here.

He retained a straight expression. "I'll try to remember that if the occasion ever arises."

"What occasion? To be honest?" Was this his subtle way of saying she'd just thrown her home, so to speak, open to a pathological liar? Julie wondered.

"No. To comment on your dress." Sparkling with humor, his eyes held hers for a second. "So, what would you like me to do?"

The words, coming out smoother than melted butter and coupled with the mesmerizing look in his eyes, momentarily distracted her. "Do?"

"In exchange for my keep?" he prompted.

"Oh." Upbraiding herself for the brief lapse, she looked down at Gabriel's hands. They looked sturdier and far more capable than the kind of hands she was accustomed to seeing. "Do those just hold a brush, or do you know your way around a hammer and screwdriver, as well?"

"Built my own treehouse as a kid." Gabe didn't bother adding that his father and his brother helped and that between the two of them, they'd done seventy-five percent of the work. He'd taken pride in wriggling out of work in those days.

The smile that bloomed instantly on her face made him want to embellish his accomplishment, just to watch it a little longer.

Julie unexpectedly hooked her arm through his, leading him toward the hallway. "Well, then, you're just the man I'm looking for."

She almost made him wish he could be.

"I said it before, but I appreciate you seeing me on such short notice."

Uncomfortable about the situation she found herself in, not the woman she was talking to, Julie hiked up the sagging shoulder of the blue paper gown. Legs dangling over the side of the examination table, she had been quick to sit up once the internal exam was concluded.

With Mike Evers finally back from his European buying trip and vacation and her new live-in artist busy rehanging the storage room door, Julie'd taken the opportunity to drive down to her gynecologist's office for an official prognosis of her condition.

The additional three tests she'd purchased yesterday had turned out to be dismally identical in their positive verdict.

Pushing herself back from the examining table, Sheila Pollack rose from the stool and snapped off her rubber gloves.

"I wasn't really very interested in eating today, anyway," she admitted. She was hours behind lunch, never mind breakfast. But that was the price she paid for her vocation. Pressing the lever with her foot, she deposited the gloves into the wastebasket's yawning mouth, then picked up Julie's chart. "And for once, not a single baby was clamoring to be born."

"Must be my lucky day," Julie murmured, feeling about as far from lucky as she'd ever been.

"Well, not quite." Sheila looked up from the notation she was making in Julie's chart. "Unless of course you want to be pregnant."

Sheila was only saying what she already knew. Still, she'd nurtured a tiny seedling of hope...

Julie looked at Sheila's eyes. "Then the tests were right?"

Sheila picked up on the plural noun. That answered that question, she thought.

"The tests were right." Sheila turned to a fresh page. "They're amazingly accurate these days. Do you know approximately when—?"

"No, not approximately." Julie could tell Sheila was about to say something, but she cut her off. "I know exactly when. Christmas Eve. Eleven-thirty. I lost my head." She said the last words quietly, more to herself than to Sheila.

Sheila did a quick calculation as to Julie's due date, then wrote it down. "Should have filled that prescription for contraceptives I've been trying to get you to take."

Julie shrugged, then tugged again at her drooping paper gown. Contraceptives were for people who were sexually active. That didn't describe her.

"Water under the bridge," she answered. "He was wearing a condom."

Sheila raised her eyes from the folder. "Want to hear statistics about that?"

"Not particularly."

Sheila set her pen on the folder. "So, what do you want to do?"

Julie looked at her blankly. "Do?"

Sheila sank her hands deep into the pockets of her lab coat. "I'm obligated to tell you that if you want an abortion, the best time is now—"

"No. You don't have to go through all that. I won't be getting an abortion."

Crossing to her, relieved, Sheila stood next to Julie and put her arm around her shoulder.

"You sound like someone preparing to face a firing squad. Having a baby is a wondrous thing. Aside from my own two, I've been on the receiving end now for a number of years and I am still in awe at the wonder of it. The miracle. Babies are tissues and cells and magic, Julie." She believed that with all her heart. "Such wonderful magic."

Hands folded in her lap, Julie stared up at the ceiling to keep the tears of fear back. Fear that any step she was to take from here on in would be wrong.

Babies were not something she'd ever thought about. There'd always been too much else in the way, too much else to take up her time. She'd taken care of her father and then herself. And along the way, she'd rebuilt the family name. That had left no time for her to contemplate being a mother.

Now she felt woefully inadequate to face the task before her. "But babies need things. Important things."

They weren't talking about money. Sheila knew that St. Claire's was on its way up. And Julie wasn't the kind to be extravagant. There was something else on Julie's mind. "What kind of things?" Sheila prodded gently.

Julie pressed her lips together. Though she rarely saw Sheila socially, when she did see her, it was as if no time had passed. Sheila Pollack bordered on being a mother confessor and confidante to her. Sheila knew all there was to know about Julie, about her past.

More than anyone else, Sheila would understand about the doubts that now racked her.

"I don't know the first thing about being a mother, Sheila. I have nothing to go on." Julie hated feeling this helpless, this lost. "I know there are books, but…"

Sheila had had a hunch that that was what was bothering Julie. It was always the good ones who worried about not being good enough. "Well, unless you have total amnesia, you probably remember what it was that you wanted most from your parents."

A soft, sad laugh escaped Julie's lips. "That's easy. Love."

So wrapped up in one another, in the art that dominated both their lives, her parents had had little time for the daughter they'd created out of their passion. A passion that had somehow managed to turn to dust.

"Exactly. It's easy," Sheila echoed. "Just love them. The rest works itself out."

It only *sounded* easy. Julie shook her head, fixing her gaze at the light blue walls. "I don't think I'm that hopelessly optimistic."

Sheila had seen it before. Julie was being too hard on herself. More than anything else, a first child inspired baseless insecurity. She gave Julie's shoulder a squeeze.

"Optimism has nothing to do with it. That's the voice of experience, by the way. Been there, done that. You would be surprised what a myriad of mistakes can be washed away with enough love. Kids don't need perfect, they need a mom who'll be there for them." From what Julie had confided to her, she knew the other woman would readily agree with that.

"I'm giving the baby only half a family." There was a time, Julie thought, when she would have sold her soul to have her mother back. But she was starting her baby out the way she'd been at twelve. With only one parent.

"The father?"

Sheila didn't normally pry, but if she had a flaw, it was

caring too much about the people whose lives intertwined with hers. Julie had said nothing about her partner, never even mentioned a man before. Sheila knew that one of the reasons she'd turned down the birth control pills was because she wasn't sexually active.

"Long gone," she told Sheila. "I don't even know where." And it was best left that way.

"Well, half a loaf is better than none," Sheila said philosophically. "And in your case, half a loaf is excellent." She smiled. "I never knew you to do anything halfheartedly. Just bring your usual amount of enthusiasm into this child's life and he or she will consider themselves one of the lucky ones."

The doubts were still feeding on one another, although listening to Sheila was making her feel a little better. "You make it sound easy."

"Loving is—when you strip away all the things that get in the way. Just open up your heart, Julie. It'll do the rest."

Getting off the table, Julie went to the chair where she'd left her clothes. "Does being a doctor make you so wise?"

On her way out, Sheila stopped at the door. She thought of Slade and the two little girls who looked just like their daddy. "No, but loving a good man does. Loving my kids does. Love's a great teacher." And she had never fully appreciated it until Slade had come into her life on a fulltime basis. "And for those fill-in gaps—don't hesitate to call me."

Julie laughed softly. "I intend to take you up on it."

It was nice to have someone to turn to. For so much of her life, she'd felt obligated to keep everything inside, to turn a brave face to the world and pretend that everything was all right. More than all right, that it was perfect when it wasn't.

"I'll get an extra line put in." Sheila winked. "Oh, and when the time comes, I have a great pediatrician for you."

Reaching into the breast pocket of her lab coat, she took out Dr. Rafe Saldana's card. She sent all her new mothers to the same doctor. Her own children numbered among his patients. "What he doesn't know about kids couldn't fill a thimble." Sheila held out the card to her.

Julie shook her head. "Give it to me just before I deliver. Otherwise, I'm liable to lose it." She took a deep breath. The exam was over, the verdict in. "I guess I'm all set."

Sheila squeezed her hand. She had to get moving before her patients began backing up on her. "Then go forth and eat healthy. I want to see you back in a couple of weeks just to see how you're doing. Sooner if you need me."

"I'll try to muddle through on my own," Julie told her, a halfhearted smile on her lips.

"You'll do more than try," Sheila assured her. "You'll do fine. I'd better hustle. The waiting room is piling up. No rest for the weary." She sighed, closing the door behind her.

"None," Julie murmured as she began getting dressed.

Chapter 4

Having taken a temporary respite around four o'clock, the rain was back with a vengeance by the time Julie returned to the gallery.

She noted with philosophical resignation that the parking lot was empty, except for two cars, Gabe's rather beat-up van with its dented chrome bumper and Mike's brand-new, sleek black Mercedes. The latter was parked the length of the lot away from the former.

Julie sighed. It was just as she'd predicted. This was not destined to be one of her more stellar weeks, neither personally nor professionally.

"Win some, lose some," she murmured to herself.

Right now, she didn't exactly feel like a winner on any front.

Parking her car directly behind the building, Julie sat in the vehicle for a moment, attempting to gather herself together. Since yesterday morning, she'd experienced shock, disbelief, despair and depression. It was time to move on to resolve.

And what she resolved, Julie silently promised herself, was not to let this new twist impede her in any way. Having a baby was a natural part of life. Women did it every day. It was just something she was going to have to take in stride.

It was just, Julie thought with a tinge of regret, that she'd thought there'd be someone striding by her side when it came to this part.

"Best laid plans..."

Annoyed, Julie roused herself. She was beginning to sound like a dusty, ancient book of proverbs, or some out-of-date fortune cookie.

Enough, she ordered sternly. No more feeling sorry for herself, no more being philosophical. Back to meeting life head-on—on her own terms, the way she always had before. She had too much to do to waste time and energy like this.

Pregnant or not, she was going to go on just as she had before, she silently promised herself. She was just going to be a little wider for a while.

And after that, she was going to learn how to be the best damn mother she could. There was no way she would ever run off on the day before Christmas Eve, breaking her child's heart.

If she had any energy, she thought, feeling drained again. It came and went in waves, this irritating flux in her energy level. And she didn't like it.

Julie turned off the engine and got out of her car. Electing not to fumble with her umbrella for the short distance involved, she hurried to the back door with the umbrella closed. She was liberally christened by the time she unlocked the door.

The door slammed shut behind her as she shook raindrops from her hair. Something else that needed fixing, she thought absently. Maybe she could get Gabe to see to the hinges next—provided he worked out.

It felt good coming inside. It felt good, Julie thought, just being here, in the gallery, where she belonged. Except for the short space of time when the gallery had passed out of her family's hands, this had been home to her since she was eight years old. No other place felt the same or even came close.

Taking off her raincoat and leaving it hanging on a wall hook, Julie wondered how its former owner was doing. Of late, she'd seen very little of him. For a man in so-called retirement, Edmund seemed incredibly hard to get hold of. In the past six months, the only time she'd ever seen him was whenever he popped in at the gallery on a whim. When she occasionally called to suggest getting together for dinner, she wound up talking to his answering machine. A machine that appeared derelict in forwarding her messages.

Probably off entertaining himself with some lady friend, she mused. In his late fifties, he was still a charmer in the Old World sense of the word.

She missed him, she thought. He was as close to a father as she'd had in a long time. Far more caring of her than her own had been.

Julie walked into the gallery's main room. The radio station she normally kept on in the background when she was here had been silenced. Mike didn't care for music. He found it annoyingly distracting.

She glanced around for Gabe, but he didn't seem to be in the area.

Looking up from the newspaper he'd been reading, Mike Evers pushed his rimless glasses up his nose and watched as Julie crossed to him. He couldn't help thinking what a fine, handsome woman she was. A pang accompanied the thought. Women like Julie didn't pay attention to men like him, no matter what sort of a car they were driving or how expensive their suits were. But he could keep on trying, he thought. Under the right conditions, princesses did kiss frogs.

She smiled at him brightly, raising a brow. "Anything?" There was no harm in asking, although she felt she already knew the answer.

He shook his head. "Not even a phone call." Folding the newspaper, he raised his eyes to hers as he ran a hand over his slightly thinning, wheat-colored hair. Mike attempted to look stern. Julie was the only person he couldn't manage it with. "You know, you really should stop taking in strays."

"Funny, that was the same word Gabriel used—Did I still take in strays."

Mike was unimpressed. Feeling uncharacteristically optimistic when Justin had finally cleared out, he didn't welcome the idea of having yet another strange face around. "Well, you shouldn't, you know."

Julie smiled. The terrain was not unfamiliar. He'd given this lecture before. "And why is that, Mike?" she asked indulgently.

Mike was several inches taller than she was, but his slight build gave him a smaller appearance. He made every effort to rectify that by raising his head and bracing his shoulders back. "Because not everyone is trustworthy, Julie," he pointed out. "What if you're here alone at night and he gets ideas?"

With great effort, Julie held back a grin. She had long since decided that Mike had had a very repressed upbringing. He was exceedingly neat, almost obsessively so, somewhat high strung at times, and very formal. But he was a dear for all that and she had worked with him for years. He had excellent taste when it came to acquisitions, periodically going to more modest galleries around the country and occasionally, like his last trip, to Europe, harvesting a small but rather distinguished crop of paintings and artists to showcase at their gallery.

Andrea Winslet had been one of his finds. Now the woman's name was on everyone's tongue in the art community. Julie trusted Mike's judgment implicitly. At least as far as art was concerned.

She smiled at Mike fondly now, touched by his concern. "That's sweet, Mike, but I can take care of myself. Really."

Julie couldn't help wondering what he'd say if Mike knew that one of her "strays" had left her in her present regrettable condition. Mike hadn't liked Justin, either, and, in that case at least, he'd been right. Undoubtedly, Mike would feel called upon to lecture her once he found out, but she could quickly cut him short. For all his verbiage, he was easily intimidated.

At the moment, having worked up a full head of steam, Mike was not appeased and not finished.

"This one looks more like a day laborer than an artist," he grumbled.

Comparing Mike and Gabe was like looking at before and after shots in an advertisement for weight training equipment. She knew Mike felt inadequate and gently overlooked the obvious. "They can't all have artistic hands like you."

Mike spread out the fingers of one hand, glancing at them with pride as if he'd forgotten about that feature. "No, I guess not." Dropping his hand, he frowned again and looked accusingly toward the ceiling. "How long is he here for?"

She looked at Mike again. "Stop making noises like my big brother and go home, Mike." Julie glanced at her watch. "It's after five, nobody's coming now." Especially not when it looked so forbidding outside. "No sense in you hanging around here."

Mike raised his eyes toward the ceiling again. Strangers on the premises always made him uneasy. Julie was far too trusting. He hadn't been in town yesterday, when this latest parasite had arrived. But he was here now.

"I could stay a while longer. Just in case."

"He'll only pounce on me after you're gone, I'm sure." The grin broke free of its restraints and took over her face, humor glinting in her eyes. "Stop worrying and go." Turning from the desk, she began to gently push Mike toward the coatrack in the corner. "I wouldn't have offered the apartment to him if I thought he was dangerous. He seems like a very nice guy."

Mike snorted, completely unconvinced. Why couldn't Julie stop playing the patron saint of artists? "The Boston Strangler was supposed to have seemed like a nice guy, too."

"Haven't you heard? I bring out the best in people." She patted his cheek fondly. "Go home."

Julie locked the door in Mike's wake, flipping over the Closed sign. And so ended an otherwise uneventful day, she thought sarcastically, glancing down at her very flat stomach.

She wasn't going to think about that now, she told herself.

Turning toward the rear of the gallery, she let her mind wander to the man she'd taken in. Preoccupied, she'd left him to his own devices yesterday and for most of today. Mike's concerns were totally unfounded and didn't trouble her, but he had gotten her thinking. And wondering.

What was Gabriel Murietta's story? How had he come to this junction in his life, ambitious, talented but obviously not overly driven? If he had been, the talent she'd seen displayed in his work would have undoubtedly gotten him somewhere in the art community by now, if not in the world of art, as well.

He aroused her curiosity.

Had she not been in her present condition, Julie mused as she turned off the lights within the front of the gallery one by one, he might have aroused something else.

But right now, handsome men with strong chins and sensitive green eyes were not very high on her interest list. She left the center light on and opened the door leading to the staircase.

She was still feeling incredibly drained as she made her way up, managing to mask it only long enough to get Mike out the door. She didn't feel up to fielding any of his questions about her health. Questioning her rationale as caretaker had been quite enough.

God, this was awful, she thought, reaching the top of the stairs. Sheila had warned her that waves of exhaustion were part of the early stages of pregnancy, but she'd hoped to bypass them.

Actually, she was hoping to bypass the whole ordeal altogether, Julie thought wearily, feeling her pocket for her key. Just wander into the cabbage patch and collect her baby when the time arrived.

The notion had her smiling.

The fact that there was a light on between the two apartments, brightly illuminating the foyer only registered belatedly. When it did, she looked up at the heretofore darkened light fixture.

So, Gabe had taken it upon himself to change the dead bulb. That was an encouraging sign. The man was obviously a self-starter, at least in a small way.

"If he meant to have his way with me, Mike," she murmured to the departed buyer, "he wouldn't have put in a light."

Julie thought of knocking on Gabriel's door to ask him how the repairs on the sticking door had gone, but decided it could wait until later. After she'd had dinner.

Except for a cupcake, she hadn't eaten all day. Dinner was definitely a priority. Her growling stomach insisted on it.

Inserting her key into the lock, she found it wasn't necessary. The door was already open. Julie frowned as she slipped the key back into her pocket. Why was it open? She'd locked her door on the way out, she was sure of it.

Though she resisted them, Mike's words echoed in her head. *The Boston Strangler was supposed to have seemed like a nice guy, too.*

Pins and needles traveled up and down her arms and spine. She debated calling the police.

And won't you feel like a fool when it turns out just to be a lapse of memory, she upbraided herself. She'd never been afraid of her own shadow before, this was not the time to start.

Blaming it on the pregnancy, the weather and Mike's prophesies of doom, Julie cautiously crossed the threshold, leaving the door wide open—a fast exit if it proved necessary.

"Hello?" Julie switched on the light in the living room. The room was uncluttered, almost Spartan, with no place for anyone to hide and leap out at her.

There was no one around.

"Hi. In here."

Burglars did not call out greetings. Taking heart, Julie quickened her stride as she followed the voice to its source, the kitchen.

She spied the long torso immediately. Boots, jeans-encased legs and a blue denim workshirt, partially undone at the waist. His face was obscured. Gabe was flat on his back, working under her sink.

Puzzled, she dropped her purse on the table, never taking her eyes off him. A wary caution still lingered. "What are you doing?"

"Unclogging your trap." Julie heard metal clang against pipe. Was that a good sound, or the sound of a five-hundred dollar plumber's bill in the making?

She squatted beside him as close as she could manage. Craning her neck, she tried to see what he was working on. "Why?"

Gabe lifted his head slightly. She saw the flash of teeth in a grin that she found oddly reassuring, since she really knew nothing about the man. "Because it was clogged."

The muscles on his arms were tensing. All of them. And a slight, quick scent of cologne drifted over to her from this angle. She found both very distracting. Julie moved her head back.

The air was less lethal here. "And how did you come to find that out?"

Twisting the wrench, he tightened the last screw on the pipe against the underside of the basin. "When I washed my hands to get off the WD-40."

Julie felt as if she were trying to follow a trail of microscopic bread crumbs back to its original source. "Okay, I'll bite, what were you doing with WD-40 on your hands?"

Gabe began to snake his way out from underneath the sink. Julie got to her feet quickly. Too quickly. With tiny pinpricks of bright lights exploding in her head, everything began to spin around her.

And then she felt strong hands on her arms, steadying her. Holding her. The tiny starburst of lights dancing before her eyes gave way and then disappeared.

She found herself looking up at Gabe, a hint of concern on his face.

"Are you all right?"

Julie sucked in a lungful of air before she trusted herself to answer.

"Yes. Just got up too quickly," she murmured, feeling foolish. And feeling oddly warm at the same time. Maybe he'd done something to the heater as well, while he'd been up here.

Gabe slipped his hands from her cautiously, watching to make sure she didn't weave again. Satisfied, he returned to her question as if nothing had happened.

"I got some on my hands when I was getting rid of the squeak in your door." He nodded toward it for added emphasis. "I noticed it when you went into your apartment yesterday."

She'd been meaning to get to that. Meaning to get to a lot of things. The fact that Gabe had so quickly should have felt like a boon, but it left her a little uncertain as to how to take all this. "And you just took it upon yourself to desqueak it."

Broad shoulders quirked slightly in response as he carelessly regarded her question. "I thought it was the least I could do." His eyes met hers. "You did say I was to do chores, didn't you?"

The quickening in her heart rate was unexpected. Julie focused on the question, not the man. "Yes, but I thought they'd be chores I'd tell you to do." She glanced back toward her door. "How did you get in?"

Gabe thought of telling her that she'd left the door open, but he had a feeling that she knew she didn't. When in doubt, go with the truth—unless the truth worked against you.

"I unlocked the door."

An uneasiness slipped over her. Had she just thrown her doors open to a cat burglar? "How? I don't remember leaving you a key to my apartment."

Distracted by the way her mouth puckered when she frowned in concentration, Gabe slipped his hands into his back pockets. "You didn't. I worked at a locksmith's shop one summer."

There, a logical explanation. She had to stop listening to

Mike. Humor curved her mouth. "And he taught you how to pick locks?"

Gabe laughed. "He didn't call it that."

She smiled, relieved that her instincts were right after all. "I see. So, am I unclogged?"

Gabe gestured toward the sink. "Why don't you see for yourself?"

Turning toward the sink, she pushed the chrome handle toward the right. Cold water poured out and went swirling down the drain instantly.

As good as his word, Julie thought. She closed the faucet, then turned and leaned her hips against the cabinet, regarding Gabe with interest.

"Unclogged, lit up—" she indicated the hallway beyond for emphasis "—and de-squeaked all in one afternoon. What more can a woman ask for?" The sharp pinch in her belly reminded her that it was long past feeding time. She took two steps toward the refrigerator, then stopped to look over her shoulder at Gabe. "I don't suppose you've eaten anything?"

He had, but Gabe saw this as a way into an invitation. And for unguarded conversation. Going through her things in the apartment hadn't yielded anything. But then, he hadn't finished.

He shrugged carelessly. "Been busy."

Julie thought of the cut of London broil in her refrigerator. Really too much for one. But just enough for two if she added a salad and a serving of vegetables. "Could I tempt you with steak?"

He almost said that she could damn well tempt him without steak, or anything else in the way, either, but he thought better of it immediately. There was friendly, and then there was *friendly*—a line that he didn't want to cross just because retracing his steps might be more difficult than he would have liked. This was a place where the truth didn't work.

The easy smile on Gabe's lips sent strange undercurrents through Julie. "Meals included with the apartment?"

Julie took the steak out of the refrigerator and placed it on the counter. She also took a deep breath before reaching for the frying pan. She had to stop letting herself get distracted this way.

"Let's just say you're not the only one who can color outside the lines occasionally. You got a little ahead of yourself and fixed things before I actually asked you to. Initiative should be rewarded. The least I can do is feed you." Thinking it safe, she spared a glance in his direction. "How do you like your steak?"

"Rare."

It looked as if they had more than art in common. She took out a box of frozen peas and dumped them into a pot. "Man after my own heart. You know, of course, it's healthier charbroiled."

The fact that she moved around the kitchen with confidence surprised Gabe. The woman didn't exactly reek of domesticity. Looking at her brought other rooms of the house to mind, not the kitchen.

"I know, but I prefer living dangerously where tastes are concerned."

Julie laughed. He had a sense of humor, which was a refreshing change. Of late, she'd found herself surrounded by people who took life exceedingly seriously and at times, that was a little wearing.

"All right, we'll take a walk on the wild side." *In more ways than one,* she silently added.

"Can I do anything to help?"

"How are you at setting a table?"

"Formal or informal?" The question had her raising a

brow in his direction. "Spent a few months working for a catering company that also ran a restaurant."

The man had hidden talents. *Don't go there,* she warned herself, laughing at her own thoughts. "You get around."

"Yes, I do."

The response seemed to sizzle along her spine.

Looking over her shoulder, she saw him go to first one cupboard, then another. "Dishes are in the one to the left," she prompted.

At least he hadn't gone rummaging through her cupboards, she thought, turning back to the counter. *Boston Strangler. Where do you get these ideas, Mike?*

Chapter 5

Julie was surprised at how "at home" Gabe seemed in the kitchen. Her own father had needed a road map to find the stove and most of the men she knew weren't much better. When she'd mentioned making a garden salad, Gabe hadn't looked at her blankly but instead had pulled out all the major ingredients and proceeded to make one as she manned grilling their steaks.

Good-looking, artistic, gregarious, and handy with a toolbox and kitchen utensils. The man seemed too good to be true.

It made her wonder what his flaw was and how deep it went.

That, she thought as she placed each steak on a plate, was her father in her. He'd always seen the dark side of everything. Of course, the way things were going lately, it wouldn't hurt her to be a little suspicious of people before embracing them with open arms.

As she helped herself to the salad, Julie looked at the

man sitting across from her for a long moment, debating how much she could safely ask without seeming as if she were prying. "Where did you study?"

"Study?" he asked, as he looked up from cutting his steak.

"Art." Julie kept her voice light, conversational. She didn't want him thinking that she was interrogating him, but by the same token, there were things she wanted to know about him. Things that would either validate or seriously negate her instincts about allowing him to take up temporary quarters here.

Since he hadn't answered immediately, maybe a little rewording was in order. "Where did you get your formal training?"

The steak had been forgotten the moment Gabe raised his eyes in response to her question. He caught himself watching the way the overhead light played off her hair. Just for a moment, he'd allowed his mind to wander.

The question had barely skimmed along his consciousness.

Regrouping, he considered Julie's question and quickly reverted to the personal history of the man he'd created. It was comprised of half fact, half fiction.

"U.C.I." Gabe had attended the California university, but it was law enforcement he had majored in, not art. Although there had been that one course he'd taken, he remembered, the one in which he'd joined other earnest would-be artists, painting life forms. He'd been forced to audit the class, unable to take it for credit because of his major.

There had been one outstanding life form in particular...

As he recalled, they'd gone together the entire fall quarter of his junior year. He'd sketched with a passion for ten solid weeks. A smile curved his mouth, interfering with his meal.

Now that he thought of it, Julie bore some resemblance to that girl. Except there was a great deal more going on behind the eyes with Julie than there had been with... Nancy. That had been her name, he remembered suddenly, pleased that he could still recall it. Not much going on behind the eyes maybe, but Nancy had things going on in other places that had made up for it.

Gabe realized that Julie was looking at him, waiting for him to tell her about his art career. He switched gears, giving her a small peek into his own life. There was no harm done as long as it fed the image.

"I picked up my first brush when I was five. Watercolors," he elaborated. God, but the steak was good. He hadn't really paid attention...had she done anything special to it? Or was it just nervous energy, making him so hungry? "The kind where you dip your brush in water and spread it over the page to watch the colors pop out." Gabe watched her eyes to see if she was familiar with what he was talking about.

A flashback zipped by her. She was standing in a toy shop, pointing to a rack filled with coloring books. Her father's fingers closed around her hand tightly as he marshaled her out of the shop.

"I wasn't allowed to have those. My father was convinced I could do it from scratch, even at five." Julie toyed with the salad. It was good, but the voracious hunger that had haunted her had receded almost from the first mouthful. She wondered if going crazy was all part of pregnancy, too. "He thought it was in the genes."

Gabe realized, as he studied it, that her face was almost a perfect oval. "And was it?"

She laughed softly to herself. "Only the artistic temperament, not the ability. Oh, and the frustration, too." Her smile was rueful and private. "I spent a long time trying and failing before I realized that painting wasn't my calling."

After her mother had left, her father had attempted harder than ever to bring out the artist he felt Julie harbored within her. For years, Julie had thought he'd turned to the bottle because she'd failed to fulfill his dreams. It was only later that she realized she wasn't the one who had brought him to that junction.

The steak became secondary. Gabe finished it almost absently, his attention intent on her. "And running an art gallery is?"

"I have a finely honed sense of appreciation for art and a good eye for both composition and what appeals to collectors. Match that up with a good head for business and you have yourself a thriving art gallery."

"The best of both your parents," Gabriel allowed kindly, toasting her with his glass of caramel-colored soda.

She thought of the way she'd discovered that her father's lack of business acumen had run them aground even before his drinking had floated them to bankruptcy. But even though it was public knowledge in some circles, she felt a certain disloyalty in exposing that underlayer to a stranger.

"Only my father," she said casually. "My mother was the artist. I don't think I got a drop of her blood, really." At this point, she could sketch and paint tolerably well, but no one was ever going to pay even modest sums of money to have one of her paintings on their wall.

As if waking from a dream, Julie blinked, slightly dazed. "How did we get started talking about me? I asked you the question."

"You're a lot more interesting than I am," he said, spearing a piece of broccoli.

The man knew his way around flattery, too. The more Julie looked at him, the more lethal she decided he was.

She was going to have to watch her step here. "Be that as it may, I know my story. I don't know yours."

"Not much to tell." He wiped his mouth, then dropped the napkin beside his empty plate. "Kid loves art. Kid wins a few cheap blue ribbons, the kind that run in the rain," he added. "But they make him feel like the next Andrew Wyeth. Kid's parents want him to be the next Donald Trump." He spread his hands. "Impasse. Parents have the money, so kid keeps up charade as long as he can. Discovery, falling out. Fatal car accident robbing kid of chance for final reconciliation." He looked properly subdued for the count of five, then continued. "Kid wanders around, feeling sorry for himself. Finds true calling never left. Tries again, this time seriously." He smiled at her as the curtain went down on his inventive little drama. "And here I am, still trying."

"You have a gift for brevity." Her mouth quirked. "Ever think of hiring out to one of those companies that summarizes long books?"

His eyes met hers. They smiled at one another before his mouth joined in. "It's crossed my mind. Especially when I've skipped too many meals."

"You left out something in your narrative."

"What?" Not knowing what to make of the comment, he waited. And silently held his breath. Did they have a problem?

"The emotion."

No problem. Relief was swift and sweet. "I've found that emotion is best left out of things. It only gets in the way."

Gabe figured that was the proper artistic thing to say. Weren't real artists supposed to be brooding? He'd never been able to pull that off himself, enjoying life as much as he did, but a touch wouldn't hurt.

Her fingers laced together, supporting her chin, Julie

looked up at him. Bemusement infiltrated her smile. "Really?"

"Really."

"Huh." She sat back, taking her napkin off her lap. She toyed with it for a moment, still studying him. "Then I guess we have more than rare steak in common."

He didn't want to dwell on common ground. That wasn't part of his assignment. "From what I hear, you don't leave out emotion."

"Oh? And what is it that you hear?" Maybe she would regret the question, but that same compelling curiosity spurred Julie on. Just what did others say about her when she wasn't around to hear?

"That this is the place for starving artists to come— young or old. That you'll give them a place to stay, a warm meal and a decent chance to reach their potential."

Once, she would have done that without a second thought. Deprived of so much on so many fronts, it was still in her nature to be generous. Empathy sent her on that road.

But people like Justin made her rethink her actions and wonder if perhaps she wasn't just being hopelessly naive. And being taken for a ride.

Reaching, she took Gabe's empty plate and then rose, taking it to the sink. "Is that what you heard, or hope to hear?"

Gabe didn't understand the question. She'd already displayed her generosity. "I'm already here. I've been here for over a day."

"That's because I wouldn't let anyone out on a night like this."

Coming up behind her, he brought his glass to the sink. "It wasn't night when I came."

Julie turned around slowly. The hot flash of electricity that sizzled through her veins at the brief contact of their bodies, brushing against one another, registered with the subtlety of a thirty-story building imploding and crashing to its foundation.

She caught her breath and forced herself not to avoid his eyes. "Don't make me out to be St. Joan. I expect something back for this."

So, there was a sexual side to her. Gabe had begun to think that maybe it had been wistful thinking on his part—not that he could do anything about it if there were, he reminded himself. Still, it might not hurt to play this line out a little, as long as he remembered to maintain his control.

The sensual smile spread across more than just his lips as it unfurled. "What?"

"Your best."

With his hands braced on either side of her, his fingers curling around the rim of the sink, for a moment Julie thought he was going to kiss her. And then she turned her head abruptly before he could, looking for something to divert his attention.

She saw her plate still on the table. She'd hardly touched her meal. She knew she should have eaten it, that she was eating for two now, as the classic phrase went. But the thought of putting the meat between her lips, so tempting before, only made her stomach twist in genuine agony now.

"You seem to like my cooking."

Gabe took his cue from her and stepped back. For a brief moment there, he'd felt incredibly drawn to her. More than just curiosity, need had been involved. He took the breather gladly.

That lapse shouldn't have happened.

"You make a mean steak."

"Want mine?" Crossing to the table, she pushed her plate to his setting.

"You're not hungry?"

She shrugged, then looked at him pointedly. "I only thought I was."

He understood. "Happens sometimes," he agreed, sitting again. "People get signals confused." Their own and other people's, he added silently. Gabe looked at the plate, thinking. It might be wise to take more than just a breather. He needed to regroup. "Maybe I should just take this back to my apartment."

Relieved, she nodded. "Maybe."

Gabe didn't like being confused. Not like this. Puzzles were one thing. They were a mental challenge. But this puzzle addressed something other than his mental faculties, and he wasn't sure just what to make of it. Or if he was supposed to.

Not on this watch, buddy, he told himself. He was here to find evidence, not make time.

But if making time might be a means to an end…

Only as a last resort, he decided. He wasn't at that point yet. There were still avenues to try, a lot of spaces to poke around in the gallery. Not to mention that computer he'd seen in her office.

His quick search, aborted when he'd heard Julie coming up on the stairs, had yielded nothing. Which wasn't to say that there was nothing to find, only that he hadn't found it yet. Not knowing exactly what you were looking for just made the search that much more difficult. But not, in his experience, impossible.

Where there was smoke, there was usually some sort of fire, even if it was only smoldering, and in this case, there was definitely smoke.

So it was a waiting game.

Gabe had never been a great one for waiting. But there was a detective's shield with his name on it at the end of this road and for those kind of stakes, he was willing to give patience a try.

Besides, he thought, stripping off his shirt and tossing it on the tiny bureau, the surroundings weren't that hard to put up with.

Julie came to mind instantly.

As for the other people…

Evers had taken an instant dislike to him, but Gabe had a hunch that was because the man thought he might have designs on Julie. Though Evers and Julie had interacted briefly before Julie had left for her mysterious appointment this afternoon, Gabe could see that Evers felt protective of her. Or maybe that was just possessive.

Not that he blamed Evers in the slightest for feeling that way. Juliette St. Claire was one fine-looking woman. The kind that would make every man's head turn as she walked into a room, no matter how immersed they were in conversation.

Those were the kind of women, in his experience, who felt confident that they could get away with anything once they set their minds to it. Including breaking the law.

"Not this time, honey," Gabe murmured under his breath.

With the evening stretching before him, he began a slow, systematic search of his small apartment. Gabe doubted if there was anything to find here, but it never hurt to cover all bases. He intended to cover every square inch of the gallery just in case.

Too bad he couldn't do the same with Julie.

A half smile curved his mouth as he thought of her. Granted it had been less than two days, but he was usually pretty good about forming accurate opinions about people. In her case, it was different. He wasn't sure just what to make of her yet. On the surface, she seemed open enough.

Friendly, warm, all those good adjectives that made a man trust a woman.

But she hadn't volunteered anything more at dinner than he already knew about her. The scant information she had given him was the same given in the thumbnail bio on the back of one of the gallery brochures.

Gabe wanted more. He wanted to get into her life, become an integral part of it so that she would let her guard down, speak more freely. Let him find out just how far she was involved in all this. Was it somehow just happening around her without her knowledge, or was Juliette St. Claire up to her pretty little neck in illegal drug trafficking?

He didn't know, but he was damn well going to find out.

It was a tough assignment, what with its potentially abbreviated deadline, but he figured he was up to it.

The reflection in the bureau mirror grinned back at him. He was thinking of the way she'd looked when he'd caught her earlier in her kitchen, her eyes a little dazed, her hair just the slightest bit tousled.

The lady had trouble written all over her in big, bold letters that were five feet tall. Five feet, three inches, he amended. And trouble came with a hell of a tempting invitation.

It was a dirty job, but someone had to do it.

"You can't do this."

The high-pitched wail had Julie hurrying from the floor of the main gallery to her office in the rear. This morning Mike had apparently appropriated it. His face was a mask of pure horror as she came running in.

Mike was clutching the telephone receiver in both hands as if squeezing a retraction of whatever he'd heard that had given him such obvious grief.

"But we'll be ruined. St. Claire's can't take this kind of

a setback. You have to—'' Words failed him as he looked up at Julie helplessly.

Mike had always been a little temperamental and high strung, but she had never seen him like this before. Concerned, she laid a hand on his shoulder. ''Mike, what is it?''

Instead of explaining, he thrust the receiver at her. ''Talk to them, make them understand,'' he pleaded as if this affected him more than her. ''They can't do this. We'll be ruined.'' Renewed horror washed over his thin, angular features. His legs no longer supporting him, Mike sank into the chair like a puppet whose strings had been severed. ''Oh, my God, we'll be ruined.''

This was melodramatic, even for Mike. Julie covered the receiver and looked at him sternly in an attempt to get him to pull himself together.

''Stop hyperventilating and tell me what's wrong.''

But he couldn't. Words had suddenly failed him, lodging instead in his throat. Mutely, he gestured at the telephone.

Left with no alternative, Julie spoke into the receiver. ''Hello? Who is this?''

An irritated voice responded. ''This is Agent Jenkins from the U.S. Customs Office. Who am I speaking to?''

Customs. She immediately thought of the paintings in transit for their upcoming show. The paintings that should have already arrived. The ones for the St. Claire gala. She was beginning to comprehend the reason for Mike's hysteria.

''This is Juliette St. Claire.''

''Oh, the owner of the gallery.'' The voice on the other end was prim and reedy. Julie couldn't easily tell if it belonged to a man or a woman. The range made it impossible to tell. ''I was just informing Mr. Evers that we are going to have to hold the paintings in quarantine at Long Beach for at least two weeks, perhaps longer.''

St. Claire's invitations had not only gone out but had been returned with enthusiastic promises of attendance. A complete new crop of collectors was about to descend on her gallery, anticipating seeing and possibly buying paintings that now, apparently, weren't going to be there.

Julie turned her back to Mike. His pained expression was distracting her. "Quarantine? Why? What happened?"

The person sighed. Apparently this was a second-run through for them. "One of the sailors on the ship bringing your cargo over from Europe has come down with what appears to be some sort of unusual virus. It may or may not be contagious and until we assess the situation, no one is being allowed off the ship at the moment."

It sounded like a scenario from some sort of TV movie of the week. But these kinds of things didn't really happen in real life. Did they? "But the paintings aren't people."

An unintelligible noise dripping with disapproval echoed in her ear. "Be that as it may, everything is staying exactly where it is, Ms. St. Claire, until such time as we feel it is safe to release. The quarantine includes the cargo. You have a few paintings at stake, we have the welfare of the country to think of. The government is not about to risk an epidemic of who knows what proportions because a buyer at some gallery is throwing a tantrum."

Julie sighed. She was surprised that the strains of "The Battle Hymn of the Republic" didn't come echoing out of the telephone to accompany the terse lecture. Of course the agent had a valid point, but that didn't change the fact that the person was being a pompous ass about it, she thought in disgust.

But she knew there was nothing she could do. She was stuck.

"I understand. Please call me the moment the quarantine is lifted." Feeling like someone who had just discovered they were working without a net over shark-infested waters, Julie hung up the receiver.

"What are we going to do?" Mike wailed.

She lifted one shoulder in a half shrug. What could they do? "We wait."

"Trouble?"

She turned to see Gabe standing in the doorway. Had he heard Mike's cry of despair all the way upstairs?

"Big time." She looked at Mike. He looked like someone who had just been told he had less than a week to live. "Although it's not as big a tragedy as all that, Mike—"

He looked up at her. "Julie, we have all those big-time collectors coming. McCaffee, Hernandez. Joseph Klein. If we don't produce the paintings they're expecting, we'll lose their patronage. Not to mention our credibility. Again."

The last word had an ominous ring to it. Gabe looked from Evers to Julie. "What do you mean, 'again'?"

Mike's face darkened. "Nothing to concern yourself about," he snapped. Suddenly jumping to his feet, he looked as if he wanted to move Gabe forcibly out of the room.

Gabe ignored him. "I'd like to help," he said to Julie.

She didn't see how. Julie shook her head at the offer. "The only way you could help right now is if you knew a few Customs officials to bribe. Most of the paintings that are to be in the gallery show at the end of the month are now tied up in Customs." She glanced accusingly at the telephone. "Indefinitely."

This was just getting better and better, wasn't it? Pregnant, with a galleryful of people arriving at the end of the month to preview empty walls. That made two strikes.

Julie was afraid to contemplate if she was in line for a third.

Chapter 6

Julie didn't have too long to think about it.

As she came to view it later, the third strike that knocked her completely out of the ballpark arrived the following afternoon via the telephone, on the heels of a marathon calling session in which the receiver had all but gotten glued to her ear.

Determined to untangle at least part of the web spun by the Customs office, Julie had been on and off the phone that was located in the main gallery for the better part of the day. Most of the time had been spent on hold, or playing Russian roulette with recorded messages that gave her endless menus, endless choices only to culminate in an endless headache. Frustrated, she hung up.

"That doesn't sound good."

Head swinging around, Julie looked over her shoulder at Gabe, biting back terse retorts that were motivated strictly by aggravation.

After sending Mike off to sweet-talk Customs, she'd put

Gabe to work on the banister early this morning. But he'd absentmindedly left the door between the foyer and the gallery open, and she'd been aware of his watching her off and on.

There was something about his gaze that seemed a little more than just cursory, a little deeper than just curious.

She was just tired, Julie told herself. Tired and imagining things.

All those creative genes had to go somewhere, she mused.

Feeling the need to regroup before she became a complete shrew, Julie blew out a long, cleansing breath before she spoke. It helped—marginally. "That's because it isn't good," she admitted truthfully.

Abandoning his tools and taking an impromptu break, Gabe got up and wiped his hands on the back of his jeans before crossing to her. "They tell you no dice?"

"'They' didn't tell me anything. I can't get anyone with a pulse on the other end of the line to talk to me for more than five seconds." Jenkins, the agent who had spoken to her yesterday, was conveniently out for the day. Everyone else down there seemed bent on giving her the roundaround.

Feeling the edges of her temper getting more frayed just talking about it, Julie struggled to reinstitute control. It was an effort doomed to failure—just like her attempts to find someone to talk to her.

"Everything's recorded. Every time I press a key, I get another damn 'menu' offering me choices. I don't want lunch, I want to talk to someone." Well, that cleansing breath hadn't lasted very long, she thought. Julie looked at him, the corners of her mouth turning up in a rueful, apologetic smile. "Sorry."

"For what?" He laughed at the idea that she actually thought she had something to apologize for. In his book this didn't even come close to a display of temper. The woman had obviously led a sheltered existence. "Blowing off steam?" Leaning forward, he brushed back a strand of her hair from her face with the tip of his finger. "Hey, news flash, you're human. You're allowed to do that once in a while. At least you didn't punch your fist through a painting."

His smile seemed incredibly soft, given the muscular portions of the rest of him, Julie thought. "Is that what you do when you get angry?"

"No, not me." He didn't want her thinking he had a temper. He wanted her to trust him so he could get the information he needed without resorting to coercion. "But I know an artist who does."

"Who?"

Absolutely no one came to mind who he could safely offer to her. Stuck, Gabe grinned engagingly. "No one you've heard of."

"If he punches out all his paintings, small wonder." With a resigned sigh, Julie turned back to the telephone, bracing herself for another trip through the never-ending maze.

Unwilling to give up the tiny crack that was beginning to open up, allowing him a small view into her world, Gabe moved around her desk so that he was in front of her again. He placed his hand over hers, noting with a touch of male satisfaction that a pulse jumped in her throat.

"Why don't I get you some tea? You look as if you could use it."

Julie retracted her hand. She stared at him, mystified. "What, do you read minds, too?"

His eyes washed over her quickly, efficiently. Stirring her. "No, just tense shoulders. Yours look as if you're carrying the weight of the world on them—and that they're about to buckle under the burden."

"Not the world," she corrected simply. "Just St. Claire's."

Because he felt a sudden desire to feather his fingers along her cheek, Gabe tucked his hands into his back pockets. "Even so…" His voice trailed off as he went into the kitchenette set up in the back room.

Julie tried not to stare at where his hands were as Gabe walked away. Or how rhythmically they were retreating.

"Well, stop worrying," he advised, continuing as if there'd been no break in the conversation. "Things always have a way of working themselves out."

She used to believe in sentiments like that, she thought. But after what had been happening lately, she was no longer sure.

Julie looked down at the mug as he set it in front of her. Two packets of real sugar, no cream. Just the way she took it. She could only remember sipping tea in front of him once. A pleased, pleasant sensation washed over her as she reached for the mug. Lifting it, she looked at him. "You're very observant."

Gabe was pretty sure she meant it as a compliment and not as an accusation. He shrugged it off. "Most artists are."

Julie thought of Justin, who hadn't even noticed this small detail, much less anything of importance. And of her mother, who hadn't even enough maternal compassion to get in touch with her after she'd buried her father. The funeral had been given publicity and was well attended. There was no way her mother couldn't have known that the man she'd once promised to love and honor had died.

"No, most artists that I've known have tunnel vision." Holding the mug in both hands to warm them, she took a long sip. "They see only what interests them, what applies to their work. Nothing more."

His eyes touched hers. The smile in them slid slowly

into her consciousness, like the tea. "Maybe my scope's larger."

"Maybe."

The telephone rang just then, breaking up the moment and what could have followed.

"Maybe that's Evers to the rescue," Gabe said, backing away.

Pulling herself together, Julie decisively set the mug on the desk. "I certainly hope so."

She picked up the receiver, a silent prayer echoing in her mind. "Good afternoon, St. Claire's Art Gallery. How may I help you?"

As soon as she heard the person on the other end say hello, Julie knew that the third strike she'd been worried about had just become a reality.

It wasn't Mike.

"Jules, is that you?"

Shock gripped Julie with its icy fingers, closing around her and making her numb as she clutched the receiver.

Jules.

Only her mother had ever called her that. Her mother, the woman who had left the day before Christmas Eve without a single word to her. Trusting instead a small white index card with the words "I'm sorry" to cover the huge gaping wound her flight had created.

Clutching the receiver in both hands, Julie could feel the blood draining from her face. In the blink of an eye, she was twelve again, walking into the kitchen, calling out to her mother. Finding only the note. Finding the house and her life empty.

She could feel a strangled cry thickening in her throat.

Gabe was about to walk away and get back to work when he saw Julie's expression. She couldn't have looked paler than if she'd suddenly been confronted with a squadron of marauding bikers.

Was there a drug dealer on the other end of the line? Maybe threatening her?

Instincts part professional, part personal, kicked in. Gabe remained where he was, his eyes on her face. Waiting. Ready.

Julie was aware of nothing and no one, save for the voice on the other end of the line.

"Yes, I'm here," she said hoarsely. "What do you want?"

Elizabeth St. Claire hesitated.

The pause was so long, Julie thought that perhaps the connection had been lost. She fought the impulse to hang up. To run.

"Jules, may I come to see you?" That soft, sweet voice had haunted Julie's dreams for more than a year after her mother had abandoned her. She couldn't brace herself enough to withstand its effect and could feel angry tears forming.

"Jules, may I come to see you?" Elizabeth waited for a reply. When none came, she added in a quiet voice that barely held the lid down on despair, "I have nowhere else to turn."

Julie wanted to say that she didn't care, that her mother had made her bed, now she had to lie in it. She wanted to say a hundred different, hurtful things to pay back in some small measure all the pain she'd felt over the years.

But all the words remained in her throat, unvoiced. Unspoken.

With effort, she tried to focus. Julie had lost all track of her mother. Everyone had. Even the detective her father had hired all those years ago hadn't been able to locate Elizabeth's whereabouts. As far as anyone was concerned, Elizabeth St. Claire had completely vanished, disappeared from the art world. Perhaps even from life itself, no one knew. She hadn't lifted a brush in fifteen years.

Longer.

Control returned, but only in half measures. Julie licked her lower lip, her throat dry. Her eyes moist with anger. "Where are you?"

"Not far from the gallery. May I come to see you?" There was a siren echoing in the background.

Julie realized with a start that she was hearing the same siren passing by St. Claire's now. That meant her mother was perhaps a block away, maybe closer.

"Why did you bother to call?" Julie demanded. She finally became aware of Gabe watching her and turned away, trying to shroud herself in privacy. "Why didn't you just turn up on my doorstep?"

She heard her mother hesitate again before saying, "Because I couldn't bear to have you turn away from me. I had to be sure you would see me."

Wave after wave of bitterness came, engulfing her, refusing to leave her alone. Refusing to let her catch her breath. Julie wanted to scream at her mother, to demand an explanation. How could a mother choose a lover over her own child?

But all she said was, "You were never one to face up to things, were you?"

"Then it's no?" The sorrow in Elizabeth's voice seemed endless. "I don't blame you, Jules. I know that I—"

Julie passed a hand over her eyes, wondering why, after all this time, she was still capable of feeling something for the woman who had abandoned her? Why the emotions hadn't evaporated? She shouldn't be feeling anything anymore. Her mother hadn't. Elizabeth hadn't even once attempted to contact her once in all these years.

Not even out of a morbid sense of curiosity.

With determination, Julie sealed herself off. "You can come," she said, her voice dead.

She cut off the connection before her mother could say

anything further. Staring at the telephone, Julie felt as if
her emotions were running in all directions at once, going
nowhere. Unsettling her beyond belief. Shredding her apart.

Why now, of all times? Why did her mother choose now
to turn up in her life? Didn't she already have enough to
deal with? A good amount of her available capital, not to
mention her reputation, was being held captive in a ship
docked in Long Beach harbor and if that wasn't enough,
she was pregnant to boot.

Since when had her life turned into a modern equivalent
of Job's?

"Are you all right?"

Gabe's voice penetrated the fog that was quickly en-
croaching around her brain. She'd forgotten he was still
standing there. Instead of answering him immediately, Julie
simply waved her hand at the question, as if to make it fade
away.

Her hand felt as if it weighed a thousand pounds. All of
her did.

The room was beginning to close in, its edges painted in
black.

"Put your head between your knees."

She realized he was talking to her, but his voice seemed
disproportionately far away. Julie tried to turn her head in
Gabe's direction, but she couldn't readily locate him. Perspiration was forming a damp crown along her forehead.

"What?" She almost had to push the word out.

His voice hovered somewhere above her head. "You
look like you're going to pass out. Put your head between
your knees." This time, it was an order.

Gabe was more than passingly acquainted with the signs.
She was going to faint dead away unless he did something.
Gently, firmly, he encircled the back of her neck with his
fingers and pressed it down, forcing her to comply with his
instructions.

Barely conscious, Julie didn't resist. She felt blood and awareness rushing down to her head. The darkness receded, and with it, the light-headedness.

Staying in that position a moment longer, Julie dragged air back into her lungs.

Gabe stood beside her, his hand remaining on her neck to keep her from picking her head up too soon. That made twice he'd thought she was going to faint, he realized. There'd been a logical explanation for the first time, but this time had to be because of the call.

"Look, I don't know who just called, but if they threatened you in any way—"

Despite his hand resting on her neck, Julie jerked her head up and stared at him. "What makes you say something like that?"

Gabe cursed his error. Covering, he lifted a shoulder in a vague shrug.

"You turned as pale as a ghost. I thought maybe it was— an obscene phone call." He grasped at the first explanation that came to mind. He couldn't very well say that he suspected her of trafficking in drugs and thought she'd just been threatened by a dealer.

A knight in shining armor—with a tool belt and a paintbrush. It made for an amusing image. Julie smiled. Life worked in very strange ways, she thought, grateful for his concern.

Taking another deep breath and letting it out slowly, Julie shook her head. "No, no obscene phone call." She looked at the telephone. "Actually, I think I would have preferred that."

Gabe was right, it had been the drug dealer. His partner, Ken McCarthy, had told him that there was a tap on the lines that came into the building. It wouldn't be difficult to verify his hunch. He glanced at his watch and made a mental note of the time. He'd call McCarthy the first chance he got.

Hoping her state would make her let something slip, Gabe pressed a little further. "If it wasn't an obscene caller who got you so upset, then who was it?"

It occurred to Julie that he was prying. And that she should tell him that it was none of his business. But Julie suddenly felt as if she needed someone in her corner. For reasons she couldn't quite make out, she'd temporarily decided on him.

"It was—" The front door to the gallery opened. Heart in her throat, Julie turned, knowing who she'd see before she looked. "—My mother."

The words hung in the air like dried mistletoe, a holiday symbol mistakenly forgotten and left behind when the ornaments had been taken down.

Julie looked at the woman who stood in the doorway, fighting feelings of compassion. Elizabeth St. Claire didn't deserve her compassion. She'd given that right up a long time ago.

Her mother was thinner than she remembered. Thinner and older. And worn. The wild, Gypsy-like profusion of golden blond hair was darker now and pulled back in a tight French twist that only emphasized her high cheekbones and her weariness.

The gray coat the woman wore hung on her like a worn regal cape. Gabe couldn't tear his eyes away. Guinevere returning to the ashes of Camelot after Arthur's death and Lancelot's retreat.

It was still raining outside and some of the rain entered with her as Elizabeth St. Claire crossed the threshold she hadn't stepped over in so many years. A multitude of emotions raced over her, fighting to take possession, fighting for position. She'd been happy here once, for a time. And here was where she'd left the one work of art she would always be proud of, always cherish. Juliette.

With all her heart, Elizabeth wanted to take her child into her arms and just hold her. Just breathe in the soft scent of her hair to assure herself that she was finally here.

Home.

Fear of rejection held her fast where she was. "Hello, Jules."

Anger raged within Julie, overpowering the young girl who wanted to throw herself into her mother's arms and tearfully demand an explanation for the years of abandonment. For the very act itself.

How many times had she envisioned her mother walking into the gallery?

How many times had she acted out the scene in her mind, with a thousand different variations, a thousand words coming to her lips?

None occurred to her now. Lifting her head stiffly, Julie returned the greeting without a drop of emotion. "Hello, Mother."

Gabriel looked from one woman to another. It was clear, even if Julie hadn't said the word, that they were mother and daughter. One was an older, far more world-weary version of the other. But just as regal. Just as beautiful. And the eyes... Between the two sets they left the sky devoid of color.

He couldn't remember when he'd been in the presence of this degree of tension before.

Taking the focus off Julie, he moved forward toward Elizabeth, his hand outstretched. "You're Elizabeth St. Claire?"

Appearing surprised and confused, Elizabeth looked at him. "Yes."

When she made no move to shake his hand, he took hers, his strong fingers wrapping themselves around her delicate ones. "It is a real honor to meet you." Playing the part, he thought of the rumors. "Forgive me, but I'd heard that you were dead."

Elizabeth's eyes shifted back to her daughter's face. There was no light there, no sign that there would ever be even a trace of forgiveness. But then, she knew she didn't deserve any.

Her voice was hardly above a whisper when she answered. "I am."

Chapter 7

As a kid, Gabe had been tormented by an older cousin who'd capitalized royally on his fear of things that went bump in the night. A long talk from an older, wiser, and protective Rafe had knocked all thoughts of zombies, werewolves and vampires out of his head. The exorcism had included ghosts, as well.

And even if he'd belonged to that small, stubborn band of true believers who felt that spirits did indeed haunt and roam the earth, the lady in front of him was one of the least likely candidates to be labeled a ghost that he had ever seen.

The only thing ghostlike about her was the haunted aura mantling her thin shoulders.

Gabe looked down at their hands. He was still holding hers and although it felt frail, it also felt very solid. "You certainly look real enough to me," he told her gently.

A hint of a tired smile barely brushed Elizabeth's lips. "The vital signs don't always have to be gone for one to be dead, Mr.—'' She spared half a glance in his direction although for the most part, her eyes were intent on her daughter's face.

Something less than hope, more than hopelessness struggled to rise there. Gabe found himself feeling sorry for the woman without fully understanding why. "Murietta. Gabriel—Gabe,'' he amended.

This was an interesting twist, he thought.

Elizabeth nodded, just marginally aware of the name he'd given her. She was watching her daughter's face, hoping to discern even a hint that there was a drop of love left within Julie's breast. Because only love could offer her forgiveness. Only the presence of love would give her the opportunity to make things right.

"Gabriel,'' Elizabeth murmured. "Like the angel.''

When Elizabeth said his name, it almost did sound celestial, he thought. Despite the circumstances, Gabe could easily see why men had been attracted to the older woman. There was something about her, even now, that drew a man's soul to the fore.

He grinned in response. "Like the angel.'' As an afterthought, he released her hand.

Stepping back, he looked in Julie's direction. Her face was rigid.

Julie felt as if she was suspended somewhere between heaven and hell, in a place with no lights, no road markers to help her find her way out.

Look at her, Julie thought angrily. *Already gravitating toward a man to help her out.*

Though she'd always tried to block them out, her father's words rang in her ears. *Your mother was a slut, ready to go with any man just to make me suffer.*

Julie squared her shoulders, her eyes hard. "Well, Mother, is this a lengthy visit, or will you be running off again without warning?''

Gabe saw that the question hit its mark. Elizabeth's porcelain complexion became almost translucent. He half expected her to sink to the floor, a fragile flower that had been carelessly plucked.

"Lengthy," Elizabeth finally said. "If you'll have me."

"If I'll have you," Julie echoed, her mouth twisting in bitterness, just as her stomach was twisting. Loyalty to her father prompted the next words. "If I'm not mistaken, I'm the wrong gender for that to happen. I suppose that denies me access to a very large club—"

Words, far more caustic than even the ones she'd just uttered, hovered on her tongue, demanding release. Demanding to be allowed to inflict at least some small measure of all the pain she'd borne.

But the slight flinch she detected in her mother's eyes aborted the rest of the words. Julie sighed. She supposed that made her a coward.

"Never mind, we'll work something out," she finally concluded.

There was none of the warmth Gabe had heard in Julie's voice previously. If anything, he would have said that her voice was hollow, devoid of all emotion. Which only told him that there was probably an entire tempest being dammed up.

He sure as hell hoped he wasn't in the vicinity when that dam finally let loose.

Gabe thought of the apartment he was staying in. Maybe he could bunk downstairs in the back room. He'd endured worse on stakeouts, it wouldn't be that much of a hardship. As long as he was on the premises, he could continue his investigation.

"Look, this isn't right," he said to Julie. "She can have—"

He was going to be noble again, Julie thought as she looked at him sharply. "No, I won't have you kicked out

of your apartment, so to speak, twice in the space of—"
Unsure of the time involved, she looked at Gabe expectantly.

"A week," he volunteered.

"A week, right." That meant he'd lived in his van around five days. She'd seen the van. That was enough penance for anyone. "You've already made your down payment on the quarters with what you fixed last night." She drew herself up, talking to him rather than her mother. "I said we'd work something out and we will." There was a spare bedroom in her apartment. It had once been hers before the gallery had been sold and the living space converted. "Given Mother's habits, I'm sure this won't be for long."

Gabe almost winced for the other woman as he looked at her to see the effect of Julie's words.

She appeared composed, though the sadness in her eyes looked as if it was deepening by degrees. "Jules, if this is causing you any hardship—"

Her mother certainly picked a fine time to be concerned. Now, when it didn't matter anymore. Where had her mother been all those years when she'd *really* needed her?

"No, *this* isn't causing me any hardship," Julie denied tersely. "*This* is nothing." Her eyes narrowed into blue rapiers, striking fast and hard. "And it's a little late in the day to be worrying about my feelings, don't you think, Mother?"

Elizabeth withstood every blow, every thrust, knowing she deserved that and more. There had been reasons she'd done what she'd done, reasons that involved Julie, but there was no use in explaining. Not that Julie would understand. Telling her would mean destroying a cornerstone of her daughter's life. It was easier bearing up to the contempt. "Jules."

"Don't call me that. You gave up the right to call me

that a long time ago." She turned toward Gabe, not really looking at him. "Mind the gallery, please, Gabe. I have to show my mother where she'll be staying."

Glancing back at the front door, Julie doubted if anyone would come. They'd passed the peak lunch hour, and it would be a while before the next wave was liable to come.

"It's pretty nasty out. I don't expect anything else will be blowing in," she told him. "If you have trouble, call me. I'll be as quick as I can." Her voice turned as hard, as impersonal as granite. "This way, Mother. I'm sure you still vaguely remember your way around."

Without turning to see if she was being followed, Julie walked up the stairs. The short climb made her feel as if she were walking the last mile to her own execution. Outside, the wind was moaning. Inside, there was only stillness broken up by the sound of footsteps on the wooden stairs.

Not a word passed between them.

At the landing, Julie headed toward her apartment. Realizing that she was standing in front of the door alone, she looked over her shoulder to see why her mother had stopped following her.

A feeling of homecoming had seeped through Elizabeth when she'd stepped through the door of St. Claire's. But the feeling was missing here. There wasn't even a hint of it. Things had been rearranged. Walls and doors had gone up where none had existed before. Where was the broad front room with its library?

Elizabeth felt Julie silently watching her. "You've changed this."

"A lot of things have changed since you left. My apartment's this one."

Elizabeth looked toward the other door before she joined Julie. "And Gabriel lives in that one?"

"Yes." The key stuck as she tried to turn it. Fumbling, she tried again. This time it turned and the lock gave. She'd forgotten to mention this to Gabe, she thought. Her thoughts were still scattering and regrouping like lost urchins in a storm.

"He seems nice." Elizabeth walked into the apartment, looking around. Grays and blues were everywhere. Her favorite colors. She wondered if Julie remembered that. She turned toward her daughter. There were so many questions. So many things she was so hungry to know. "Is he your—?"

Julie resented even the smallest personal question. Her mother had no right to ask questions, no right to any information about her at all. Her mother had been the one to cut off communications, not her. The one to keep the lines down. She'd been alive all this time and never so much as a word.

Damn her.

"Artist," Julie snapped. "He's an artist, Mother. Just someone down on his luck and trading work for a place to stay."

Where had you been all this time, Mother? Why didn't you have the decency to call, to ask me how I was? To tell me you were alive?

Turning to face Elizabeth, her hand fisted on her waist, Julie demanded, "Any other questions?"

Elizabeth shook her head, retreating. "No."

The look she saw on her mother's face threatened to cut through the anger she felt. But she wasn't going to fall for the act, Julie promised herself.

Turning away, Julie led her to the spare bedroom. Opening the door, she remained outside. "You can stay here if you'd like."

Elizabeth pressed her lips together. Her eyes filled with tears as she remembered. Remembered so much. Remembered what she had surrendered because there was no other way. She kept her face averted, not wanting Julie to see. "Thank you."

The expression of gratitude was meaningless to Julie. "Well, I've got work to do." She began to back out of the room.

Leaving, she was almost at the outer door when she heard her mother's voice. "Jules, I'm sorry."

Julie stiffened.

Sorry. As if the word was enough to wipe away everything. Enough to wipe away years of pain. Once, it might have been. But not any longer. Now it would take much more before the rent was mended. She doubted if it ever would be.

"Fine," Julie said crisply, turning toward her mother. "Well, we got that out of the way. Now, if you'll excuse me—"

"Yes, of course." Elizabeth hesitated. "You're a lot like him, you know."

Julie tightened her hand on the doorknob. "A lot like who?"

"Your father."

That made her turn around again. Julie's eyes narrowed as she regarded her mother. "How would you know?" she demanded, her anger spilling over, scalding her. "You weren't around to know what he was like, what he became because of you. But I was." Her hand was wrapped so tightly around the doorknob, she was surprised she didn't snap it off. "And I had to take care of him. He was that helpless without you, that destitute. I never got a chance to be a teenager, Mother. To enjoy what you had enjoyed. I had to grow up fast because you couldn't grow up at all."

Each word felt like a knife piercing her heart, Elizabeth thought, reopening wounds that had never properly healed. "Juliette—"

She wasn't going to stand here and let her mother fill

her head with excuses and lies. There was no point, anyway. What was done was done.

"I have to go," Julie repeated, clamping down on her emotions again. "There're towels and extra linens in the closet." Julie waved in the general direction. "Food in the refrigerator. Help yourself to whatever it is you want."

With that, she left.

And because she felt like crying, she forced herself to get hold of her emotions before she went back downstairs. With a start, she realized she could have saved herself the effort.

Gabe was at the bottom of the stairs, working. Belatedly, she realized that he had probably overheard a great deal more than she would have wanted him to. As if she wasn't uncomfortable enough...

He moved out of her way as she walked past him.

Gabe watched Julie as she made her way to the desk in the front. Toying with a decision, he threw the wrench into the toolbox. It landed on the other tools with a warning clatter as he crossed to her.

She made him think of someone lost. Someone who needed to be held.

Hooking his thumbs in his belt loops, he looked at Julie until she finally raised her head. "You were pretty hard on her, weren't you?"

Julie was right, her mother had already managed to weave a web around Gabe. It didn't take long. She felt a tinge disappointed. She'd have thought he wasn't that much of a pushover.

"Hard on her? Hard on *her?*" she demanded incredulously. "How about how hard she's been on me? How hard she made my life? You have no idea—" Abruptly, Julie stopped. No way did she want to go into all that. "Don't butt in where you don't belong."

He had every intention of butting in. He needed to get

close to Julie, and this seemed like the perfect opening. If the look in her eyes served as partial motivation, he didn't consciously admit it to himself.

"You're right. I don't have any idea. But I do know she's your mother, and we only get one of those when we go around in life."

Julie's mouth nearly fell open. If anything, she'd expected him to take up the damsel-in-distress's fallen colors, be her champion. Not get nostalgic about Mom and apple pie.

Just how many curves was this man going to throw? "This from a rebel?"

Gabe played that angle, though no one had had a more loving upbringing than he and his brother. His mother had been part saint, part magician and probably one of his best friends, even when it hadn't been cool to admit the fact. He'd been well into his teens before he realized that everyone wasn't as fortunate as he and Rafe had been.

"Maybe it's because I am a 'rebel' and went through it that I can say this. Don't say things you might not be able to take back when you come to your senses and want to."

"What makes you think I'd want to take them back?"

"Because you're a caring person." He refused to rise to the challenge in her voice. He wasn't about to trade hot words with her. The thought of hot words momentarily dragged his thoughts in other directions, to other, hotter exchanges, but he reined them back. "Because you're not the kind to bear a grudge."

Her mouth hardened. "Try me."

He'd like to. Until this second, seeing her with fire in her eyes, Gabe hadn't realized just how much he'd like to. But those kinds of feelings would only ultimately get in his way. He had to remember to keep a very tight rein on himself and only use the moments, and the emotions that were in them, to his advantage. To the investigation's advantage, he amended.

There was something just a little off-putting about the utilitarian slant. He ignored the slight bad taste that rose in his mouth.

Instead, he smiled down into her face, and moved aside the one wanton strand that insisted on straying into her eyes. Funny how something so simple stimulated him.

"Later."

The word whispered along Julie's skin like a promise. It took effort to pull her head back, away from his touch, but she did.

The very last thing she needed in her life right now was one more complication.

She rose to her feet, and found that there was no breathing space between them. She created some, part of her wishing that she didn't.

"Don't lecture me as if you know me. You don't know the first thing about me."

"Wrong." Unwilling to retreat, Gabe followed her as she began to move through the gallery. "There's your reputation, remember? I say they were right on the money about you." When she turned to look at him quizzically, he added, "I'm a pretty good judge of character."

"I don't know about that." Julie involuntarily glanced toward the stairs. "You're on her side." Crossing to the rear door, she closed it, and with it, blocked the view of the stairs leading up to the apartments. To her mother.

He turned her around to face him, surprising her at the familiarity of his touch. At the way something inside her responded even in the middle of what she would have called an argument.

"If I'm on anyone's side, Julie, it's yours." His eyes touched hers. "I just know what it's like to leave things unsettled."

She raised her chin like a warrior. "They're settled."

"Can you honestly look at yourself in the mirror and still say that?"

Her temper broke loose of its confinement.

"Look, she walked out on me, I didn't walk out on her. She was the one who ran off with her lover and never even had the decency to try to get in contact with my father or with me. She never even so much as hinted that she was sorry. Never came out of the woodwork when my father died to even attend his funeral—or to be there for me when I needed her."

Fed up, furious, she realized that she was almost shouting. With effort, she lowered her voice, but not the level of her emotions.

"Things are settled, all right, and she was the one who settled them." She looked toward the telephone. It was time she got back to work. Her mother had disrupted enough. "Now if you'll excuse me, I have a gallery to try to save." Pushing past him, she went to her desk and sat.

Julie got halfway through dialing the number to the Customs office when she stopped, muttered something unintelligible and not very flattering under her breath and hung up.

Turning her chair around to face where he'd gone back to working, she looked at Gabe. "Look, I'm sorry. My emotions are a little off lately."

Gabe paused, the smile on his face absolving her of the need for any further apologies. "That's okay. We all have our bad days."

"How about a bad month?" Frustration filled her voice. Frustration not just over the situation, over the deadlock on the phone she couldn't break, or her mother's sudden, untimely, knocking-her-for-a-loop return, but at the fatigue that kept assaulting her. Like a hijacker lying in wait, it would pop out of nowhere, take hold and then squeeze all the energy right out of her.

Sitting back on his heels, he studied Julie's expression. "Just how important are those paintings on the ship?"

Where was all her enthusiasm? Julie demanded silently. She'd been so determined just before her mother had appeared. Even though she wanted to, she couldn't lay all the blame at her mother's feet. This was the work of hormones, pure and simple. Hormones that were ravaging her and making her life miserable. Someone should have outlawed hormones a long time ago.

"Does the word bankruptcy mean anything to you?"

Gabe let out a low whistle. "That bad?" It was an easy enough thing to check. He'd have McCarthy run a credit check on St. Claire's and on Julie. Desperation would be reason enough to get involved with drug traffickers.

"Close." Even as she elaborated, Julie tried not to dwell on the actual significance of the words. "I have most of my available cash flow, not to mention a tidy sum that is best left untouched, invested in those paintings. Or rather, the sale of those paintings plus the new buyers that the paintings would attract to the gallery."

As an artist, Julie conceded, he probably had no concept about the financial measures that were involved. To him, it undoubtedly all ended with the sale of a painting. "A whole new caliber of collectors. The kind of buyers my father only dreamed about when he bought St. Claire's to begin with."

"And all that will be lost if you don't get the paintings here on time?"

"Let's say collectors like having something to collect. They get a little testy about being drawn away from the comforts of their homes for no reason. I'd be cast in the role of the little boy who cried wolf. In this case, the 'wolf' would be the paintings."

"Postpone the show."

If it were only that easy. Julie shook her head. "Can't. I have to make a least a couple of sales to pay off an installment on the note I floated to get those paintings."

Though he was free with his money when he had it, Gabe never spent what he didn't have. He couldn't understand what possessed people who did. "Why extend yourself that far?"

"If you don't risk, you don't win. I wanted to bump St. Claire's up a notch, and Mike thought these paintings would do it. He was very excited when he called me from France about the new paintings." The excitement had been contagious. He'd gone off with the intention of finding one, perhaps two paintings. Instead, he'd returned with twenty after she'd wired him the money. Like the optimist she inherently was, Julie kept a positive attitude about it. "He's generally right in his assessments."

She sounded so sincere when she spoke, Gabe was tempted to believe her. Believe that there was nothing else going on at St. Claire's but the show, the sales. But he knew that there was something else going on. Too many things pointed toward it.

Were the paintings being held up in Customs part of it? Or were they just the camouflage to get the right people together for a more lucrative, darker purpose? Right now, he didn't know. The best way to go was to make the paintings available.

If worse came to worst, he could probably ask the captain to pull a few strings and have Customs agree to release the paintings. It was a last resort, but maybe it could be arranged if Customs could be convinced that it meant bringing down a drug ring and cutting off a major source.

She looked anxious to get this resolved. He backed away. "Well, then, I'd better let you get back to your work."

The way Julie felt right now, facing more recordings and

more menus did not hold out an allure. She watched him pick up a hammer. "How's the banister coming along?"

He ran the flat of his hand along the railing. "I should have it fixed in another half hour."

Julie forced herself to draw her eyes away from his hand. And her mind away from wondering how that hand would feel gliding along her skin just like that.

She sat again. "If you're not doing anything else after that, I'd appreciate you taking a look at my lock. It's suddenly sticking."

Sticking wasn't the problem, Gabe thought. When he'd worked open the lock, he'd slipped and inadvertently jimmied it. He hadn't had the time to rectify the error before she'd arrived.

"Sure thing," he promised with a smile. With any luck, he'd be able to poke around a little more before she came upstairs.

Sometimes things worked themselves out to his satisfaction.

Chapter 8

Gabe carefully moved the paintings in the back room one by one, placing them against the far wall. Julie had decided that she wanted shelves installed all along one wall, and he couldn't even get close enough to the wall to make measurements.

It occurred to him that each painting represented someone's unrealized dreams. He'd almost cleared the space when he stumbled across a half-finished painting. Because of its incomplete state, there was no signature, but there didn't have to be. Gabe recognized the style, the composition and the strokes. It was one of Elizabeth's.

He wasn't in awe of artists, regarding them without the reverence some had attracted, but as the age-old saying went, he knew what he liked. And he liked Elizabeth St. Claire's work.

"What a shame you stopped," he murmured, putting the painting aside again.

He thought of bringing the unfinished work to Julie's

attention, but then decided against it. After only a short time here, he'd formed the opinion that Julie was the type to be on top of everything. She was undoubtedly aware that the unfinished work was here. And it wasn't part of his job to bring mother and daughter together. They were going to have to accomplish that on their own.

His job was to spy. It was beginning to feel that way, with all the dark undertones that the word implied. He was spying on her. Spying to gather information that would exonerate her. Or incriminate her. So far, it was leaning to the latter, and he found himself chafing against the evidence.

Rummaging through the desk in her office, he'd uncovered a list of guests she'd invited to the showing. Prominent was the name Klaus Von Buren, a known drug dealer of growing proportions. No incriminating evidence had ever seemed to be enough to support the charges against him. The man, apparently, was encased in Teflon.

But even non-stick coatings eventually wear thin. Over time, things began to stick. Maybe Von Buren's time had come, Gabe thought.

Certainly his and Julie's hadn't. Surprised by the stray thought, he blocked it out.

Looking around the room, Gabe realized that he hadn't come across the two paintings he'd brought with him as his cover. Curious, he went out into the gallery to see if Julie had hung them there. Odd that he wouldn't have noticed.

But there was nothing to notice. The paintings weren't anywhere in the gallery.

Busy talking with Mike, Julie was distracted by Gabe's entering the main gallery. She looked in his direction. "Can I help you find something?"

He was about to shake his head, then thought that it

would look better if he were to seem curious about the fate of his paintings.

Crossing to her, he assumed the proper sheepish/brash expression suited to an artist impatiently standing on the threshold of "discovery."

"I noticed you didn't hang either one of my paintings up. Did you change your mind?"

Julie smiled. She was surprised that it had taken him this long to notice. For an artist, he was strangely and pleasantly devoid of all ego. It was a really nice change. "No, I didn't. I've decided to save them for the show."

Mike's eyes widened in astonishment behind his rimless glasses. This was the first he'd heard of her plans. "The big show? The one we're having at the end of the month with the paintings from Europe?"

She didn't have to look in his direction to know the look that was on his face. "The way it looks right now, it might just be a very little 'big show.' Gabe's paintings might be the only new ones we have to display."

"You can't do that." His protest was embedded in a whine.

"You don't think they're good?" It was intended as a serious question on her part. Although Mike had let her know in no uncertain terms how much he disliked having Gabe on the premises, he hadn't said one word about the paintings. She had come to believe that they had similar views when it came to spotting potential.

"I really didn't pay that much attention to them."

Julie took his hand. "Well, then, come and pay attention."

Things like social amenities had never stopped Mike from speaking his mind. And, to his credit, Julie knew prejudice had never interfered with his giving an honest appraisal. All impressions to the contrary, Mike Evers was impartial when he looked at a painting, somehow being able to magically separate his feelings from his judgment.

So when she brought him over to where she'd temporarily stored Gabe's work and waited for his verdict, Mike stood back and looked from one painting to the other before giving his opinion.

"I'll agree they have a certain flair, a certain exuberance that manifests itself somewhat intriguingly." He spared a condescending glance toward Gabe. "Although personally I would suggest a little more attention be paid to form."

He was hedging. "Give me a yes or no answer," Julie prodded.

Lips pursed, Mike studied the paintings more intently. "All right, yes. I suppose it wouldn't do any harm displaying them during the show." That said, he had to qualify his approval. "But I'd suggest placing them somewhere toward the back."

"Best for last?" Tongue in cheek, Gabe couldn't resist needling the man a little.

Mike drew himself up haughtily, squaring shoulders that were his mostly through the courtesy of a good tailor. "Hardly." In his opinion, the work was far superior to the artist, and Gabriel Murietta badly needed to be put in his place. "After feasting on the main course, a little after-dinner mint might be enjoyed."

"After-dinner mints, eh?" Amusement lifted the corners of Gabe's mouth.

It was a dangerous smile in Julie's opinion. Maybe he wasn't as devoid of ego as she'd first thought.

Accustomed to dealing with artistic temperament, Julie easily slid in between the two men. Ever the peacemaker, she turned toward Gabe.

"I love mints. They serve a very useful function. But I was thinking more along the lines of dessert myself." She heard Mike make a small, strangled noise that sounded just this side of mocking. Typical Mike, but she wasn't sure just how Gabe would react to large doses. Better safe than sorry. "Mike, why don't you go back to the Customs office and see if maybe you can't shake someone's tree down there? Maybe they'll get tired of being bothered and just give us the crates to get rid of us."

"You've got that right." He took his umbrella from the stand. The rain, no longer fierce, nevertheless showed no signs of letting up. It had been raining steadily now for more than a week and it didn't help his mood. "Every last one of them is evolutionarily stunted." The door shut behind him, punctuating his disdain.

Gabe turned to Julie, an incredulous look on his face. Talk about being pompous. "What the hell is 'evolutionarily stunted'?"

A smile curved Julie's mouth. "That's just Mike's way of being superior."

Gabe had another word for it. "He'd better watch out or someone is not going to notice that he's wearing glasses and volunteer to rearrange his face."

Julie studied Gabe's face. There was sensitivity there, but it was coupled with strength. She doubted if anyone ever made the mistake of underestimating him. "Like you?"

"Me?" Gabe pretended to be surprised by the assumption, though he wouldn't have minded putting a scare into the little snob. "No, he doesn't faze me. I grew up with an older brother and a houseful of cousins coming and going. I've got a hide you can't pierce with an elephant gun."

What was that like? Julie wondered. To be surrounded by teasing, loving siblings and relatives instead of living in an adult world, treated, for the most part, like a forgotten, unnecessary appendage? She would have loved to have the opportunity to find out.

Not possible. There was only the present. And the future,

which was looking pretty shaky from all directions at the moment.

"If I didn't know better," she said to him, "I'd say that sounds suspiciously like a challenge."

"No one to challenge here." Gabe saw what appeared to be a hint of disappointment in Julie's eyes. Something stirred within him. Something he would have rather left alone. "A man would be a fool to risk being thrown out on his ear for making an unsuccessful pitch to the lady who was generous enough to take him in."

Julie tried to read between the lines, to see this as nothing more than a harmless flirtation. But even that could be dangerous.

Despite her common sense, she found herself taking another step along the tightrope. "So it's already a forgone conclusion that the pitch would be unsuccessful? Is that how you keep your elephant hide intact? By not venturing out on the range?"

Gabe tried to remind himself that they were only exchanging banter. That there was nothing behind the words. That the curiosity about her, about the way she'd feel beneath his lips, beneath his body, had no place here. "If I ventured, would I be stepping into quicksand?"

"Depends on your definition of quicksand." The teasing tone faded. Something turned very still inside her as Julie looked up into his eyes. She could hear her heart beating. Could he? "I guess you're just going to have to venture out and see."

His smile was warm, promising. Filling corners. "Maybe I will."

It was time to retreat. Before she discovered that she was standing on nothing but air and plummeted to her death. "In the meantime, why don't you tell me what you're working on?"

"Working on?" Why was she asking him that? Gabe

had already given her the receipt for the lumber he'd bought at the barnlike hardware store this morning. "The shelves you wanted. It's going to take me a little time—"

She laughed, shaking her head. "Not that, your *work*. Your real work." When he looked at her blankly, she stressed, "Painting."

"Oh." His mind scrambled for a plausible reason to give her as to why he hadn't yet put brush to canvas. "I'm waiting for inspiration to hit me."

"A muse to sit on your shoulder?" she suggested, tucking her tongue into her cheek.

She saw right through him, though luckily not all the way. "Something like that."

Laughing, she cupped his cheek in a gesture intended to only reflect friendship. But contact insisted on something a little more. "My suggestion would be to meet that muse halfway and sketch a few things until something catches fire for you."

His hand covered hers before he could think to restrain the reaction. Suddenly aware of what he was doing, Gabe dropped his hand.

Something had already caught fire for him, but he was trying very hard to ignore it. Off duty, if he'd come across someone like Julie in one of the places he enjoyed frequenting, they would have already been well on their way by now to enjoying one another in every sense of the word.

The attraction, the chemistry, had all been there from the moment he'd walked into the art gallery.

But she wasn't someone he'd met during his off hours. He was very much on duty here, and she was his assignment—or rather, checking out her connection was his assignment—and until such time as she turned out to be uncontaminated, he couldn't risk getting personal. Couldn't even think about getting involved.

Thinking had very little to do with the matter at hand.

And sometimes, things just happened with or without permission. He had a very strong feeling that this might just be one of them.

"Maybe I'll do that," he drawled. If he demurred any more, she might become suspicious, or at the very least, try to get him to come around.

"There're empty canvases in your apartment as well as in the storage room."

"I noticed." He'd moved at least ten of varying sizes when he cleared the space to put up the shelves.

"Feel free to help yourself to one," she invited. "There's an easel in there someplace, too." Julie saw the quizzical look on his face. "It belonged to my mother."

He thought of the woman upstairs. Their paths hadn't crossed since that first day, but Gabe didn't feel right about using something that belonged to her without permission. "Won't she mind?"

In her present state, Julie doubted that her mother had enough emotion within her to mind anything. "I don't think she'll be making use of it anytime soon."

When he'd looked into Elizabeth's eyes, Gabe had had the distinct feeling that the woman was haunted by something. "Might be good for her if she did."

Julie's mouth hardened as she stepped away from Gabe's paintings and walked back toward her desk. "A lot of things might be good that never happen. If my mother had wanted to paint again, she wouldn't have waited until she came back here to start."

"Maybe she came back to start," he suggested. Julie turned to look at him in disbelief. Gabe elaborated. "Maybe the memories here are good ones for her and she's trying to recapture that."

"I don't think you should try adding psychologist to your résumé," she advised coolly. "If the memories were that good, she wouldn't have left in the first place."

She seemed determined to try to hate her mother. He had a feeling that what she was looking for was something to hang on to, something to point her in the right direction. He wasn't sure why he felt he had to give it to her. "Sometimes we don't know what we have until we lose it."

Julie looked at him with interest. Was there someone in his past, a woman he'd loved and lost, or walked away from, only to regret it? It occurred to her that she still didn't know very much about him. Usually it took very little for her to become well entrenched in someone's life history. For all his friendliness, Gabe was rather close-mouthed.

"Speaking from personal experience?"

Gabe wasn't. There wasn't a single woman in his past he regretted no longer being with. But he thought better of denying it. He might hold her interest more if she thought he was. "And if I am?"

Julie wanted to make it clear to him that she was a friend, someone he could trust. Someone he could turn to if he needed to. "I might be interested in hearing about it sometime."

His grin erased any serious moment in the making. "No woman likes hearing about another woman."

Julie winked. "I'm not your average run-of-the-mill woman."

No, she wasn't, he thought. She wasn't an average anything.

The bell that went off when the front door was opened interrupted them. They looked in unison as the small woman slipped out of the gallery.

Julie glanced at her watch. Three. "Like clockwork," she murmured. Since her return, for the most part her mother kept to the rooms upstairs. But she left the building at the same time each day.

Curious, Gabe looked back to Julie. "Where does she go every afternoon?"

She shrugged the question off, trying very hard to appear careless. "To hell and back, I would imagine." The front door opened again. Turning, she saw a well-dressed older couple enter. "Ah, customers. Off to earn the mortgage payment."

Gabe watched, fascinated, as she crossed to the couple, a sunny smile emerging on her face. All thoughts of her mother appeared to have been erased.

Could she turn it off and on like that? Or was that just something she wanted him to think? Not having anything to guide him, Gabe let the question go for the time being.

With Julie occupied, Gabe returned to the storage area, then made his way out the back door. It might prove handy to know just where Elizabeth St. Claire went each day around three.

Grabbing an umbrella he'd unearthed in the room, he hurried off in the direction he'd seen the woman take and got lucky. Elizabeth was only a block ahead of him. Because she walked so slowly, he had to curtail his own gait not to catch up to her.

Two blocks later, he saw her slip into a church. Its side draped in dropcloths and buffered by a scaffold, the building was only partially through an extensive retrofit and renovation program. The church was one of the oldest buildings in the city.

Gabe counted to ten before he entered the church himself.

The outside noise seemed unable to penetrate the soft tranquillity within the church. For the most part, it was empty, with only a few people scattered here and there amid the two long rows of pews. Keeping to the side, he passed a confessional, its light dimmed, before he finally saw her. A lone figure lost in prayer at the altar.

He stood and watched her, a part of him waiting to see if Elizabeth was meeting anyone here. After five years on the force, Gabe was a cop clear down to his bones. He viewed very little without at least a trace of suspicion. He'd given up a large chunk of his youthful idealism, losing it on the battlefield in the war against crime, against violence and against drugs. He figured it was worth it, but there were times he missed taking things at face value.

No one met her.

Elizabeth didn't stay long. Perhaps fifteen minutes before she rose from her knees. Making the sign of the cross, she retreated from the altar. A look of recognition followed by one of surprise filtered through her eyes as she approached the rear of the church and saw him.

"I miss the altar railings," she said wistfully. "They used to have altar railings."

"Progress isn't always a good thing," he agreed, falling into step beside her. "Mind if I walk you back?"

She smiled at him with an expression that made him think of Julie. "I'd like that." Elizabeth gathered her coat to her as he opened the door. The chill went right through her. "Did Julie send you?"

Holding the door open for Elizabeth, he waited until she stepped through before joining her. "No, curiosity did. I noticed you leave the gallery every day at the same time."

With him beside her, he noticed that she walked a little more briskly now than she had earlier. "Very observant. I always liked that church. I find it very soothing being there."

"You painted it once." He'd been thorough in his homework. *"The Haven."*

"Why, yes, I did." It always surprised Elizabeth when someone was familiar with her work. Fame was something she'd never wanted. All she'd ever wanted to do was sit in a corner somewhere and be allowed to paint. But Miles had had other ideas. And when the fame had come, what little happiness there had been between them disappeared. "How nice of you to remember."

She seemed so unassuming, it was hard for Gabe to reconcile the fact that this was the same woman who had launched such a furor with her abrupt disappearance. "Why don't you paint anymore?"

The sadness in her eyes deepened. "I have nothing more to give. To paint, you have to want to say something, to give something." She regarded the people on the street around them before turning to look at Gabe. She would have gladly traded her life for any of theirs. "I feel very empty inside, Mr. Murietta."

"Gabe," he corrected softly. He found himself moved. And sympathetic. "When something's empty, you just have to find things to fill it with."

The simplicity of the statement made her smile. He meant well, but he was so young. So untried. "It's not like an empty refrigerator, Gabe."

"Maybe not a refrigerator," he agreed. "But empty vessels can be filled again." Stopping at the corner, he pressed the pedestrian light and waited for the signal that allowed them to cross. It gave him time to study the petite woman beside him. "You just have to want to try."

Maybe that was the key to it. Elizabeth had given up wanting a long time ago. "Maybe I'm too tired."

"You came back," he pointed out.

They walked across quickly. The gallery was just ahead. The wind started picking up even more. "Apparently just to cause my daughter grief."

"My guess is that she just needs time to work things through." It wasn't difficult for Gabe to figure out what Elizabeth was thinking. That Julie didn't love her anymore. But he had seen the struggle in Julie's eyes when her mother had first walked into the gallery. Julie was battling a great many emotions. "You can't cause grief if there's no love."

Elizabeth stopped and looked at him for a long moment. The softness around her mouth reminded him of Julie again. "Where did you gain such insight at your age?"

He wanted to say that he'd come by it honestly, from his parents. Sometimes resisting the lessons that somehow left their mark anyway. But he knew it wasn't the right thing to say here. It would only remind her that she hadn't been there for her daughter.

"I'm a fast study. And knocking around can do that for you."

"You're lucky. All knocking around did for me was leave black and blue marks." She ran her hands up along her arms. The chill didn't leave. "Julie's lucky to have you."

He didn't want her misunderstanding the relationship. "I'm just passing through, Ms. St. Claire."

"Are you now?"

The smile on her face told him that she felt she knew otherwise. He was probably reading too much into it, he thought.

She looked up at the door of St. Claire's as if arriving here came as a surprise to her. "Well, here we are again. Thank you for walking me back."

"My pleasure, Ms. St. Claire."

"Oh, Elizabeth," she corrected. "Please."

He smiled at her. "Elizabeth."

Glancing toward the door when she heard the bell, Julie froze for an instant when she saw them walking in. The last time she'd seen Gabe, he was on his way to the back room to work on the shelves. What was he doing outside with her mother?

"Excuse me, could you tell me a little about this artist?"

The customer's question brought Julie's attention back to the gallery. But only in part.

Because there was no way to ask Gabe what was going on without appearing as if her interest went beyond casual friendship, Julie held on to her questions until that evening. She'd avoided being alone with her mother, coming up only after she was certain her mother had long since gone to bed.

But tonight was different. Tonight she wanted answers so she asked her mother to have dinner with her. It took her more than half an hour before she could find a way to approach the subject. Half an hour spent in relative silence while sharing a meal neither one of them really tasted.

"I saw you with Gabe this afternoon. What were you two talking about?" The words felt as stilted as dried sticks in her mouth. She could talk to anyone else, but when it came to her mother, she couldn't string five coherent words together.

"Just life in general." Rising, Elizabeth cleared away her dish and reached for Julie's. Julie pulled her own plate away and took it to the sink. "He seems to be very insightful." She paused, wondering if she was overstepping another line. It was hard to tell just where she was supposed to remain. "He's very nice."

Was her mother pretending to take an interest in her life? Julie felt something rebelling inside her. "He's just passing through."

The similarity in phrasing made Elizabeth laugh softly to herself. "That was what he said."

So don't let yourself become attracted, Julie warned herself sternly. Shifting the subject away from Gabe, she looked at her mother. "Why haven't you painted?"

She rinsed off her plate. "He asked me the same question."

Julie removed it from the drain board and wiped it instead. "And what did you tell him?"

Elizabeth wiped her hands on the small dish towel. "That I don't have anything to give."

Anger filled Julie. Anger that came from nowhere and made her feel as if she were going to explode. "How do you know until you try?"

"You just know."

"Or think you do," Julie contradicted. "In any event, it makes for a handy excuse to hide behind, doesn't it, Mother?"

The accusation stunned Elizabeth. "I'm not hiding from anything."

But Julie knew differently. All the things she'd never said to her father, she said now. "Oh, yes, you are. You and Father were a pair, you were. Both hiding from life, from taking responsibility for your actions." She clenched her hands at her sides, remembering. "For the repercussions your actions had. You left that up to me to deal with."

Elizabeth became aware of the pain in her daughter's eyes. It sliced through her like a rapier-sharp carving knife. "Oh, my darling, I'm so very sorry. I never meant to hurt you."

The funny thing was, Julie believed her, but knowing didn't help. She could feel tears welling up within her. "You probably didn't even realize you were. I wasn't important enough to you to enter your mind."

"Don't say that," Elizabeth ordered, distressed that Julie should think this way. "You were, you were the most important thing in my life, Jules."

But Julie refused to believe her. Actions spoke louder than protests. And Elizabeth had abandoned her. "Don't stand there, lying to me. I'm not a little girl anymore. I won't stand for it."

Julie pulled back when her mother reached toward her. Upset, she strode away quickly. She needed to get out. To be alone.

The door slipped from her hands and slammed behind her. She didn't care.

Hearing the commotion, Gabe opened his door and saw Julie's back as she hurried down the stairs. A moment later, he heard the front door opening and then closing. What the hell was she thinking, going out this time of night? Didn't she realize it wasn't safe to roam around? Concern for her safety made him increase his speed. This time, he grabbed his jacket before he followed. It got cold here in the evenings.

Chapter 9

Julie had no idea where she was going, only that she needed to get away, to burn off some of the charged emotions that were ricocheting around so wildly within her, threatening to explode.

She had put three blocks between her and St. Claire's before she realized that it was misting again. She could feel the moisture accumulating along her skin, her clothes, her hair, sinking in deeper and deeper.

Dragging her down.

Or were those just her feelings, getting heavier, threatening to weigh her down completely?

It felt as if everything was getting worse, not better. She was pregnant, without a clue as to what lay ahead of her. She was tottering on the edge of possible financial ruin because she'd overextended herself on Mike's say-so. And her mother was back, bringing with her all the old unresolved conflicts Julie had finally managed to bury in the years since her father's death.

Oblivious to where she was going, Julie pushed on in the direction of a strip mall. The lights within the stores that lined the block were dimmed because of the hour. She didn't notice.

Tears burned in Julie's eyes and she blinked them away. Why did her mother have to come back now, of all times? Why couldn't she have come earlier—years earlier? When it would have helped.

When it would have mattered.

Julie had spent six long years since her father died, learning how to stand on her own two feet. In that time, she'd completed her education, saved enough money to buy St. Claire's and make a go of her life.

Had she gone through all that only to end up here, waiting for her life to go up in smoke? To disappear as if it had never even existed?

A sob caught in her throat. She felt as if everything was crumbling around her.

Like a missile fired underwater, she torpedoed ahead with little regard for the people or the streets she passed.

Her mind spun around, catching on fragments of thoughts. What would she do if she lost St. Claire's? If there was only Edmund Raitt involved, she knew that things could be worked out and the art gallery would remain hers. Edmund had sold St. Claire's to her for a down payment of a single dollar. He'd often said he was only "minding" the gallery for her until she could reclaim it again.

But there was a second mortgage on St. Claire's now, and the bank did not have Edmund's patience or his kindness. They wanted returns on their money. Dreams were not considered bankable collateral.

The paintings held up at Customs were, but if she couldn't get her hands on them in time, it wouldn't matter.

Frustration beat savagely in her breast, feeding on helplessness.

Darkest before the dawn, she thought. But right now, dawn seemed a million years away.

"Hey, honey, why don't you come in out of the rain? I've got something here to get you nice and warm."

Startled, Julie looked around, taking in her surroundings for the first time. Somehow, she'd managed to wander into an alley.

The man talking to her stepped out of the darkened doorway. The muted streetlight played across his flushed face. She smelled alcohol as he came closer. Tall, heavyset, his eyes glinted insolently as they raked over her. Obviously intent on a private party, he held out a bottle to her.

Averting her eyes, Julie quickened her pace.

The man was faster. He grabbed her by the wrist and jerked her around to face him.

"Listen to me when I talk to you, bitch," he snarled into her face.

The next second, he found himself flying, and then concrete was shredding his pants' leg and chewing into his flesh. Howling in outrage and pain, he scrambled up to glare at the man who'd sent him sprawling. "Find your own!" he shouted.

Gabe's arm tightened protectively around Julie's shoulders as he moved her behind him. His eyes never left the other man. "I already have."

Rage discolored a face that had grown bloated and blotchy from years of drinking. "In your dreams, you son of a bitch."

Taller and heavier than Gabe, the man charged at him, hands outstretched. Pulling Julie over, Gabe sidestepped the attack.

The next moment, as the heel of Gabe's boot made contact with his stomach and blood filled his mouth from a well-placed blow to his jaw, the belligerent drunk fell for the second time, shrieking.

"Leave my mother out of it," Gabe warned evenly.

With his arm around her shoulders, Gabe hurried Julie away before the drunk could get up and come back for more. *All strength and no brains,* Gabe quipped silently. He was well acquainted with the type.

Urging her forward, Gabe didn't stop until they were clear of the alley and on a well-lit street several blocks over. He glanced back to make sure the other man wasn't following them.

Of all the dumb stunts, he thought, banking down his annoyance.

Gabe peered into Julie's face to make sure she was all right. He was pretty certain he'd gotten to her in time.

It took him a second to realize that he was trying to curb his temper. "Did he hurt you?"

She shook her head. The air was only just now returning into her lungs. Julie wiped the mist from her face, annoyed with herself for being so recklessly careless. "That was stupid," she said vehemently.

She'd get no argument from him about that. "I'm glad you said it. Saves me the trouble." Even so, waiting a beat, the words wouldn't stay banked. "What the hell were you thinking?" Exasperation edged his voice. "Don't you know any better than to go wandering off into dark alleys by yourself at night?"

"Yeah, I do." Dragging her hand through her wet hair, she blew out a breath. The dampness was beginning to penetrate even deeper. She felt cold.

"You're shivering." Stopping, Gabe took off his jacket. Then, as Julie stared at him in wonder, he slipped it around her shoulders. Pulling the ends together to maximize her coverage, Gabe avoided looking into her eyes. He had a feeling that if he did, he might do something stupid like kiss her. The object was to befriend her, not seduce her.

Right now, though, he felt more like the one being seduced.

"C'mon." Wanting to get her back home and dry, he slipped his arm around Julie's shoulders and coaxed her in the right direction. "So what happened?" he pressed. "What made you suddenly take off into the night like that?"

"I'm not sure." Julie felt her face flush ruefully at her embarrassment. Another emotion, more potent than the first, whispered along the fringes of her soul. She struggled to ignore it. "The world felt like it was closing in on me. I had to get out to clear my head."

"You almost had it cleared clean off your neck. That guy back there was one step removed from a cave dweller."

"I know." The dust began to settle from about her brain. Gabe had been magnificent back there, his movements fast enough to almost be a blur. "Where did you learn how to do that?"

"I discovered Bruce Lee when I was a ninety-eight-pound weakling." Gabe smiled, remembering how pathetically awkward he'd been in the beginning.

"Bruce Lee? Isn't he dead?" Julie asked after a second.

The martial arts master had died more than twenty-five years ago. "The magic of celluloid, video and laser disc will keep Bruce Lee around forever, the patron saint of scrawny, picked-on kids everywhere." Gabe decided there was no harm in letting her in on this part of his life. It didn't get in the way of anything. "I got tired of having my big brother defend me. I rented some videos, found the training manual on Jeet Kune Do—that's the martial arts program he came up with—in the library and studied very, very hard."

For months, it became almost a religion to him, learning the moves, the mindset. After that, years of training followed. He'd conned Rafe into helping him. When his parents had discovered what he was up to, they'd paid for lessons. He could teach it himself now, if the need arose.

"It obviously paid off." She smiled at him. The more she learned about him, the more incredible he seemed. "Artist, locksmith, carpenter, superhero, you're the closest thing to a Renaissance man I've ever met."

Uncomfortable with what he saw in her eyes, with his deception, he shrugged the compliment away. "That sounds a lot nicer than jack-of-all-trades."

"A jack-of-all-trades isn't supposed to be good at any of it, according to the rhyme. You are." She paused for a moment. "Thanks for coming to my rescue." She surprised him by stopping and kissing his cheek softly.

Something deep and wanting quickened inside him. He shut it away, denying its existence. There'd only be complications if he released it.

"I couldn't very well stand by and let him maul you, could I? Not when I'm so close to being part of my first show." He saw the light extinguish in her eyes. A sadness hit him square in the pit of his stomach, as if he'd just killed something and was now watching it die. What had he said? He touched her shoulder, needing the contact. "What's the matter?"

Julie thought of Justin. Of being used. Of the dangers in letting herself care a little too much. And it was already beginning. But she'd never been the type to do things by half measures and it was against her nature to divorce herself from people.

"Nothing." Julie looked at him as they walked back to the gallery. "How did you happen to be there, anyway?"

The truth was always easier to deal with and more convincing, Gabe thought. It would help lay the foundations for the lies that were to follow. He tried not to dwell on that, but forged ahead. "I followed you."

"Why?"

That, at least, was easy enough to explain. "Because I thought you were upset. I heard you and your mother, uh...talking."

"You mean, you heard my mother talking and me shouting," she said with a half smile.

"Something like that," he conceded. "At any rate, I heard the front door slam and I thought you might need a shoulder to cry on." He thought of her headstart. He'd had to move quickly to stay just behind her. "You walk fast for a woman in high heels."

"I was sprinting more than running," she admitted, then sighed. "Trying very hard to outrun this feeling inside me."

They sidestepped a couple hurrying to their car. It was beginning to actually rain now. Gabe and Julie stepped up their pace. The gallery was just up ahead.

"Maybe you should try dealing with it instead," he suggested.

"I am—in part—" She shook her head, more to herself than at anything he'd said. "But I'm not getting anywhere."

Reaching St. Claire's, Julie fumbled in her skirt pocket for the key. Shivering, she dropped it. Gabe picked it up and opened the door, letting her walk in first. Closing it behind him, he flipped the lock into place, then bolted it.

The light from the street lamp outside pressed itself against the blinds in the windows, finding cracks through which to squeeze. Tiny spotlights pooled on the floor around them.

He wanted to hold her.

Restraining himself, he took her hand and placed the key

into it, then closed her fingers around it. He held her hand for a moment longer, looking into her eyes.

For the first time in his life, he wished he wasn't a cop.

"You'd better go upstairs and get out of those wet clothes," he advised. "You don't want to add being sick to the list of whatever's bothering you."

Julie nodded, but somehow she couldn't get her feet to move just yet. Instead, she remained where she was, looking up at him, wishing with all her heart that her life had arranged itself differently. That she was free to do what she wanted to, instead of being hemmed in by responsibilities.

"Thanks again for saving me."

He slipped the jacket from her shoulders. Wet, it was only adding to the chill. It felt a lot as if he were undressing her, he suddenly realized. The thought sent hot, pulsing waves shooting through his extremities. It was difficult to find his tongue.

"My pleasure. I meant what I said earlier—about a shoulder to cry on. If you want to talk—"

Julie wanted to, oh so very much. But she couldn't. It was her problem, all of it. Sharing wouldn't make it any less, any better. But his offer of friendship touched her. "Thanks, but it's too complicated. I don't want to involve you."

She was talking about the drugs. Gabe ignored the sinking feeling in the pit of his stomach. Was she sorry now that she was in the middle of this? Had concern for the financial stability of her gallery sent her into the embrace of the drug world? He couldn't picture her a wanton criminal, motivated only by greed. There had to be another reason for what she was doing.

He couldn't resist touching her, just her face, just for a moment. "Maybe I want to be involved, did you ever think of that?"

The question whispered softly along her skin, arousing a

need so great that it threatened to overwhelm her. Knowing she was being foolish, Julie pretended that he was talking about something else.

About them.

What would it be like to have this man hold her? To have this man kiss her? "You have no idea what you'd be letting yourself in for."

The touch became something more. Ignoring all the warning signs, all the alarms that were going off inside his brain, Gabe tilted her head back. "There's something to be said for being surprised."

And then, because he couldn't resist any longer, he kissed her.

And told himself it was just to maintain his cover, just part of the performance he was giving.

That his head spun and his blood rushed was only testimony to how well he immersed himself in the role, how well he played the part.

He told himself all sorts of lies, just to continue kissing her.

His arms almost seemed to have a will of their own, closing around Julie and bringing her to him so that the heat from his body could penetrate hers. So that he could warm her the way she warmed him.

Julie felt the sizzle, the quick jump of electricity, traveling through her veins, shifting to his. Joining them just the way his lips joined them. The sigh that escaped her lips, grazing his tongue, was one part pleasure, two parts desire and a hundred percent hunger.

Forgetting about the child she was carrying, about everything, she surrendered herself to the kiss. To the man. Rising on her toes, Julie encircled her arms around his waist.

Lights went off in her head. Beautiful, sparkling lights that dazzled and bewitched. That ignited. She wanted him to take her, to make love with her. To her. To make her feel, just for a little while, that nothing else mattered but this wondrous feeling that had spun out of nowhere to capture her.

He wanted her.

It wasn't fair, it wasn't right. And it wasn't part of the deal.

With effort that was so difficult, it was almost wrenching, he pulled his mouth away from hers. When he did, Gabe was surprised that he didn't see puffs of smoke rising between them. He'd certainly felt the fire taking shape.

"You'd better see about getting out of those clothes," he told her quietly.

Before I strip you of them right here. Gabe bit back the words that begged for release, held back the desire that did the same.

The extent of his reaction, of his desire, left him shaken and unsteady. Desire had never clutched him in such a vise-like grip before.

He let her go up the stairs first.

Confused, she looked back at him. "Aren't you coming?"

Gabe remained where he was, regret battering at his soul. He wondered if they gave the Purple Heart along with the detective shield.

He nodded toward the rear of the gallery. "I think I'll just work on the shelves some more." Although maybe breaking up huge slabs of concrete with a sledgehammer might be more beneficial in releasing the tension he was suddenly experiencing.

Gathering her dignity to her, she nodded. It was better this way, of course. The last thing she needed was to get involved with someone while she was pregnant with another man's child.

She should have been glad that he wasn't some libido driven artist, that he was levelheaded.

Should have been, but wasn't.

"I'll see you in the morning," she murmured. "Thanks again."

Gabe ran a tentative finger along his lips. He should be the one thanking her. "Don't mention it."

He turned away, heading toward the back. It was going to be a hell of a long night.

"Do you have any idea what time it is?" The sleepy voice on the other end of the line made the indignant demand in his ear.

Ken McCarthy's annoyance didn't do much to soothe his own. It had taken three rings to wake his partner. With each one, Gabe's agitation seemed to increase tenfold until it felt almost insurmountable.

He shifted the receiver to his other ear. "Yeah, late. The big hand is on the twelve, the little one is on the three."

"Very funny. What do you want? You know you woke up Maureen."

Gabe snorted. There'd been little chance of that. "Your wife slept through the last major earthquake. You told me so yourself."

"All right, all right, so what's so important that you couldn't wait until morning to call me like a decent human being?"

Working on the shelves, Gabe had had time to reassess the situation around him. He'd deliberately put the personal element out of his mind and concentrated on the investigation. The one that threatened to go nowhere unless he got things moving.

"I need you to find a way to get Customs to release those paintings to the art gallery." He'd already told McCarthy about the paintings that were being held in quarantine.

"And while I'm on it, do you want to wear glass slippers to the ball, or will you be wearing your running shoes instead?" Dropping the sarcasm, McCarthy demanded, "How the hell am I supposed to get Customs to move on that?"

"That's your problem." If he had an answer to that, he wouldn't have called with the request. "That's why you're the backup man in this operation. Talk to the captain. It's a big department. Somebody has to know someone who owes them a favor."

Though there was an unspoken competition between each and every department of law enforcement, there were times that it was necessary for one hand to wash the other. Gabe was banking on it now.

"Tell me again. What's so important about getting the paintings released?"

"I've got a feeling that they're a crucial component in this operation." He thought of the invitation list. "One of the so-called collectors coming to the show is Klaus Von Buren." He heard McCarthy's low whistle of appreciation. At least he had his full attention now. "If there're no paintings, there's no show. No show, no collectors and maybe no drug shipment being exchanged. We need to see what they're up to. Von Buren isn't about to drop in on a moderate-size art gallery just because he feels like slumming."

"So then the St. Claire woman is in on it." It was a statement, not a question.

Gabe felt his jaw tightening. He was a cop first, he reminded himself. The desire to protect her was something he was going to have to work at ignoring. "I still don't know, but it's beginning to look like she's involved in some way."

Exhausted, McCarthy didn't bother stifling a yawn. "Okay, I'll see what the captain can do. First thing in the morning. Anything else?"

There was a list of things, but he mentioned only the most important for now. "Yeah, find out what you can about Elizabeth St. Claire."

"The mother?" Gabe could tell he now had McCarthy's attention. "You think she might be involved?"

He didn't know, but her sudden appearance after all these years seemed rather odd. Or timely, depending on the view. "Suspect everyone, isn't that what they taught us?"

This time, McCarthy bit back the yawn. "I dunno, I slept through that class. I'll just take your word for it."

The calls couldn't be allowed to run too long. Cell phone signals were the easiest to tap into. He had to get going. "I'll try to call you tomorrow."

The huge sigh on the other end told him that McCarthy had heard.

Terminating the call, Gabe hid his cell phone inside the closet, then turned off the light and lay down on the bed. Outside, the rain scratched against the window. He thought of the way Julie'd looked earlier, wet, lost. The way she'd felt in his arms when he kissed her.

The promise of her body lingered hauntingly in his consciousness.

Who are you, Julie St. Claire? Are you really what you seem—that warm, generous, feisty woman I see? Or am I letting myself be blinded by that smile of yours?

It was a long time before he fell asleep.

Chapter 10

Maybe the gallery was to blame. Gabe wasn't exactly sure just how it began, or even really why. He certainly hadn't felt the urge to paint in years. His life had gotten far too busy for that.

Yet as each day passed, an unfamiliar desire seemed to slowly dribble into him until he finally became aware of it. A desire to leave his mark on a virgin field of white. To leave his mark on a canvas.

Because it was necessary to add the subtle details of an artist's life to perpetuate his cover, Gabe had asked Julie if it would be all right with her if he brought the easel up from the back room and set it up in his apartment. Her response was that he didn't even have to ask.

Any way he looked at it, Gabe thought, the lady was magnanimously generous. As the days went by, he was having more and more difficulty reconciling the idea that Julie St. Claire was somehow a shill for a covert drug operation.

Yet she seemed too intelligent, too on top of things to be a dupe.

He decided to reserve his judgment and just continue doing what he'd been doing, keeping his ears and eyes open and reporting back even the slightest thing that seemed out of the ordinary.

Bringing the easel upstairs, Gabe had set it up in the front room. That way, it looked as if he wanted to capture the brilliant afternoon light, making use of it. Gabe's actual intent had been nothing more than to make it appear as if an artist were inhabiting the rooms.

Certainly he hadn't meant to begin painting.

The verbal groundwork he'd laid made it seem as if he were in the midst of searching for a subject to paint. That should have bought him some time and leeway until the actual show took place.

But without his looking for it, the subject presented itself to him. Teasing his mind, asking to be given life and breadth. Each time he passed the easel with its ready canvas, it called to him. Demanding his attention. Demanding his hand. Almost without thinking, he'd taken a few passes at the empty canvas with his pencil.

The sketch lines that emerged bore a haunting resemblance to the woman whose hospitality he was attempting to turn to his advantage.

Advantage.

He was taking advantage of Julie without her even suspecting it.

The thought bothered his conscience, something that had taken on a life of its own ever since he'd arrived here. Not wanting to deal with it, he shut the feeling away.

But he couldn't shut away the urge to go a little further with his sketch, to add a little dimension to the lines. One stroke led to another and another, until he found himself looking into Julie's face.

The eyes were wrong, he thought, even for a second rate sketch. They didn't begin to capture the life, the zest that was there.

Studying the sketch, Gabe frowned. If anything, the eyes appeared to be accusing as they looked back at him. The way Julie had looked at her mother that first afternoon.

Sighing, wondering what the hell he was even doing, Gabe began to rub away the eyes with the edge of his fisted hand.

"Is that me?"

He swung around, startled.

He looked guilty, Julie thought. Embarrassed. A boy caught with a handful of cookies from the jar that lay shattered at his feet. She had no idea why it should, but it charmed her.

Crossing to the easel, she tried to look at the sketch with a discerning eye rather than through the eyes of a very flattered woman.

"Your door was open," she murmured, half apologetic, half bemused, studying the sketch. "I couldn't help looking in when I saw you were working." She realized what was bothering her about the work. She looked at him, a little confused. "This is different from the paintings you showed me."

Trying to appear blasé, Gabe shrugged as he damned himself for myriad oversights. He shouldn't have given in to the impulse to work on the sketch. He hadn't meant to remain in the apartment, only to get something and then return downstairs. But the canvas had called to him like a siren's song. The pencil had just leaped into his hand, the same way the need to sketch her had suddenly commanded his attention.

What had he been thinking? Of course she'd notice that the styles were different. That was her job, to see things like that. See the difference between Rafe's paintings and the one he was doing. While their approaches were very similar, there were still noticeable differences. For one thing, Rafe was precise. Gabe's strokes were like his life— all over the place.

Shrugging, Gabe shoved his hands into his back pockets. He wanted her out of here before she could begin asking questions. "I was just fooling around..."

It was the first time Julie had ever seen him act as if he were unsure of himself. So this was the heart of the man, she thought. His work. And he felt exposed because she'd come across it at the very beginning stages.

Even so, what she saw appealed to her. There seemed to be more heart here than in the other two paintings. More raw emotion. She hadn't been wrong, he had a great deal of potential.

Julie raised her eyes to his. "You fool around very nicely. I'm flattered. I'm also intrigued by your different approaches."

Gabe's mind raced, searching for a plausible explanation. "My work is a reflection of what's going on in my life at the time. When I did the landscapes, everything was settling into a comfortable niche." He looked at her. "That niche is gone now. I see things differently."

She understood that. To her, art had always been an outward expression of an inner emotion. She liked the fact that they had similar philosophies, at least about art.

Lingering, Julie felt reluctant to leave. Outside this apartment, demands were waiting to be made on her. Problems looking to her for solutions. And her mother was only a few yards away. As of yet, Julie hadn't come up with satisfactory solutions for any of it.

For whatever reason, his apartment felt like a haven to her.

Julie remained awhile longer. "I'd be willing to sit for

you, if you like. Starving artist, starving model," she murmured, more to herself than to him.

The offer surprised Gabe. And, he had to admit, it appealed to him. He told himself he was only going along to do what was necessary to perpetuate the role he'd assumed, but the truth of it was he wanted to paint her. He'd never really wanted to paint anything before, but he wanted to paint her.

"You're hardly a starving model," he pointed out.

Julie thought of the show that was breathing down her neck. And the paintings that still weren't in her possession. "It might come to that." She sighed.

The distress he saw in her eyes affected him more than he thought it would. "Still no luck?"

She laughed softly. "Lots of luck, all bad. The Customs office refuses to budge until they're cleared by the board of health, which in turn is waiting to see if the rest of the crew comes down with the same disease or if, by some freak happenstance, the unfortunate sailor is an isolated case. In either case, I might not get my hands on those paintings until after the show."

Annoyance scratched its way to the surface. "And there doesn't seem to be a damn thing I can do about it. I'm still making phone calls, but so far, I can't seem to find anyone to help me and I'm running out of time." Mike was still getting nowhere with his repeated visits down to the harbor and it seemed to Julie that she now spent the better part of her day with the telephone receiver hermetically sealed to her ear, trying one extension after another, being bounced from one recorded bureaucratic message after another.

"How about now?" Gabe heard himself asking.

"Now?" The expression on her face told him that she wasn't sure what he was suggesting.

Since she'd bought his explanation without challenging

it, Gabe felt he was on relatively safe ground again. He tested it a little further.

"For the sitting. Jeff's downstairs, minding the store." He saw her begin to protest. "Maybe your mother can pitch in if it gets too busy."

Julie laughed at both the thought of her mother helping out and his phrasing. "You've never really hung around a gallery, have you?" He shook his head in response. "I didn't think so. 'Too busy' usually means there are more than three people milling about on the floor, looking up at the paintings. You make it sound like the last-minute Christmas rush at Macy's." She let out a breath. "No danger of that happening." It was almost time to close up. Jeff could do that. She felt herself weakening.

"Then there's no problem, is there?" he asked, carrying in a stool from the breakfast nook.

The sitting would be a good opportunity to talk to Julie in a relaxed atmosphere. More like, pump her for information, Gabe amended. That had an ominous sound to it, but that didn't make it any less necessary. He glanced at her. If it hadn't been for the tip, this would have been the last place he would have tied to a drug ring. If anything, the people here could be seen as a little quirky, but definitely not dangerous.

But the tip was there, on the table, and he had to do something with it. Prove it or disprove it. And he'd found it was always easier to assume that there was guilt until something convinced him otherwise.

Right now, he was seriously hoping for something to convince him otherwise.

Gabe set things up. If she asked to see the painting, he'd already decided to tell her that he didn't like a work in progress being viewed. That would keep the charade going for as long as he needed it.

There was another minor protest from the area that he

assumed was his conscience but he ignored it completely. He'd taken an oath when he'd put on his uniform. The oath didn't get amended just because one of the alleged "bad guys" had gorgeous legs, hair the color of light honey with the sun trapped in it and skin that looked as if it was the softest surface known to man.

Julie stepped back and closed the door as he set down the stool. She looked skeptically at her clothes. She was wearing a cherry red jumper and a billowing, sleeved, white blouse. Fine for the gallery, but not exactly something she wanted immortalized. "Like this?"

"Why not?" He stopped to survey her clothes. A smile played on his lips. "I could, of course, paint you nude if you prefer."

She'd been taught to separate the two. Standing nude in front of an artist was different than standing nude in front of a man. But somehow, here the lines between the two had blurred for her. She couldn't quite divorce one from the other when it came to Gabe.

Afraid he could read that in her eyes, she covered deftly. "What I'd prefer," she confided, "is to be painted as a Greek goddess." She stretched out her arms, getting into the spirit of the part. "With a flowing white tunic and flowers in my hair." She tossed her head for emphasis. Blond hair brushed against her shoulder invitingly. "Aphrodite before she became jaded."

Gently, he guided Julie back so that she could sit on the stool. "I didn't know that Aphrodite became jaded."

"Very much so." She thought of her parents. And of her mistaken feelings toward Justin. "She would have had to, finding out that love wasn't as pure among the mortals as she'd intended it to be."

Something in her voice caught Gabe's attention. Tilting her head a little to the side, he skimmed his fingers along her throat. The need to touch her was suddenly overwhelming. He satisfied himself by arranging her hair. "She's a goddess. Goddesses always take things in stride. They're above disappointment."

Why did she feel as if her breath was backing up in her lungs? He was just posing her, nothing more. "Don't read much mythology, do you?" Julie was surprised to discover that she'd whispered the question.

The desire to kiss her was strong, but Gabe resisted. He couldn't risk messing things up just because his hormones were suddenly getting short-circuited.

Arranging her hands in her lap, he stepped back to study what he'd done. "I'd say a red jumper is a good compromise between nudity and a flowing white tunic."

For a moment Julie had thought he was going to kiss her, but the moment was gone and she was grateful. And maybe a little sorry. But mostly grateful, she told herself firmly. She didn't want to make the same mistake again. "You have some imagination."

"Don't all artists?"

Standing behind the easel, Gabe paused to gain his perspective. The light embraced her, making her seem almost golden. Like the goddess she'd longed to impersonate.

Once, Julie would have agreed that all artists had imaginations. Wonderful imaginations. But she'd learned otherwise as she was growing up. "I guess. Although some were limited."

There was that note again, the one that was so impossibly sad. Gabe began to wonder about her personal life. There were huge gaps in her history when it came to that. She always seemed to be so busy running the gallery and helping artists that there appeared to be nothing else in her life. Looking the way she did, he figured that had to be an omission. He'd get McCarthy to see what else he could pull up to fill in the obvious gaps.

He tried to sketch her eyes again. "Who?"

"Nobody you know."

And nobody she wanted to talk about, he guessed. That wasn't hard to pick up. Okay, that was fine. It probably didn't enter into his true purpose for being here, anyway, and that was all that mattered, he reminded himself. He was here to break up a suspected drug smuggling ring, not find out who her date for the prom had been.

The eyes were still wrong. He decided to leave them for now and just sketch the rest.

"How are you and your mother coming along?" Glancing down for a beat, he frowned when he looked up at her again. His pencil hovered in midstroke. "You moved your head."

She lowered it slightly to approximate the way he'd posed her. "You asked the wrong question."

She'd done this before, he thought. Probably a dozen times from the ease with which she returned to the pose. He wondered if there were any sketches of her amid her mother's work.

Or if she'd posed for a lover.

The question had snuck up on him and he banished it just as quickly. "Sorry."

"No," she apologized. "I'm the one who should be sorry. I keep snapping at people when I shouldn't."

The flush that came to her cheeks was infinitely appealing. Committing it to memory, he meant to give it life later when he was working in colors.

"So it's agreed, we're a sorry lot." Raising his brow, he looked to see if he'd managed to coax a smile from her. When he saw that he had, the amount of pleasure that spilled through him surprised Gabe.

He'd made her smile, Julie thought. It wasn't the first time, either. There was something appealing about that. About him. He had a way of taking things down to a common denominator, making things seem not quite as serious, as insurmountable, as they appeared. It was a nice quality to have. After the show was over, she was going to ask around to see if any of her friends knew anything about him. Maybe even contact Cassidy in France, since Gabe had mentioned him.

. She was letting her mind drift again, Julie lectured silently. Sitting perfectly still, she fixed her eyes on the heating vent in the ceiling. After a moment, she answered the question he'd originally asked. "Things with my mother are going as well as can be expected, given the circumstances."

Her mother was keeping her distance, keeping out of her way. In the days since her mother's return, Julie had seen her less than a handful of times. She purposely kept herself busy in the gallery, leaving the upstairs quarters to her mother. As far as she knew, except for daily walks at three, her mother didn't really leave the apartment.

Keeping his mind on the conversation, Gabe tried not to get lost in her hair as he sketched it. "Exactly what are the circumstances?"

He'd asked the question before. Julie debated telling him that it was still none of his business, but the need to connect outweighed the need to keep the hurt private.

It wasn't all that private anyway, she reminded herself. Other people knew about it. Once it had been the talk of the art community, even though her father had tried to hush it up. If he stayed around long enough, Gabe would hear it from someone. She figured it might as well be her.

"My mother ran off with another man fifteen years ago." From the corner of her eye, she saw Gabe look up at her. She fixed her attention on the vent again, staring at it as if her very life was focused there. "I came home from school the day before Christmas Eve to find a four-by-five index card propped up against an empty vase on the kitchen table.'' She felt her stomach twisting as she remembered. "All it said was, 'I'm sorry.'"

Sketching quickly, he tried to capture the look he saw entering her eyes. Haunted. And haunting. "How did you know it was with another man?"

"Everyone knew. Simon James," she said the name of a man she'd trusted. A man she'd thought of as part of the family. "I always thought he was just a friend of hers. Obviously I was very naive."

Though it hurt to give voice to the past, it was also oddly therapeutic. She'd never really talked about it before. Not to anyone. Certainly not to her father. At times, dealing with this had made her feel completely cut off from the rest of the world. But talking to Gabe connected her, she realized.

"My father was devastated. He'd worshipped the ground she walked on." She remembered how afraid she'd been when her father had found out. Afraid that in his grief he would kill himself rather than live without the woman he loved. In a way, she supposed he had anyway.

"He hired a detective to find her and bring her back, but after nine months, the man gave up. He'd followed my mother down to Mexico City, then lost the trail. He even gave my father part of his money back." She sighed. "That was how sorry he felt for him."

"What was his name?"

"Henderson—no, Harris. Jim Harris, I think. Why?"

"No reason." With broad strokes, Gabe drew in the folds of her sleeves. "Just curious." He'd have McCarthy run the name through the computer; see if the man was still around, still practicing. Get his take on the story if he was willing to talk. It wouldn't hurt to fill in as much as they could. "What did your father do when Harris couldn't find her?"

He fell to pieces, she thought. A loud, bombastic man, he eventually became a shell of his former self.

"He tried to make a go of St. Claire's for a while, but his heart wasn't in it anymore. She'd ripped it out." Did that come out sounding as bitter as she thought it did? she wondered. "He'd bought the gallery to showcase my mother's work. Without her, he just wasn't interested." Not in the art gallery, not in life. Certainly not in her. "He would sit up here, night after night, anesthetizing himself. At first it was a bottle of rare wine, then brandy, and then it stopped mattering. The evenings got longer and longer, the days shorter, until he stopped going down to the gallery altogether. He pretty much drank himself to death." Her lips twisted. "Because of her."

Gabe worked furiously to capture what he saw before it was gone. "What about you?"

"Me?" The question pulled Julie out of the past's grip. She didn't understand. "What about me?"

"You, his daughter," he elaborated. Gabe knew that it might have been a corny sentiment to express, but he also knew that no matter what was going on in his parents' lives, they never lost sight of the fact that they were responsible for the two sons they'd brought into the world. "It sounds to me that he seemed to have forgotten that he had a daughter to take care of. You were how old when all this started?"

Fiercely protective of her father, of his memory, Julie grudgingly volunteered the information. "Twelve."

Twelve. Little more than a child, Gabe thought. Too young to have to instantly grow up and face that kind of reality. "Seems to me he had an obligation to you that should have come before his feelings of being hurt."

Julie's eyes narrowed. He knew nothing about her father. Nothing about her mother. How could he presume to pass judgment like that?

"My mother had that kind of effect on men, on people in general," she amended. "Made them forget about everything and everyone else."

From a very young age, Julie had always known that she couldn't hold a candle to her mother as far as her father was concerned. Her mother was the talented one, the beautiful one. And when her father had finally accepted the fact that Julie had no talent, that she couldn't begin to paint the way her mother did, he'd lost total interest in her. It had been to her mother she'd turned whenever she needed someone. Until her mother wasn't there any longer.

"Besides, I could take care of myself. I always did." She'd had to for the most part. "They were very much wrapped up around one another when I was growing up. At times, it was hard to know where one started and the other stopped."

There was another side to it, a side Gabe wondered if she was blocking out. He debated mentioning anything, then decided to push the conversation up another notch and risk it. "What about the arguments?"

She blinked. "Arguments?"

He heard the denial in her voice and knew that she was aware of what he was talking about. "I remember reading somewhere that there were violent arguments between your parents. That the police had to be called in a couple of times."

Julie remembered how embarrassed she'd been by it. How embarrassed her mother had seemed. And how smoothly her father had talked the police away from the door.

"Raised voices, nothing more. It's a quiet neighborhood. People don't always understand artistic temperaments. My father would push, my mother would rail. They were very impassioned people."

She was lying, Gabe thought. Covering for one or both

of them. Or maybe her memory was distorting the facts he'd glossed over in preparation for the assignment. The woman across the hall didn't strike him as particularly impassioned. He would have used the word regal to describe her. Something else to follow up on, he thought.

This had nothing to do with drug trafficking, he upbraided himself. But maybe it might hold the key to why she was involved in it. For now, that was enough.

"So I take it having her live here is awkward for you." From the sound of it, there'd been no fence mending, no reconciliation of any sort. Just two people avoiding one another and the past.

"Awkward doesn't begin to explain it."

"Then why take her in?" She looked restless. Any minute, she'd probably get up. He began putting in the finishing touches to the sketch. Something to work with later if he felt like it.

His question surprised Julie. Subtly, she shifted again and felt something crack in protest along her spine. Wasn't it too early to feel this kind of discomfort? Backs were supposed to ache toward the end of a pregnancy, not the beginning.

"I thought you were the one who said I shouldn't turn her away."

"That's my approach to it," he reminded her. His eyes were smiling as he raised them to hers. "But you're not me."

She shrugged. Maybe she should have just turned her back on Elizabeth, but it wasn't in her. She probably would have taken Justin in, too, if he found himself in the dire straits her mother was in. Julie hadn't asked any questions, but the first night her mother had volunteered a tiny bit of information. She hadn't painted a stroke since she'd left St. Claire's. Simon and she had long since parted company and all she had in the world was on her back. Only a monster would have turned her out.

Julie didn't feel like going into details such as how she'd opened her closets to her mother when she found out Elizabeth had nothing else to wear. It wasn't any of his business.

"She doesn't have any money. So for the time being, this is where she'll stay. I want to hate her," she confessed. "But—"

"But you can't." Another woman in her place would, Gabe thought.

"Maybe I'm not passionate enough to come up with emotions as powerful as that."

Finished, he put down his pencil, then crossed to the woman he'd felt compelled to capture. "I think you're very passionate." It was there, in the set of her chin, the look in her eyes. He wanted to hold her, but he held himself in check.

"How would you know?" The laugh barely emerged before it faded away, erased by what Julie saw in his eyes.

"Artists know these things. It's called instinct."

Too close, she thought. This was getting too close. She was allowing it to get too close. Abruptly, she rose from the stool.

She gave Gabe the impression that she was running. From what? "Where are you going?"

"Downstairs." She waved vaguely behind her. "It's all the time I have right now."

She was lying. Why? And why did she suddenly look so nervous? Had he touched on something, said something? "What are you going to do downstairs?" He glanced at his watch. "Jeff's probably closed the gallery by now."

"Oh, well, I could go over the books, look to see if maybe I've miscalculated..."

She was turning from him and he should have let her.

Should have, but didn't. Something had him catching her arm and turning her back to him. She looked unsettled. Maybe even a little afraid, he thought. Of what?

"You're running off."

She tried to sound casual. "Happens when your life is in fast forward."

"Did I make you uncomfortable just now?" He wanted her to feel relaxed in his presence, not on her guard. "Because if I did, I didn't mean to."

Julie felt like an idiot. "No, it's not you. Sorry—" Hearing herself, she stopped. "I keep saying that, don't I?"

"Yes." Very gently, Gabe skimmed his fingertips along her jaw. If there was something softer than her skin, he wasn't aware of it. "You don't have anything to be sorry for."

Then, because the moment seemed to freeze around them and threatened to remain that way unless he did something, Gabe cupped her face in his hands, looked down into the eyes that haunted him and sampled the lips that had been tempting him all this time.

Chapter 11

This was wrong. Completely wrong.

The words echoed within Julie's brain like rain on a metal roof. You didn't kiss one man while carrying another's child in your belly. What kind of a woman did that make her?

A lonely one, she realized.

With all the commotion going on around her, with all the people she knew, all the business that passed through her doors, she was lonely. Lonely for the right touch, the right caress. The right man.

The right man wasn't Gabriel Murietta, she told herself.

But right now, words and common sense weren't penetrating, weren't even making a dent. Like arrows shot through a tank filled with gelatin, they weren't even close to hitting their mark.

All she wanted was this. This warmth, this heat, this passion to singe her mouth, her soul.

Only for a moment.

Nothing would come of these stolen moments. Julie was as sure of that as she was of tomorrow arriving after today.

And if nothing was to come of them, then there was no need for confessions, no need for penance or even guilt. This wondrous feeling enveloping her would stop, all too soon, taking the thrill, the rush, away with it. Leaving her alone again.

So for now, for the singular, shining moment that it existed, she would enjoy it and pretend that she was free to do so.

Did she taste this sweet because she was forbidden fruit, or was that sweetness, that heady intoxication, a product all her own? For the life of him, Gabe had no answer, and all too soon, he didn't even have the question.

All there was for him, was desire—all-consuming, passionate desire. As it surged, questing for even more, Gabe pushed her up against the door. With the barrier at her back, he pressed his body against hers. Raising her hands high above her head, his fingers lacing with hers, his mouth slanted over hers again and again as Gabe absorbed all that was her. And felt the fire growing inside him.

The fire that had only one way to be quelled.

He had to stop, while he still could, Gabe upbraided himself. Now, before desire overpowered him and he overpowered her.

He had no right to do this. No right to ravage her mouth this way. It was wrong, damn it, totally wrong for him to allow this to happen.

How did something so wrong feel so right?

He felt his body scream in protest as he pulled away. Breathing came at a dear cost.

"You'd better go," he told her. With effort, Gabe stepped back. The space between them felt as if he'd just created a huge chasm. A gaping emptiness that threatened to swallow him up whole. "Before I won't let you."

Shaken, Julie dragged air into her lungs, unable to catch her breath. He was right. Right for so many reasons. She should go now, before this went any further. Before she crossed a line she couldn't readily step over again. She was pregnant. He was a penniless artist just passing through. She'd made this mistake before.

Nothing was as it was before.

This time, there was no champagne to cloud her head, no feeling of abandonment and excruciating loneliness to push her into his arms. There was only desire.

She couldn't make herself leave.

Gabe saw the need in her eyes and knew he had to be the stronger of the two. Knew, too, that for the first time in his life, he wasn't. He couldn't be. She had to be the one who walked away.

She made no attempt to even turn away.

"God help me, but I'm going to be damned for this," he muttered with a surrendering groan, bringing his mouth back down to hers.

Somewhere deep inside her head, Julie could have sworn she heard the beginning strains of the "Hallelujah Chorus."

With a wild rush forward, exhilaration seized her as she threw her arms around Gabe's neck, her soul into Gabe's hands.

There was nowhere else to be but here, no time other than now, no consequences to face until such time as when sanity returned from its holiday. Julie surrendered and felt as if she'd won.

She'd never felt this way before, never felt a need to outrun something, to take passion quickly before things arranged themselves to snatch it from her.

Never felt as if she would die if she didn't make love with a man before. This man. Here. Now. While her body burned for him.

Her lips sealed to his, she searched for the buttons of his

shirt with trembling hands, undoing them with jerky motions that felt foreign to her. If she could have stopped and stepped back, even for a second, she wouldn't have recognized herself. But this wasn't about self-recognition, this was about passion, about being bathed in feelings, about wanting and glorying in being wanted.

She didn't step back, and she didn't stop.

Julie was breathless even before she began, air entering her lungs in small, greedy snatches. Finding no room because all of her was filled with desire.

This had never happened to him before. It was as if he had jumped into a car with no steering wheel, no brakes and no way out. There was no way to take control, nothing to do but hang on for the ride and pray that when the drop finally came at the other end, he'd survive it.

Right now, he didn't even care. Later he would think, would analyze, would worry. Would regret. Now he only wanted to enjoy. To taste her mouth over and over again, to nibble on the shoulder he'd just bared, to suckle on the breast he had just cupped. To breathe in the scent of her that swirled all around him, more intoxicating than any perfume he'd ever encountered.

Eager to feel her, to touch her softness and discover for himself if it felt like silken cream, he undressed her in a flurry of material, hoping he hadn't torn anything, not sure if he had or not.

Blind to everything but her.

The bra he'd pushed down to her waist snagged on his calloused hand as he tried to unhook it. It took him a minute to even realize what had happened and why it wasn't coming undone. Biting back a curse, he worked to dissolve the union without tearing the delicate lace.

He flushed ruefully, feeling like a clumsy teenager. That was a new sensation for him, too. "It would have been easier if you'd posed nude."

She sucked in her breath as the last of her clothing fell away. Her skin tingled in anticipation. "Maybe next time."

The answer came of its own accord, with no thought, with only hope to put it together. It surprised her far more than him.

There wouldn't be a next time, she promised herself.

But there was a now and she wanted to make the very most of it.

Eager, she pulled his belt out of its restraining loop, undid the snap at his jeans. Her nails slid over legs that were muscular and hard as she urged the denim material down. Her fingers tangled in his dark briefs, clutching at the fabric as he pressed his mouth to her throat.

She bit back a moan as sensations, bright and glowing, pierced through her.

And then it began. A spiraling journey into ecstasy.

His wondrous mouth was evoking responses the likes of which she'd never experienced as they crisscrossed her flesh. She could feel herself throbbing, moistening. Aching.

Julie arched her body against Gabe's, greedy for the sensations to continue, to grow. To absorb her. She twisted and turned as they burst through her, linking themselves into other sensations that came in their place and grew even larger.

What was he doing to her?

Why couldn't she even stand up anymore? Why were her knees bending, sinking, sending her down to the floor as if they'd suddenly turned to blocks of ice left in the blazing sun?

He touched. He teased. He explored. And very quickly drove himself crazy. Because even though he was the one touching, teasing and exploring, he wasn't in charge, wasn't master of her fate or even his own.

What he was, was caught in a fiery trap that threatened to consume him.

And he didn't give a damn.

As long as he could die this way, it didn't matter.

He couldn't satisfy himself, couldn't get enough. Like a child let loose in a candy store, filling his pockets with every confection he came across, Gabe fascinated himself with every inch of her. Fascinated himself with subtle curves, dark, tempting tastes, and secret places of wild responses. He'd never grown this excited pleasuring a woman before. It was as if he could feel everything she did and felt it for the first time.

Tottering on the brink, his body begging for the surging release, Gabe held himself back with more strength than he ever believed he possessed. He watched, awestruck, as rapture took hold of her, then sent her plummeting down to earth again.

When she gasped his name, it echoed in his mouth, danced along his tongue.

He began again.

He felt her body quicken against his as he touched her, deftly turning arousal into wild culmination. She shuddered, her body slick and sweet, and he groaned, held fast by the very action he had created.

This was crazy. He was crazy.

It didn't matter. The investigation, the suspicion—nothing mattered. He just wanted her.

Wanted to have her, to lose himself deep within her body, her scent.

Within her.

Unable to hold back even a heartbeat longer, he took her on the floor. Though he wanted to, he couldn't even summon the strength to carry her to a proper bed.

There was nothing proper about this. Nothing at all.

He didn't care.

He wanted—really wanted—to give her the option of saying no. But he was terrified that she would, terrified that at the very last moment, she would change her mind and then his sin would be even greater than it was now. Because he couldn't let her go.

Eyes fixed on orbs so blue his own ached to see them, Gabe brought his body over hers, shadowing it for a split second. Searching for the answer he wanted. Not knowing what he would do if it wasn't there.

But it was.

What he saw in her eyes was an emotion twin to his own, to the one beating within his chest, within his heart.

If there was any question left, she silently answered it herself, raising her hips to his. The battle was lost without a shot.

With a strangled cry comprised of one half endearment, one half passion, Gabe sheathed himself within her. Joining them. And destroying hastily constructed bridges that led to safe retreat.

The rhythm swept over them, a timeless rhythm as old as the sea, as new as tomorrow. It urged them up toward the summit faster and faster until, breathless, spent, they reached the goal together. Stars exploded over both of them, their bodies sealed together, drenched in stardust and sweat.

With a sigh that came from the very bottom of his being, Gabe couldn't remember when he'd felt so exhausted. Or so content. He gathered Julie to him and let the euphoria blanket him.

Knowing that all too soon, it would be snatched away. Would she hate him once she knew that everything he was was a lie? Trying to block the thought out, he kissed the top of her head.

With her cheek pressed against his chest, Julie felt Gabe's heart beating against her skin. If there was ever a more comforting sound in this world, she'd never heard it.

She lay there, listening. Feeling.

Her brain felt as if it had been tossed into a blender. But that was all right. She didn't want to think. Her thoughts would only intrude and ruin everything, taking away the bright packaging around what she was feeling right at this moment. Happy, protected. Safe. And beautiful.

When she felt Gabe kiss the top of her head, she raised it just a little and looked at him. The euphoria continued to wrap itself tightly around her. A bemused smile curved her mouth as her eyes danced. "What just happened here?"

He laughed, curling her wayward strand of hair around his finger. "You don't know, either?"

Very slowly, she shook her head from side to side. The sly smile that appeared on her face took the same steady route.

"I guess we might just have to conduct the experiment again to make sure of the results." She had no idea what possessed her to say that, only that the motivation came from deep within her. As did the desire that was beginning to whisper along her body again.

Groaning, he laughed as he tightened his arms around her.

"If we do it right now," he warned, kissing her mouth quickly, "the only one who'll evaluate the results is the M.E. doing the autopsies on us. We almost set the place on fire."

She pointed to the fixture in the center of the ceiling. "There's a sprinkler system in place. I had St. Claire's refitted when I took over."

"I don't think they make sprinklers for this kind of thing."

Lifting his head, which seemed to be the only part of him he could actually move easily, Gabe glanced toward the open door to his bedroom. He should have at least had the decency of making love with her on the bed. With a groan, he fell back to the floor. "We didn't even make it to the bedroom."

She was just glad that the front door had been closed. The bedroom had seemed a million miles away once they had gotten started. Julie couldn't help the grin that quirked her mouth. "Something to shoot for."

He looked at her for a long moment. Then gently framed her face with his hand. "Is it?"

The laughter faded from her lips, to be replaced by something she wasn't entirely sure of. A feeling she'd never really experienced before. She resented it stealing the laughter from her.

"I don't know. This isn't exactly something I normally do…"

Her voice trailed off. Guilt rippled through her. If he knew she was pregnant, he'd think she'd just fed him a line. Worse, a lie. But making love wasn't something she did. Not like this, with passion and abandonment. As if her whole heart was involved.

And certainly not so quickly. She'd only known him less than a month.

The words replayed themselves in her mind. She'd only known him less than a month.

Suddenly, she didn't have to wonder what he thought of her. She knew. Self-consciousness fell over her like a heavy coat of iron mail. The euphoria, so precious, so delicious, was completely gone, deserting her in a heartbeat. As if it had never even existed.

Stricken, Julie sat up and looked around for something to drape over herself quickly. She was no longer nude, but naked, and there was a world of difference between the two states. She needed to get out of here. Now.

"I know that," he said quietly, seeing the change in her. Guilt whipped him like a cat-o'-nine-tails, ripping into his flesh. Damn it, she was already having regrets. He hadn't meant to turn this into something sordid. He hadn't meant to do it at all.

Except that she'd been so damned enticing. So damned beautiful.

Just as she was now.

Distracted, wanting only to get away, Julie shoved her arms through his shirt. It was the first thing she could find. She whirled around in his direction, holding the shirt closed against her. "What?"

"I know it's not something you do."

Apologies weren't things that came easily to him. But he needed to clear the air while this was still fresh. If they waltzed around it, pretended it didn't exist, it would only get that much more difficult with each passing hour. At the very least, it would jeopardize the operation, and he couldn't allow the fact that he had messed up to affect the lives of others.

"Look, if I forced myself on you, I'm—"

She stopped gathering her clothes together and stared at him, stunned. "Possessed of an incredible ego, I'm sure."

That shot the apology to pieces. It was Gabe's turn to stare at her. "What?"

Self-consciousness gave way to indignity. It made things tolerable and gave Julie something to rally behind. She was always better at rallying.

Dropping her clothes in a heap, she stepped over them and knelt in front of him. There was fire in her eyes. "Let's just get something straight. This isn't a turn-of-the-century melodrama." She poked a finger at his chest to emphasize her point. "I didn't faint at your feet, and you didn't ravage me. What happened here did *not* happen against my will."

At least, she amended silently, not in the way he meant. It had happened against her will only because she felt it wasn't fair to either him or the baby. And maybe, in a small way, it wasn't fair to her because she knew that her feelings had been involved. And nothing good could come of that.

"You did not overpower me. Did not force yourself on me." Fired up, she poked his chest each time she made a point. "Did not—"

Gabe grabbed her hand before she had a chance to bore a hole in his chest and wrapped his fingers around hers. Laughing, he shifted the mood again. "Anyone ever tell you that you're gorgeous when there's steam coming from your ears?"

Still on her knees, Julie backed off a little. "Okay, maybe I came on too strong just now," she conceded, "but—"

Sitting up, he cupped her face and brought it closer to his. "I love a strong-willed woman."

Kissing her, he caught her lower lip between his teeth ever so lightly and nipped it. He heard her quick intake of breath, saw the rigidness fade from her body. Very gently, he pushed his shirt from her shoulders until it pooled at her waist. His eyes wicked, he pulled it away from her and tossed it aside.

Unable to help herself, to talk any more sense into her head now than she had been able to the first time, Julie leaned forward and kissed him hard on the mouth. And raced straight back into the arms of insanity.

"Be gentle with me," he said, burying his hands in Julie's hair. "I bruise easily. It's this delicate skin of mine..."

His skin was bronzed and far from delicate-looking. "Shut up and kiss me."

He dragged her to him, her body splayed across his. Already he could feel his body responding to the feel of hers. "Always willing to obey a strong-willed woman." He smiled into her eyes. "I'm just putty in your hands."

She ran her hands over his body. The man was a rock. "Funny, you didn't feel like putty."

"The industrial kind," he teased just before he covered her mouth with his again.

Chapter 12

She was gone when he woke up.

Rousing himself, Gabe stared at the empty place beside him on the bed. They'd finally made it to his bedroom on the third try.

He smiled to himself, remembering.

Who would have ever thought a woman as small as she was would have that much energy? Or create that much energy within him? By his count, they'd made love four times within one night. He couldn't remember ever being with a woman who had aroused him enough to want to make love with her half that many times, much less crave more even though he was enveloped in the most bone-draining exhaustion he'd ever experienced.

And he wanted her all over again. Gabe ran his hand over the space where she'd spent what had been left of the night when they were through with it. The sheets were cool. He was surprised they hadn't been singed in the foray. The lady was something else, all right.

The words replayed themselves in his mind. Something else. And it was that "something else" he should be keeping his mind on, not his libido, not passionate embraces and warm flesh touching flesh.

He knew that McCarthy would have thought him certifiable, but he'd already crossed the line, he reasoned, trying to assuage his conscience. As long as no secrets had been given away, no harm would be done. At least, not to the operation. If Julie were clean in this, she would never forgive him. But whether he'd made love with her once, twice, even four times, her anger would be the same.

The self-inflicted lecture did no good.

Gabe pulled her pillow to him and inhaled. Her perfume or whatever it was that was so distinctly Julie still lingered there. He let it fill his head for a second longer before he made the effort to pull himself together.

Sitting up, he tossed the pillow aside.

He hadn't really expected to find her beside him when he woke up. Hoped, but not expected.

And maybe, just maybe, he was a little relieved, as well. Though he was as good as they came at shutting away his emotions and thoughts when the need arose, he was beginning to seriously doubt that he could pull it off this time, not feeling like this.

This was a completely different set of circumstances than he'd ever been confronted with before. None of the old parameters applied anymore. It made him feel as if he were free-falling without a parachute, without a clue where ground zero was.

Or even *if* it existed.

He needed a few minutes to pull himself together, to carefully replace the facade he was supposed to be wearing. To be someone else other than Gabe Saldana, undercover Vice cop.

With a deep sigh, Gabe scrubbed his hands over his face. A hell of a fix, anyway you looked at it, he thought.

The scent of coffee, drifting slowly in, finally registered, telling him that his first impression was wrong.

Julie was still here.

Getting up quickly, Gabe eschewed underwear and pulled on his jeans, hurrying to the tiny alcove that served as a kitchen. He dragged his hand through his hair in lieu of combing it. He needed a shave and a shower to feel human, but his need to see her outweighed those necessities.

He refused to consider the implications.

The kitchen, hardly large enough to be thought of as a nook, looked brighter just for having her in its midst. Julie was up, dressed and cooking. And looking as clean and delectable as the first slice of some forbidden, powdery and rich confection. He wondered how she would look with whipped cream adorning her—and how she would like having it licked off...

He had to keep reminding himself about the forbidden part. So far, he wasn't doing a very good job of remembering. Shifting gears mentally, he began to seriously think along the lines of proving Julie innocent instead of finding evidence to tie her to the trafficking.

Despite the fact that he was barefoot, Julie heard him coming. She had been listening for him. Frying pan in hand, she turned toward the doorway to see Gabe standing there, hair still falling in his eyes, stubble darkening his face. His jeans were slung low on his hips, and he'd forgotten to close the snap. She had to hold tightly on to the pan to keep from dropping it.

You would think, Julie mused, that after last night's marathon, she would have been sated. More than that, she should have gotten her fill of lovemaking for the next few years.

Should have. But hadn't.

Seeing Gabe like this made her want to make love with him all over again. The realization surprised her. She'd never been a creature of appetites before.

But there was something about Gabe, something that transcended all her good sense, all her well-ordered principles. Transcended and blew them apart until there was nothing left but smithereens.

And she couldn't quite make herself care that they were.

Julie flushed, not exactly certain how he would act toward her, or how she would, or should, respond. They weren't lovers, but last night had been more than a one-night stand. At least to her.

"I was going to be gone by the time you woke up," she confessed before reaching for an egg and cracking it into the pan. "Then I thought maybe you'd like a good breakfast for a change."

Uncertain what had prompted her, she'd glanced in his refrigerator and seen only milk, cereal and cold cuts for sandwiches. That was what had convinced her to steal back into her own apartment and bring back the eggs she was making.

He came up behind her, warning himself to stop. She was supposed to be *his* enemy and he hers until proven otherwise by something besides his instincts.

That didn't seem to want to penetrate anymore. Gabe nuzzled his face against her neck. Another assault of perfume almost made him feel light-headed. "Know what I'd like even more than breakfast?"

Her heart jumped at the question. She was pregnant, the owner of a prestigious art gallery, and a level-headed, responsible businesswoman and her heart jumped like some carefree teenager's at his question. Astounded, she didn't even try to make sense of that. Something inside urged her to enjoy it while she could. Before it was gone.

She covered Gabe's hands with her own, absorbing the feel of him. Letting it warm her. "Do I get three guesses?"

He laughed, the sound seducing her ear. "If you need three, then apparently I didn't do such a good job last night."

She turned in his arms to face him, electricity racing through her veins as her body brushed up against his. "Oh, was that what it was? A job? You expect to get paid?"

Even as she teased, a tiny part of her couldn't help but think of Justin and wonder if this was a case of déjà vu. Justin had been smooth, too. Smoother than Gabe, actually, if she were being impartial.

But not sexier. Or more inventive. Or more wonderful...

Yup, she had definitely regressed to being a teenager, she thought, completely unashamed.

The grin in his eyes teased her, as did the one on his lips. "Sure, as long as I get to exact the form of payment."

Her arms laced around his neck, she cocked her head. "And that would be?"

"Guess." And then he laughed. "Is it me, or did we just have this conversation a minute ago? Never mind, I talk too much."

His mouth took hers captive with quick, darting kisses that grew longer and longer with each pass until Julie found herself within a kiss that drew her out of her very core.

Somewhere along the perimeter of her mind, the part that could still function and identify sounds nudged at her consciousness. She thought she heard something. It took her a beat before she could put a name to it.

"Ringing," she said with a sigh against his mouth.

All he could think of was carrying her back to his bedroom. "You hear bells, too?"

The question made her laugh even as she felt her heart hugging him. "Not bells, bell. The telephone." She pointed to it on the wall.

All Gabe's systems went on alert. The moment evaporated instantly. When she reached for the receiver, he pulled her away from it.

Surprised, Julie looked at him quizzically. With effort, he pretended to still be in the grips of what had been unfolding between them.

"Must be a wrong number." He kissed her neck. "I'm not expecting anyone. I haven't given this number out to anyone." Which was the truth, but he had a feeling that McCarthy had it anyway. His partner might have seemed sleepy-eyed, but he was on top of things.

The telephone continued ringing. "How can you stand not answering it?"

He dragged his hands slowly down the length of her, hating that he was doing it to distract her. "I've got better things to do."

Her laugh washed over him as she pulled free. Darting clear, she grabbed the receiver. "Hello?" All she heard was a subtle click on the other end of the line. Julie stared at it accusingly, then replaced the receiver. "They hung up."

"See, wrong number. Told you." He took her back into his arms. Her body fit against his, tempting him. Making him crazy. "Now, where were we?"

"Burning breakfast," she yelped, looking around his shoulder. Darting past him, she pulled the frying pan from the stove. It was too late. The sunny-side-up eggs were burnt around the edges and sealed to the pan. She frowned at them, then looked up at Gabe. "Not exactly what I wanted to feed you."

He shrugged carelessly, helping himself instead to the pot of coffee she'd brewed. He poured a cup as he watched her dump the eggs in the trash.

"That's okay. I'm not a big eater in the morning, anyway." He look a long sip and tried to ignore his conscience. "So, what projects do you have on tap for me today?"

Running hot water on it, she quickly scrubbed the burned remnants from the pan.

"I'm holding a small show tonight after the regular gallery hours." She'd had so much going on lately, she'd forgotten the lesser show. It had been in the works now for a month. "I could use a hand rearranging the paintings. And I need to bring out the table from the storage room," she added as an afterthought. Shaking water off the pan, she placed it on the rack to dry, then wiped her hands.

He raised a brow. This was the first he'd heard of another show. Had she rearranged things because of the quarantine? No rumors had reached the department about rescheduling the drop.

"You bribing them with food?" he asked casually.

"Better." She replaced the towel, hanging it up on the hook on the wall. "With wine. Some of the art dealers and collectors in the area won't deign to attend anything less than a five-star showing unless you promise to liberally lubricate their palates."

That translated to a lot of drunk drivers. He made a mental note to pass the word on to McCarthy. "I'll remember to stay off the roads tonight."

Julie shook her head. She knew she should get going. There was a lot to do today. Even so, she kept lingering, mentally bartering for a few more seconds. A few more minutes.

"Most of them come with assistants who turn into designated drivers." Her mouth curved in a humorless smile. "I once drove Stanley Armstrong home myself, to keep him from driving into the ocean. Although now that I think about it, it might have been more merciful for everyone that way." He'd tried to force himself on her. In his state, he couldn't have successfully forced himself onto a stool, but his wounded ego had caused him to write several caustic columns about some of the artists she showcased.

The name was familiar. He should know this one, Gabe thought. It took him a minute to make the connection. "Stanley Armstrong, the art critic?"

If she noticed the brief pause, she gave no indication.

"The same. He won't be coming to this one." It was far too small for him to bother with. She hadn't even sent him an invitation, knowing he would have certainly turned it down. "He'll be attending the show next week, though. If there is a show next week," she amended. An entire week, and no positive communication in sight. She tried not to dwell on it until she could do something about remedying the situation. "So, if you're not too busy—"

Draining his cup, Gabe put it down on the counter. "My muse is going to be at her day job today." He grinned at her. "I'm free."

She could swear she felt her heart flutter in response. Why hadn't she met him before Justin? Why hadn't she held herself in check and not allowed self-pity to get the better of her so that she hadn't wound up in Justin's bed was even a better question.

A better question, but one with no answer. What was done was done, and there was no way she could undo it. At least, none she was willing to take.

It was time to go before she gave in to temptation again and allowed last night to replay itself. She grasped the door-knob. "I'll see you later."

With that, she left his apartment.

Gabe gave her a couple of minutes to make sure she wasn't suddenly returning, then going to the closet, he pulled out the cell phone to call McCarthy's home number.

The receiver on the other end picked up on the third ring. "McCarthy residence," a high-pitched voice announced importantly.

Not knowing which one of his partner's three kids had

answered the call, Gabe took a blank stab at it. "Margaret?"

"It's Shawn," the hurt voice on the other end corrected. At eight, Shawn took the honor of being the only other male in the family very seriously.

Gabe could just picture the boy, his wide mouth drooping, his shoulders sagging. The spitting image of his father when McCarthy was insulted. "Sorry, Shawn, I've got a cold in my head. I can't tell voices apart right now. This is Gabe. Is your dad there?"

"Oh, hi, Uncle Gabe." Gabe could hear the bright smile in the boy's voice. All was forgiven. Shawn thought Gabe was the last word in "cool." Unlike his father. "Yeah, he's here."

Gabe waited a beat, but nothing followed. "Could you call him to the phone?"

"Oh, okay."

Listening to the small, squeaky voice turn into a bellow as Shawn yelled for his father, Gabe shook his head in understated fascination. Dealing with kids brought in a completely different set of parameters. They were painfully literal.

Several seconds went by before Gabe heard the receiver being passed from one hand to another. "McCarthy here."

Gabe didn't bother with preamble. McCarthy would figure out it was him fast enough. "Did you just call me?"

The question brought out McCarthy's testier side. "No. What do you take me for, a rookie?"

He hadn't thought so, but nothing else had immediately presented itself. "Sorry, someone just called the apartment and I couldn't pick it up. Julie was here."

"Oh, so it's like that, is it?"

"No, it's not like that," Gabe snapped guiltily. It didn't help things to have McCarthy laugh that way, making it into a sordid undertaking, underscoring the deception. "It's not like anything. Go back to your breakfast."

"Please, any excuse in a storm. Maureen is trying to make eggs Benedict. Actually makes you figure that maybe the traitor got a bum rap. Glad you called, though. Got some news you'll be glad to hear."

About to hang up, Gabe stopped and propped the receiver between his ear and shoulder. Anything to get his mind off what he'd allowed to happen. And what he wanted to happen again. "Go ahead, I'm listening."

"The captain called in every favor he had coming to him. You've got your paintings."

He wasn't sure how he felt about this. As a cop, he should have been glad. It meant the investigation could proceed. As a civilian who'd just made love to an incredible woman, he didn't know. If this went forward, and she was implicated...

"The quarantine's been lifted?"

McCarthy was surprised at the lack of enthusiasm. He figured Gabe would have been happy to hear this part. It made what he had to say even more difficult. "Let's say it's been bent a little. Your girl'll have her paintings for the show. Satisfied?"

No, he wasn't. Gabe wasn't going to be satisfied until he managed to prove that Julie had nothing to do with it. And if she did...

He didn't want to go there.

"It'll help," Gabe conceded.

They'd been partnered from the first. Before that, they'd gone through the academy together. Gabe was godfather to his youngest. McCarthy figured he knew about as much as there was to know about Gabe Saldana and what he didn't know wasn't worth knowing.

That was why he felt he had the right to say what he

was going to say about the suspicions that were creeping in. "Watch yourself, Gabe."

"What's that supposed to mean?"

"It means that I worry about you, okay? And that I'm too old to break in a new partner at this stage of my life." McCarthy sighed, then lowered his voice so that no one else at home could hear him, not even Maureen. The woman couldn't hold on to a secret with a lasso wrapped around it. "You wouldn't be falling for this woman, would you?"

Gabe laughed shortly. "I know better than to jeopardize an operation."

It was as far as McCarthy intended to press the issue, but the wording far from satisfied him. "If *I* didn't know better, I'd say you were evading the question."

Gabe understood what his partner was doing, and he was grateful. "But you do know better, don't you?"

"Yeah."

McCarthy sounded uncertain, but with a safety net below him again, Gabe wasn't about to pursue the matter. "How about what I asked you to look into? Her mother, the other two employees? Evers and Connolly."

That had been a lot easier. Credit checks usually were. McCarthy's voice returned to normal. "Clean as far as we can tell. Nobody seems to know very much about the mother. My guess is that she came back because she's got nowhere else to go."

"Yes, so she said." Sometimes an apple was just an apple and not a poisoned offering, Gabe thought philosophically. And after talking to Elizabeth St. Claire, he'd decided that she was probably just a lady down on her luck, nothing more. "Anything else?"

He heard the rustle of papers. McCarthy religiously wrote everything down in a beat-up notepad he carried in his back pocket.

"Just that none of them seem to have a bank account. The mother and Connolly don't have anything current going, and Evers closed his out six months ago. Might be significant, might just mean that he's got bills to pay he can't stay ahead of." McCarthy sighed. "Not an uncommon thing these days."

Gabe thought of the suits Evers wore and the new car in the lot. That sounded about right.

"Okay, thanks. And tell the captain I appreciate the effort."

"He says you owe him your firstborn for this."

"Then he's going to be disappointed." There wasn't going to be a firstborn. He had a feeling that he'd just encountered the one woman he would have been willing to spend the rest of his life with and one way or another, that just wasn't going to happen. Not after next Friday.

"Gabe? There's something else."

They knew each other's habits. McCarthy's was to save the worst for last whenever he dreaded saying it. Gabe froze. "What?"

"I don't know how to say it—"

"Just spit it out."

"It's your dad, he's in the hospital."

Every nerve ending within his body galvanized. "What happened?"

"They think it's his heart. He wasn't on the job or anything."

"What happened?"

"He had chest pains. Your brother was with him. Rafe made him go to Harris Memorial last night." McCarthy didn't have to be told what was going on in Gabe's mind. "You can't risk going there right now," he warned. "But I thought you'd want to know."

Gabe felt hollow. "Thanks."

Ending the call, he stared at the phone. His first impulse

was to leave everything and get down to the hospital as fast as he could. But McCarthy was right, he couldn't risk being seen outside his role right now. Not this close, not after all the pieces were being pulled together.

But damn it, this was his father. What if—

He was about to press Rafe's number when the kitchen phone rang again. Swallowing a curse, he shoved the cell phone into his pocket and picked up the receiver.

"Hello?"

There was a pause, as if the person on the other end of the line was trying to decide if they had dialed correctly. And then a deep male voice asked, "Is Julie there?"

Preoccupied, Gabe struggled to clear his head. "No, who's this?"

"Do I have the right number? Is this the St. Claire Art Gallery?"

Impatience ate away at him. He hardly heard the question. If his father's condition was serious, McCarthy would have said so, he told himself. He had to go with that until he was free to do otherwise. His father wouldn't approve of his dropping his end of an investigation because he was concerned about his health.

Gabe forced himself to focus on the man on the other end of the line. "Technically, this is the apartment above the art gallery. If you hold on, I'll see if I can get her." She was probably downstairs by now, he reasoned.

"Great. Tell her to hurry." The man tacked on a dry laugh. "This call's expensive."

It was unreasonable, but knowing that didn't stop Gabe from taking an instant dislike to the man on the other end. "Who can I tell her is calling?"

There was a second pause on the other end. "Just tell her an old friend."

The hell he would. "She's going to want to know more than that."

This time, the laugh had a touch of self-importance to it, as if the caller was placing himself in an exclusive echelon. "Don't know her very well, do you? Just hurry up."

Gabe banked down a sudden surge of anger at the high-handed attitude. It wasn't up to him to screen Julie's calls. It was up to him to break up a drug ring any way he could. He wasn't going to be a help to anyone if he kept losing sight of that.

"Yeah, hang on." Gabe set the receiver down on the counter then paused to return his cell phone to the closet. The bulge it formed made it far too conspicuous in his pocket.

Deciding to check to see if she was in her apartment before going downstairs, Gabe went across the hall and knocked on the door.

It opened almost immediately. Wearing a pale gray suit with a short, form-fitting skirt and an electric-blue blouse that brought the color of her eyes out even more vividly, she looked every inch the businesswoman. And he wanted to make love with her.

He found his voice with effort. "There's a call for you."

She looked back at her own telephone. "I didn't hear anything ringing."

Gabe shook his head. "No, it's on the other line." He jerked his thumb toward the apartment behind him.

"That's odd." The separate line had originally been put in by her when she'd lived in the apartment. After she'd bought the gallery, she'd never bothered having it switched off. Julie shut the door behind her. "Everyone usually calls the gallery or my private number."

He caught a whiff of her perfume as she passed and felt his stomach tighten.

With your brain, he chastised himself, following her back into his apartment. *You're supposed to think with your brain, not with any other part of your anatomy.*

Picking up the receiver from the counter, Julie placed it tentatively against her ear. "Hello, this is Julie."

"Julie, finally." Satisfaction rang deep in the man's voice. "I was beginning to think I'd made you up. Julie, it's Justin."

Chapter 13

Gabe saw Julie become rigid right before his eyes, like someone steeling themselves for an ordeal. Who was the man on the other end of the line? What did he mean to her?

Julie's hand tightened on the receiver. She'd thought that Justin was gone from her life forever. Complications came crashing in on her. With her mind scrambling to restore some sort of order, she tried to think.

Her heart was in her throat as she asked, "Where are you calling from?"

"No 'hello'? No 'I've missed you, Justin'?"

There was a mocking quality to his voice, as if her discovering that he'd been using her had all been just a big joke at her expense and didn't matter. What had possessed her to *ever* think she had anything in common with this man? She'd had to have been out of her mind.

"Hello," Julie snapped, purposely ignoring his second prompt.

There hadn't been a single moment where she'd missed him, not a one. If she missed anything at all, it was the illusion of being cared about. But that, she knew, had been missing from her life for a very long time.

"Where are you calling from?" she asked again, her voice a little firmer, a little sterner. If Justin was calling to pressure her for money, he was very much out of luck.

"San Francisco. But I can be there in a few hours— Unless, of course," he added knowingly, "you've already filled my space."

The referral was obviously directed at Gabe. Aware that he was taking this all in, Julie covered the receiver. "Would you give me a few minutes?" Her eyes indicated the door.

Gabe masked his reluctance as he nodded. "Sure."

Who the hell was she talking to? Was it someone connected to the drug deal, or someone from her past? In either case, there'd been something far too familiar in the man's voice for Gabe's liking.

Closing the door behind him, he remained in the tiny foyer between the two apartments. He vehemently regretted not getting a third tap. They'd gone through all the right channels to put a tap on the line coming into the gallery and the one feeding into her apartment, but it had never occurred to either him or McCarthy to put one on the private line in his apartment. Julie had assured him that it was never in use.

So who was it that was calling now? The last "tenant"? The last lover?

The flash of jealousy came and went. He didn't have time to behave like an adolescent. There was an investigation in progress and he'd already compromised it enough as it was.

Fighting frustration, Gabe was reduced to trying to listen through a door that muffled everything on the other side.

Julie waited until she saw Gabe leave and close the door.

Furious, she took her hand off the mouthpiece. "There is no space to fill, Justin, because you never *had* a space."

The laugh on the other end rankled her. "What do you call Christmas Eve?"

There was no hesitation.

"A mistake." That was what she'd said when she sent him packing and he'd thrown the incident in her face. "Still feel that way, huh?" But it was obvious that he didn't want to believe her.

"More than ever." The surprise of his call began to wear away. Her thoughts settling a little, Julie took a deep breath. She knew what she had to do, what she had to say. This made her as uncomfortable, but that didn't negate the fact that it was the right thing to do. Whatever else he was, Justin deserved to know that he was also going to be a father. "As a result of that mistake, I'm pregnant."

"The hell you are." Justin spat the words out.

She didn't have to see him to know that he was stunned. "Hell might be what I'm going through, but I *am* pregnant."

"It's not mine."

In her heart, she'd known he would deny it. She expected nothing better of him. No questions after her health, no concern as to where they went from here. Right now, for Justin it was every man for himself.

"Yes it is." A calmness had slipped into her voice. She was in control again.

"Then get rid of it."

She recoiled from the coldness in his voice. "No."

"If it's half mine, I say get rid of it," he insisted.

"This isn't up for a vote." It was a struggle to keep her voice even. The man was loathsome. He was talking about a child the way he would a bag of garbage. "And even if it were, *you* don't get a say in this."

His voice was hostile, wary. "What do you want from me?"

She thought it was an ironic question, coming from him. "You're the one who called me."

"Oh, I get it. I get it," he repeated, his voice quickening. "Very clever. You're just saying this to get rid of me. You think that if I think you're pregnant with my kid, that'll make me permanently disappear out of your life."

"Would it?" She already knew the answer to that. If it wasn't so sad, it would have been funny, listening to him backpedal.

"You're not pregnant, are you?" The knowing edge was gone again.

"Why don't you come around in September and see for yourself?"

"You can't pin this on me." The defensiveness had returned.

She was tired of this game, and she didn't feel like going around about this again. "I'm not trying to pin anything on you. I just think you should know, that's all. And for the record, I'm keeping the baby, but I want no part of you."

"That makes it mutual."

She heard the receiver being slammed down in her ear. She let out a long breath. Well, that had worked out rather well. Justin had obviously called to put the touch on her, to perhaps regain the roof over his head, this time indefinitely since the blinders were off. She'd been spared having to put up with that awkward confrontation. She didn't take on the part of the heavy very well.

Julie glanced down at her stomach. She had a feeling that it was safe to assume that Justin was permanently out of her life. A sense of immense relief slowly washed over her. She'd done her duty and told the father. That he wanted no part of the information was a bonus, something she could only be grateful for.

She saw Gabe's shirt on the floor, the one he'd worn last night. It was still on the floor where he'd tossed it after taking it off her.

What about your other duty? her mind whispered. *What about telling Gabe that he'd made love to a pregnant woman last night?*

It wouldn't matter to him, she thought. Because she didn't matter to him. Not in the way it counted. Last night had been a wondrous thing, but not a forever thing. Men like Gabriel Murietta did not stay in a woman's life. They made their way from one woman to another, giving as much of themselves as they were able. Never enough to remain.

And since he wasn't staying, she didn't have to tell him anything, she rationalized. He'd probably be on his way before she ever began to show.

Like a valiant soldier, determined to defend the fort to the death, she ignored the pang that thought brought with it.

Trying very hard not to feel anything, Julie picked up the shirt and placed it on the stool. There was work to do.

But as she walked past the easel, she couldn't help stopping to look at the painting propped up on it. She looked more ethereal than real, she thought. Did he see her that way?

Probably not. Just artistic license.

The smile that curved her lips was more sad than happy.

"You've got a show to pull together," she told herself in a stern whisper. "And no time to wallow in emotions. Look where they've gotten you already. Pregnant and confused."

Unconsciously squaring her shoulders, Julie crossed to the door and opened it.

"Everything all right?"

Engulfed in her thoughts, she hadn't realized that Gabe was still standing there, waiting for her. Had he heard anything? A quick sweep of his face indicated that he hadn't.

Still, the guilt she was trying so desperately to purge, or at least bury, came flying back to color her cheeks and bore large holes in her peace of mind. Telling herself that it didn't matter, that she owed no one any explanations, didn't help.

"Yes, why?"

Gabe went with instincts and placed a hand on her shoulder. She was more rigid than a rock formation. "You looked upset in there when you took the call." He looked down into her face. "You still look upset."

She shrugged off his concern and his hand, moving to her side of the foyer. But retreat was a luxury she didn't have time for right now. "Just someone I knew once, calling to see if there was a spot for him."

"On the gallery walls?" She was lying. Gabe watched her eyes and knew there was more to it than that.

Julie took the excuse he handed her. "Yes, on the wall. I told him we were full up right now."

She turned away from him, still telling herself that it didn't matter if he knew the truth or not. That her brief encounter with Justin and the baby they had created had no bearing on anything that was happening now. No bearing whatsoever.

"C'mon, we have work to do."

Without looking back, Julie quickly sailed down the stairs.

Gabe wasn't convinced and damned himself again for failing to get a court order for a tap on that line. He was going to have to ask McCarthy to look into that for him.

The phone was ringing by the time they entered the main gallery. Jeff, newly recovered if not energized, had the receiver before she could reach it. "St. Claire's Art Gallery, how may I help you?" He listened for a moment, his wide, open face registering amazement. "Wait, wait, she'll want to hear this herself."

Without another word, his hand clamped over the mouthpiece, Jeff excitedly thrust the receiver into Julie's hands.

She couldn't tell if it was good excitement or bad excitement. Right now, Julie didn't think the odds were in her favor, but she was hopeful anyway. She supposed that was what made her an optimist at bottom.

Morning sickness allied itself with nerves in her stomach, attacking with a vengeance. Taking the receiver, she refused to throw up.

"Hello, this is Juliette St. Claire."

Unable to wait and have information rationed out to him, Gabe took Jeff aside. "Who's on the phone?"

It never occurred to Jeff to tell Gabe that it was none of his business. Unlike Mike, Jeff had taken a liking to him. It really wasn't in Jeff's nature to dislike anyone.

"That's *Artist's Today.*" He evoked the name of a trendy, well-known publication that catered to the serious collectors. Though he'd begun in a whisper, the volume of his voice increased with each word. "They're sending one of their writers to cover the show next week." Hand fluttering to his chest, Jeff sucked in a deep breath to steady himself. "This is so great. It's going to *really* put us on the map."

Julie hung up just as Jeff made the declaration. The look on her face was far less enthusiastic than Jeff's. "On the map," she echoed. "One way or another."

Jeff's wheat-colored brows drew together in a puzzled wavy line over the bridge of his slightly turned-up nose. He didn't understand why Julie looked so somber. "What do you mean?"

This could be the kind of break she had been hoping

for—if only the pieces would all come together instead of eluding her.

"If those paintings aren't released from Customs, I'm not going to have anything to show that writer except for what I already have." She waved her hand around the paintings that were hanging there. They were all good, but they weren't the kind of cutting edge paintings the magazine was looking to expound on. The ones in quarantine, she'd been assured, were.

"How about your mother?" Gabe suggested.

"What about my mother?" she asked, turning to look at Gabe.

The possible solution had just suggested itself to him and he thought it might be worth a shot. "I'd think the reappearance of one of the art world's most promising artists after a fifteen-year absence might be considered newsworthy."

She dismissed the idea with an impatient wave of her hand. This wasn't going to bail her out. The magazine, the critic, and the collectors were all coming to see her European coupe, not a weary woman with emptiness in her eyes.

"My mother was considered a 'promising' artist more than a decade ago. I'm afraid that no one's interested now."

No one was interested, or *she* wasn't interested? Gabe wondered. "Don't be too sure. The mysterious is always interesting. And a lot of people would want to know what she's working on now."

Why was he always so quick to side with her mother? Julie wondered. Was there more here than met the eye? She looked at him for a long moment. "Or who."

Gabe would have thought her to be more forgiving than that. This was a side he hadn't expected. "That's not fair, Julie."

She regretted the accusation the moment she'd said it, but stubbornness forbade Julie from saying that, or taking it back. Instead she dug in. "A lot of things aren't fair. Running out on a family isn't fair." Julie raised her chin, daring him to dispute what she was saying. "It happens."

Was it hurt that was putting words into her mouth, or a desire for revenge? Gabe wasn't sure. "Running out works both ways, you know."

Her eyes grew into small slits. "Meaning?"

This was none of his concern, yet everything he was wouldn't let him drop it. "Maybe you're running out on her."

Why was her mother the victim, the one who merited concern? What about what she'd gone through? Julie wondered. Why was she the one who always had to take it on the chin just because she knew how to rally? To pick herself up and keep moving? She was sick of the discrimination.

"I'm here, aren't I?" Julie demanded. Out of the corner of her eye, she saw Jeff backing away, obviously stunned to hear her getting angry. She didn't care. She was hurt beyond words, and she couldn't make the bleeding stop. "I've taken her in, haven't I?"

"Physically," he pointed out. "You're still abandoning her emotionally."

She blew out an angry breath. What right did he have to lecture her? Did he even have a clue what she'd gone through "emotionally" herself? "Physically is all that counts."

"Is it?" The question was barely above a whisper. His eyes held hers. "I think you know better than that."

She did, but she didn't need him pointing it out to her. And right now, she had neither the time nor the temperament for this.

"If you're through with the morality lectures, Mr. Murietta, I've got some work to do." Julie deliberately turned her back on him and marched into her office.

Though her back was to him, Gabe inclined his head in mock submission, allowing nothing of what he felt to show on his face. Not trusting his temper to stay under wraps at the moment, he walked out of the gallery, taking care not to slam the front door and shatter it in his wake.

He was angrier than he could ever remember being and didn't have a clue why his temper had risen to such a degree.

Needing to cool off, he got into the van and drove.

The artificially cheerful room was quiet, except for the intermingling sounds emitted by machines and the low drone of a television show in which a Hollywood police detective was giving chase to a voluptuous, female suspect.

With a full head of iron-gray hair and a still powerful build, the man's presence seemed almost incongruous with his surroundings. There was an IV intrusively taped to his arm and various tubes running here, attached there, monitoring vital signs and carefully taking readings. The man appeared to be dozing.

Gently picking up the remote control from his father's bed, Gabe aimed it at the screen and shut the television set off.

"Hey, I was watching that."

"You never did have any taste in programs."

The older man's eyelids fluttered open, and he focused eyes that were a vivid green. As vivid as his son's. He smiled broadly, wiping away the years, before they returned encased within the frown that quickly followed.

"What are you doing here?"

Gabe pulled up a chair. It was late. Julie's mini show was about to start. He had already talked twice on the phone to Rafe, but he wanted to come to check everything out for himself. There'd be no peace for him otherwise.

He placed a hand over his father's and took comfort in

the fact that it still looked as powerful as ever. He could remember thinking that his father's hands were as big as bear paws when he was a kid. "Sneaking in to see my old man."

John Saldana's frown deepened. "You're not supposed to be breaking cover."

Gabe shrugged carelessly. But he'd been careful. No one at the gallery knew where he was going. And there'd been no one following him as he drove down Newport Boulevard. He'd made certain of it.

"All I'm breaking are a few hospital rules. It's after visiting hours."

John squinted at the clock that hung near the door. "How did you get in?"

Gabe winked at him. "I know a nurse."

John laughed shortly. It hurt his chest. Damn tubes, he thought. They'd had one traveling down his throat earlier, until he'd threatened to rip it out himself.

"You know a lot of nurses. Maybe you can spring me," he added hopefully.

Rafe had told Gabe that things looked good for a release by tomorrow afternoon. Getting up, Gabe lifted a clipboard that was hanging off the base of the bed. The notations on the top sheet made no sense to him. But the upward progress on the graph looked promising.

"And maybe I should tie you to your bed." Gabe hung up the clipboard again.

Weak, John still felt restless. He hadn't had a sick day in the last thirty years. This was a lousy way to break his streak. And he didn't like being the topic of discussion, especially where weakness was concerned. "Who told you?"

Gabe met the accusing look in his father's eyes with humor. He was relieved beyond words to see that his father still retained his stubborn streak. "McCarthy."

"Might have known." John snorted. He remembered Kenny McCarthy from the days when the policeman had been a young boy, hanging around his house and playing with Gabe. "Kid always was a blabbermouth."

Gabe couldn't help the grin that came to his lips. It had been a lot of years since Ken McCarthy had probably heard himself referred to as a kid. Then he sobered slightly. "I talked to Rafe."

"He probably made it out to be worse than it was."

"No, he was factual, as always." If anything, Rafe had been immensely upbeat. "Said you had a little episode."

John scowled. "Yeah, of indigestion."

That wasn't what Rafe had said. He'd called it a minor myocardial infarction. A minor heart attack. His father's first. "They have a different name for it." Gabe nodded in the general direction of the door and the hospital personnel beyond.

"Doctors." He said the title in the same tone someone might mention a plague. "Always trying to make things seem like life-and-death situations."

No, nothing had affected his father's sunny disposition, Gabe thought with relief. "Unlike us cops, eh, Dad? We just stroll through things."

For the first time, John smiled at his son. A sparkle returned to the green eyes. "Don't get smart with me."

"Okay," Gabe agreed, suddenly feeling as if something was choking his windpipe. Emotion probably. His gut had been twisted in a knot ever since McCarthy had told him about his father this morning. Fighting with Julie hadn't helped, neither had the fact that it had been over nothing, completely baffling him. "I'll leave the smart part up to you."

A gray brow rose in an inquiring arch. "Meaning?"

"You're going to give up all that rich food."

John groaned as he rolled his eyes. "That'll be just like dying."

"Not quite. You get to keep your family on this plan—and they get to keep you." He sympathized with his father, but not enough to give in. "You don't have to give up taste to give up fat."

John had already heard enough of that to last him a lifetime. His own doctor had been after him for years now, claiming that he had to slow down, take things easier, watch his diet. Making him feel old. "You sound like a damn commercial."

Gabe refused to rise to the bait. "I'll sound like anything you want, Pop, as long as you give me your word you're going to change your habits." The stubborn look in his father's eyes told him he needed something to put him over the top. After a beat, Gabe played his ace. "Rafe said Mom's crying."

"Oh, why'd you have to go and tell me that?"

They both knew that Carol Saldana rarely, if ever, gave in to tears. That she had was testimony to how serious the situation might have been. "To get you to feel guilty."

John huffed as his scowl darkened. "Well, you did it."

"Good. Then my work here is done." Gabe bent over his father and surprised John by kissing his forehead. Their eyes met and held, pregnant with so many things that remained unsaid for far too long. Too long. "I love you, Old Man, and I want you sticking around for a good, long time, telling me how I'm screwing up."

Funny how he'd thought the raspiness in his throat was finally gone and now it was back again. John grasped his son's hand. "Deal."

The handshake was firm, Gabe thought. His father was going to be all right. This had just been a warning, one that was going to be heeded even if the family had to take turns playing John Saldana's bodyguard.

It was getting late. He should have been at the gallery by now. Gabe slipped his hand away. "I've got to go."

John nodded. "Don't get caught, kid."

"Never happen."

As he walked out, Gabe heard his father cursing the detective on the screen, muttering that he'd just broken six rules of procedure.

Gabe grinned as he closed the door behind him. But his thoughts turned serious as walked to his van. After battling the fear that his father might not make it through the day, Gabe decided that maybe Julie needed to mend a fence of her own before it was too late. And if he could do one thing to atone for his lies, this would be it.

Chapter 14

Where *was* he?

Like a person in the clutches of a nervous habit, something she was definitely *not* accustomed to, Julie kept looking at her watch every few minutes. Expecting to see Gabe come walking through the front door every time she looked up.

But he didn't. He was conspicuously absent from the gallery.

Not that anyone but she would have noticed. The show, small by the standards that she had set for the upcoming invitation-only gala, was by all appearances a rousing success. It seemed that everyone who had received a verbal invitation had contacted someone else, and the art gallery was filled with twice as many people as she had anticipated. This was the kind of turnout every art gallery owner hoped for. The best part was that there were more than just one or two interested in buying paintings by the artist she had decided to showcase.

Maybe that was why it felt so unbearably stuffy in here, she thought. Though the red dress she was wearing was light, she felt as if she was going to begin perspiring at any minute.

Making her way through the crowd, she lowered the temperature setting a little. Any second now, she expected people to begin turning shades of golden brown, like end products from a toaster oven.

Wandering back to the throng, she saw Malcolm Meyers standing in front of a particularly large painting, staring at it as if trying to decide whether to digest it or acquire it. "It does catch your eye, doesn't it?" she asked, easily slipping in next to him.

The wide face behind the graying, close-trimmed beard widened a bit more in a smile. "Almost as much as you do, Juliette. What's the asking price?"

Very subtly, she pointed to the numbers written neatly below the title.

Malcolm shook his head. "Too small for me to see. Read it to me."

Obligingly, she quietly quoted the amount. She knew that if it were tripled, Malcolm wouldn't even blink an eye. He was one of the lucky ones, able to buy whatever, and at times whoever, he took a fantasy to without having to even think.

Cocking his head, Malcolm studied the painting a little closer.

"Done," he declared. "I'll take it." He winked at her. "Before he gets too big, and his asking price goes through the roof." Amused by the irony of his comment, he chuckled to himself, his stomach jiggling beneath his two-thousand-dollar suit.

This was going to make Adam Hewett very happy, she thought. The young artist spent a lot of time doubting his own abilities. It had taken a great deal of convincing before she could talk him into the show.

"Very wise of you, Malcolm. You have a very good eye for talent."

Pleased at the compliment, Malcolm snorted. "For investment, Juliette," he corrected. "You have the eye for talent. Your father, if he were still alive, would have been very proud of you."

Julie sincerely doubted that. But she smiled at Malcolm and obligingly thanked him for the compliment.

"You're very welcome." Malcolm's eyes swept over her in less-than-fatherly appraisal, though she was young enough to be his daughter. "You know, I'd still love to get together over dinner sometime and discuss my collection with you. Perhaps have you point out a few more sound investments for me."

It was an old game. She had been dodging Malcolm's thinly veiled propositions for four years now. She was grateful that he had never become insistent. It would have ruined a very lucrative association.

"I'd love to," she assured him. "But I am very busy these days. I'm going to have to check my schedule before I can give you an answer."

He accepted the evasion, amusement in his small, brown eyes. "You have my card."

Julie inclined her head. "And your check, soon I trust."

"Now if you like." Opening his jacket and digging into his breast pocket, Malcolm produced his checkbook.

Julie led him to a desk where he could comfortably write out the check. This time, when she glanced around the gallery, she was looking for the artist. Though Adam had a shock of blond hair and was as tall as a rail, it took her a few moments to find him.

When she finally saw him, he was talking to Gabe. And her mother.

Julie wasn't sure who she was more surprised to see. Gabe, who had somehow slipped in without her noticing, or her mother.

Elizabeth had turned down her halfhearted invitation to attend the show when she'd made it earlier. Feeling obligated to extend the invitation, Julie had been relieved when her mother had refused. Having Elizabeth visible and mingling with her patrons would have created too much tension for her, as well as drawn away from the star of the show.

So far, the only one who seemed to have noticed that her mother was here were the two men talking to her. But that might have been because she'd only just come down, Julie guessed.

"There you go, little lady." Malcolm ripped the check away from others and handed it to her. "You know where to send my painting."

"Indeed I do." She subtly glanced at the check to verify the correct amount before she tucked it away into her desk drawer. With a turn of her wrist, she locked the drawer and slipped the key onto a chain around her neck.

She could feel Malcolm's eyes on the key as she slipped it down the neckline of her dress. Her eyes meeting his, she smiled.

"For that amount, you get the honor of meeting the artist himself." Tucking her arm through his, she turned Malcolm in the right direction. Julie raised her voice as she looked toward Adam. "Adam."

When the artist turned to see who was calling him, she gestured him over.

But it was Gabe whose eyes hers involuntarily met with. She damned herself for being so nervous, for worrying that he'd walked out permanently because they'd had heated words.

She couldn't help wondering what was he saying to her mother.

"Would you come here, please?" She waved to the artist again. "I have someone here you might like to meet."

When Adam finally reached her, Julie made the proper introductions and then excused herself, leaving the two men to talk as she made her way through the milling bodies. It took her a couple of minutes before she could join Gabe and her mother.

As soon as she was in her mother's presence, she could feel herself changing. Stiffening. It was something that happened without any thought on her part. Involuntary, like her eyes shutting when she sneezed. Would she ever get over that?

Her smile was forced as she looked at her mother. "I see you've changed your mind, Mother."

Dressed in a soft, dark green dress that was reminiscent of a time when life moved more slowly, Elizabeth smiled at the man standing beside her. The famous line about relying on the kindness of strangers played itself across Julie's mind. It suited her mother to a *T*.

"Gabe persuaded me to come down."

Julie had a feeling she had him to thank for this. She really wished the man would stop interfering in her life. Her eyes shifted toward him, her smile still tight. "You've been busy, I see. When did you get here? I didn't see you come in."

Discovering that she'd been looking for him aroused more emotions than Gabe felt like exploring right now. The natural assumption was that she needed another pair of willing hands. A less likely thought was that she'd somehow caught on to his real purpose for being here and wanted to keep close tabs on him. As close as he wanted to keep on her.

The truth, he figured, was probably somewhere in between.

Gabe nodded toward the rear of the gallery. "I came in through the back."

Going upstairs to change into something a little more suitable for the show, he'd played a hunch and knocked on Julie's door after changing clothes. When Elizabeth answered, he'd asked if she was attending. Coaxing her, he'd turned a no into a yes. He told himself it was to add a further diversion and distract Julie from catching on to him. But again, the truth was not so cut and dried, he thought, remembering the vow he'd made after visiting his father.

He supposed that made him the voice of her conscience. He could think of worse things to be.

Gabe nodded toward the crowded gallery. "Looks like you have a hit on your hands."

There was no point in being annoyed at him. Elizabeth's reappearance was going to be noticed by someone sooner or later. She might as well deal with it now and get it over with.

Julie turned her attention to the well-dressed patrons wandering through her gallery, sipping champagne and sampling talent. Edginess turned to gentle pride.

"It does, doesn't it?" She glanced over toward Adam, who was still deep in conversation with Malcolm. For the first time in memory, she saw a glowing, boyish smile on the artist's face. "I just hope this doesn't go to his head. His success is progressing a little faster than I anticipated."

Elizabeth's gaze followed her daughter's. "Adam seems like a level-headed boy. I don't think he'll have trouble adjusting to having a few dollars in his pocket," she said softly.

A sense of competition reared its head and while she was ashamed of the way she felt, Julie still couldn't help the sudden feeling of irritation. "When did you get to be such an expert on Adam, Mother?"

Elizabeth seemed oblivious to the harsh note in her

daughter's question. "Not an expert, dear. It was just an observation. Gabriel introduced us just now."

But before she had a chance to say anything, a large, florid-faced man approached them. He had the air about him of someone who believed that he took center stage wherever he went and whenever he chose. He wasn't far from wrong. As the leading art critic on the West Coast, he commanded respect and more than that, fear.

At the moment evoking fear appeared to be the furthest thing from his mind. His hands were extended toward the woman he'd focused his piercing gray gaze on. There was just the slightest touch of awe in them.

Julie told herself she should have been amused. She wasn't.

"I couldn't believe my eyes without coming closer to make certain." Close enough now for even a myopic rodent to see clearly, the man continued staring. The wit that so many feared suddenly seemed to turn to worshipful mush. "It *is* you. Elizabeth, my dear, how have you been?" Their hands joined; he didn't even entertain the idea of releasing hers. "*Where* have you been is the better question." He raised both her hands to his lips for a respectful kiss. Finally releasing them, he reclaimed one and tucked it through the crook of his arm. In doing so, he turned his back on Julie without directing a single word toward her. "You have to tell me everything. Does this mean you'll finally grace us with another painting? It's been too, too long, darling."

Like a pirate greedily glorying in his booty, he walked off with Elizabeth.

Gabe looked at Julie. "Stanley Armstrong?" he guessed. No one else could have been so cartoonlike and still carried it off.

Julie laughed shortly under her breath. *Mother was holding court again,* she thought. "None other. Larger than life. It says so on his business card. Probably on his Christmas cards, too.'' Armstrong's appearance was a surprise. He wasn't expected to attend this show. She hoped that didn't mean he intended to skip the big one. If there was a big one.

A sense of déjà vu pervaded her. Suddenly feeling alone in the crowd, Julie turned toward him. ''Personal business all taken care of?''

It sounded like a harmless enough question. But Gabe knew a paranoid undercover cop was a living undercover cop. Why was she asking? He kept his expression mild. ''What makes you think I was taking care of any personal business?''

Julie shrugged, already dismissing the question. Wishing she could dismiss other things as easily. She hated this feeling clinging to her. She wasn't in competition with her mother. They were worlds apart. Worlds different.

And she had a living to make, she reminded herself sternly.

''Just a guess,'' she murmured to Gabe. ''You were gone for a while.''

Why was he looking at her like that? As if he was trying to decide something. Did he think she was being possessive? That was the last impression she wanted to create. Because it just wasn't true.

''Sorry, didn't mean to sound as if I was prying.'' Julie warned herself against protesting too much and making the matter worse. She shrugged. ''Just making conversation.''

But it wasn't conversation. It was curiosity, and it was pricking at her something fierce. All she knew about Gabe was what he had told her.

The same as with Justin.

But there was a world of difference between Gabe and Justin. Justin had been obsequious from the beginning, almost pandering toward her. Gabe had just been…Gabe. There was no better explanation for it. Unlike a typical starving artist, he hadn't given the impression of being brooding or needy. The only thing he'd been to excess was sexy, but she doubted he had any control over that.

The thought made Julie smile. She felt a little better.

"So," she said brightly, changing the subject and gesturing around the gallery, "what do you think?"

He wasn't sure if she meant the show, or something more specific. He took a stab at it. "I think Adam's very happy."

That he focused on the artist rather than the show was telling to her. Gabe was undoubtedly identifying with Adam and probably a little jealous of him, as well. It was understandable, although she had a hard time attributing something so mundane as jealousy to Gabe.

"We could have a show for you someday. Soon. Provided you give me more than two paintings to work with." She thought of the one in his room. And what had followed after the sitting. She roused herself before she went too far down that road. "By the way, I had an offer for one of your paintings today."

His expression froze around the edges as he looked at her. "I thought you weren't going to hang them until next week."

It wasn't quite the reaction she'd expected. "I changed my mind." On impulse, she'd had Jeff hang both up just before the show had started. A splash of variety had been her excuse. She'd really just wanted to see people's reaction to his work. She had a feeling she wasn't quite as impartial anymore as she should be. "The buyer's willing to pay the asking price, but I thought I'd ask you first. It's just a formality—"

"No."

"No?" She blinked. It was every artist's dream to sell, to have others want his or her work. "No, what?"

Gabe thought quickly, hunting for something plausible

to tell her. Selling the paintings hadn't been part of the deal he'd made with Rafe.

"I'd like it to be up for a while before it's sold."

"You don't know which one it is."

Gabe shook his head. "Doesn't matter." He stopped, knowing that he wasn't making any sense to her. Aside from self-expression, selling was what this was all about. He slanted a look toward her. "Does that sound pompous to you?"

Julie smiled at the insecurity behind the question. It was nice to know he was human after all. "No, just a little possessive. Like a father who can't let go of his children just yet." She could understand that without having taken part in the process. Loving something that's a part of you.

Like the baby she was carrying, she realized, the thought sneaking up on her.

She laid her hand on his arm. "Don't worry. I'll tell the buyer I couldn't reach you. Take your time."

Turning away from him, she looked around, unconsciously searching the crowd until she saw Elizabeth and Armstrong. They were in the center of the gallery, deep in conversation. A few people had gravitated toward the outer fringes of the tight circle they created.

Gabe followed her line of vision. He had a hunch that was what had drawn her attention. "She'll be all right."

Caught, she looked away. "I wasn't worrying about her."

"No?" The grin on his lips told her he thought she was lying. "Then why were you looking at her and Armstrong so intently?"

"Was I?" She was the soul of innocence. "I was just thinking, that's all. My eyes strayed." Then, mercifully, she saw Mike waving to get her attention. From the pleased smile on his face, she guessed that there was another buyer in the wings. She moved away from Gabe. "Well, mingle, absorb, listen. Think of it as your dress rehearsal,'' she added in parting.

Gabe stood watching her weave her way back through the crowd. Her red dress adhered to every curve, swaying enticingly with every movement.

Damn, he had to stop thinking with his body parts and start doing it with his head. Or at the very least, with his badge, he admonished himself.

Still, no matter how he sliced it, Julie was by far the most diverting sight in the art gallery.

Diverting or not, he had a job to do. Gabe picked up a fluted glass filled with champagne and did as Julie had instructed. He mingled and absorbed, but for an entirely different reason.

Thanks to the laptop and portable printer hidden in his closet, Gabe was familiar with the faces of all the major drug dealers on the West Coast. He scanned the crowd from time to time to see if any of those dealers had turned up for this show as he exchanged banal pleasantries with the other patrons.

And hated what he was doing.

It was past twelve before the last of the guests finally left St. Claire's. Julie looked around at the scattered empty glasses left in every conceivable place. For a fleeting second, she debated gathering them up. She hated coming down to chaos first thing in the morning, but she was far too tired to face the task right now.

Making up her mind, Julie kicked off her shoes and locked up.

She had sent Mike and Jeff to their respective homes more than an hour ago. The gallery was almost eerily quiet. Gabe was probably upstairs, she mused. Directing her steps toward the rear of the gallery, she took an earring off and rubbed her ear. She didn't know if it was sore from the weight of the earring, or from having to listen to Armstrong prattle on at length tonight.

He'd been enthusiastic about her mother, completely ignoring the fact that he was attending the first show of a promising young artist and that his attention should have been focused on that.

Fat chance.

As always, her mother had drawn the spotlight around herself like a tight shawl. It was something Julie had seen, time and again, during her childhood. Experiencing it again evoked no warm memories from the past. It had the complete opposite effect.

Julie stopped a few feet short of the upstairs door. She thought of going up to her apartment, of possibly having to talk to her mother. She wasn't in the right frame of mind for that right now. Feeling the way she did, she knew she might say something she would regret at a less emotional time.

Time.

She needed time. But that was something that seemed to have such a very high tariff these days. And right now, it was in very short supply. She hadn't had enough time to adjust to her mother's return—to adjust to the pregnant state she found herself in. Not enough time to negotiate the release of the quarantined paintings.

And it was definitely the wrong time to fall in love with a sexy stranger.

Turning on her heel, she crossed back to the front of the gallery, slipped on her shoes and unlocked the door. Checking her pocket for the key, she reset the security alarm and went out.

There was a beach located not far behind the houses across the street. That was part of the appeal and beauty of St. Claire's location. It enjoyed both the wealth of the close-by Newport Beach society and the bohemian, free spirit that went with being on the cusp of a beachfront community.

Right now, she needed the solitude of the beach.

At this time of night, there was very little traffic running along the junction of Pacific Coast Highway where St. Claire's was located. Hurrying across the wide street, Julie made her way to the beach.

Though it was February, the evening was seductively mild. Spring was on its way. The ocean would be cold, but all she wanted was to feel sand between her toes and perhaps ground herself a little.

Julie slipped between two houses. The beach lay just beyond.

Taking off her shoes, Julie closed her eyes and sighed as her toes made contact with the sand.

"Planning to make sand castles next?"

Heart in her throat, she whirled around. Gabe. She might have known. She began to walk down the long stretch of beach. Very slowly, she breathed in and then out, trying to steady her nerves.

"Have you decided to become my guardian angel?"

Gabe fell into step beside her. Good thing he'd decided to watch the street from his window. His first impulse on seeing her cross the street was that she was going to meet a contact. The idea that she was "dirty" still haunted him.

"Maybe. I'm beginning to think you need one." He looked around. There appeared to be no one in view. Maybe this was just a harmless stroll, after all. "I thought we already had the discussion about you not running around by yourself at night."

Julie grinned. Maybe it was hopelessly old-fashioned of her, but she liked this protectiveness about him. Liked the fact that someone actually thought of her as needing protection. "That was through alleys. This is the beach."

"And people don't get mugged on the beach?"

Shoes in one hand, she threaded the other through his arm. A feeling not unlike contentment began weaving through her. The tension slowly leeched out. "Not when they have six-foot-two guardian angels with broad shoulders."

"Six-three," he corrected. "But you're evading the question."

"Rather nicely, I thought," she agreed. Mischief curved her mouth. She was feeling giddy without a clue as to why. "Guardian angels aren't supposed to argue."

Gabe inclined his head toward her. Enough to catch the scent of her perfume again. He felt his gut tightening. And fought to ignore the longing that came in the wake of the scent.

He liked the feel of her arm linked with his. Liked it too much, he thought. And that wasn't good. But for now, he left his arm exactly where it was and tried not to think about kissing her.

"They don't like to publicize that part too much," he confided in a stage whisper. "Obviously you've never read *Paradise Lost* by Milton."

"*Paradise Lost,*" Julie echoed. So he was well read along with everything else. "You keep surprising me. But then, I'm forgetting you're a Renaissance man." She looked at the moon strumming long silvery fingers along the water. "I needed some air after the show."

"Just air?"

"Air, sand, ocean." She waved her hand at the beach, taking it all in. "Who could ask for more?"

Gabe could, he thought. He could ask for something more than he had. For things to be different. To be free to feel what he was feeling.

"People always ask for more, Julie," he told her quietly. "It's the nature of the beast."

"So now I'm a beast?" She couldn't even manage to

sound playfully offended, she was too amused. "The Angel and the Beast. Has an interesting ring to it."

He laughed and pulled her to him for a quick hug. Any longer and all bets would be off. "How much champagne have you had?"

"None. I try never to mix alcohol and business. Although I wanted one," she allowed. "After I saw my mother latch on to Armstrong."

Turning to look at her, he arched his brow. "Seems to me the latching was the other way around. I was there, remember?" The wind was playing with her hair. Reaching over, he gently combed his fingers through it.

Julie felt as if the air had stopped in her lungs again. Why did he always have that effect on her?

"You always seem to be there." Turning away, she dragged in a breath to sustain herself. "What did she have to say?"

"About?"

Impatience had her shrugging. This was difficult for her. "Anything. The show, the gallery." Julie's voice lost momentum. "I don't know."

"Why don't you ask her yourself?" he suggested. When she made no answer, he added, "Why don't you let the past go, Julie?"

"Because I can't—I try." Frustration stole away all the right words. She tried anyway. "Maybe I even want to, but every time I start to open my mouth, the words don't come out. My mother—" She knew she wasn't making any sense, wouldn't be able to make any sense. And he'd just think she was this hateful person who bore a grudge. She didn't want him thinking of her that way. "Never mind. It's just too complicated."

But Gabe wanted her to get it all out. Stopping, he turned her so that she'd look at him. "Tell me. I'm not going anywhere."

For now, Julie thought. But he would. Everyone always went, always left her eventually. Her mother, her father, people she counted on. It was just a matter of time. He'd leave, too.

"But I am," she said brightly. "Back to the gallery."

"Julie—"

She was determined. "You can stay here, if you'd like. I'm suddenly tired, and I have a long day tomorrow." Tugging her hand free, she quickly made her way back.

Chapter 15

"You know, you're never going to resolve whatever it is that's between you and your mother unless you face it yourself."

Gabe's words followed her as Julie made her way out to the sidewalk in front of the two houses. She tried to ignore him, ignore the fresh wound to her conscience that his words evoked. It was an effort doomed to failure from the first.

Jabbing at the pedestrian button on the long, metal column of the traffic light, Julie whirled around to look at Gabe just as he came up behind her.

"Maybe I don't want to resolve it, did you ever think of that? Maybe I just want to forget about it, to pretend it never happened." More than anything, she wished that it were possible.

Gabe had no idea why he had the insight into her mind that he did. Why he could see this so plainly when everything else seemed so obscure. But he knew she didn't mean what she said.

And maybe, just maybe, knowing that was beginning to color his perception of everything else.

"What about your mother—are you going to pretend she never happened, either?" he asked quietly. "Then how do you account for the woman in your apartment?"

Because his voice was so infuriatingly calm, Julie felt like shouting. But she didn't. She settled for a muffled growl. "I don't. I ignore her."

The light changed and Julie sprinted across the wide thoroughfare.

He was right behind her, his footsteps echoing hers. "You just intend to keep running?"

"I'm not running." Realizing that she was, at least literally, she slowed her pace as she reached the opposite sidewalk. "Exactly. I'm trying very hard to survive right now, that's all." St. Claire's was only a few doors down and she made her way quickly toward it. "I didn't need this added complication in my life." She spared him a fierce glance before she unlocked the front door. "I didn't need *any* of it."

Gabe moved quickly, having the feeling that she'd close the door on him if he lagged a step behind. "And by 'any' you mean—"

Flipping the locks and reactivating the security system, she turned toward him and sighed. "Let's just drop it, okay?"

That was twice she'd insisted on being evasive tonight. He followed her to the rear door and the staircase that lay beyond. "Careful, you keep tossing aside issues right and left like that, you're going to get a reputation as a litter bug."

The analogy brought a smile despite her best resolve. Julie looked at him before leading the way up the stairs. Gabe was taking an awful lot on himself, considering that they were still relative strangers in all but the physical sense.

"A little tall and muscular to be Jiminy Cricket, aren't you?"

He laughed as they reached the landing. "They were going for a brand-new interpretation."

Why did he keep making her want to smile when she should be telling him to butt out and mind his own business? What was it about this man that made him so damn appealing and got under her skin so?

"Why don't you just quit while you're ahead and stick with the guardian angel gig?"

"Can't." Even when he told himself he should. "A man's grasp should extend his reach, or what's a heaven for?"

"For retreating to."

She didn't mean that. Gabe saw right through her. "You're not the type to retreat, Julie." Unable to keep his hands away from her any longer, he allowed himself the smallest sample. He caressed her cheek. "You're the type who forges on. Who conquers things."

Julie could feel it beginning. Could feel her blood begin to stir. "Right now, I don't feel very conquering-like."

"What do you feel like?" The question was hardly louder than a whisper, moving seductively along her skin. Undermining every single resolve she'd so carefully locked into place.

What did she feel like? Like being conquered, she thought. Like having the conscious decision of making love with Gabe ripped out of her hands so that she wouldn't feel guilty about it. So that she could point to being overwhelmed by him as an excuse.

Because she wanted him so badly right now, she could hardly form coherent thoughts. Valiantly, she took refuge in a lie. "I'm too tired to feel."

"You went out on the beach because you were too wound up to sleep, now you're too tired?"

His eyes were laughing at her. They were beautiful eyes, she thought. Mesmerizing eyes. She sank a little deeper. "The beach'll do that to you."

Gabe pulled her into his arms, their union a foregone conclusion. "Know what the beach does to me?"

The question hung suspended in a warm, inviting haze that hovered all around her. "What?" Julie had to concentrate to push out the word.

"Makes me want to go swimming." Very lightly, he pressed a kiss to one temple. "Swimming in your eyes." He anointed the other temple.

She was melting, she thought. There was no alarm attached to the realization. "Watch out for the shallow end."

"There is no shallow end." He moved his head back to look at her. At her eyes. "They're so deep, they're bottomless."

And that was just the way Gabe felt right now, as if he'd fallen into a bottomless pool. As if he were going down for the third time.

Drowning in her eyes.

All the good intentions, all the promises he'd made to himself broke apart and dissolved like tufts of cotton candy thrown on the water.

He was compromising everything. Himself, his principles, his investigations, and God only knew what else, but knowing that didn't stop him. He just couldn't seem to help himself. Couldn't make himself stay away.

The lost look in her eyes pulled him to her as nothing else could. The only thing he wanted right at this moment was to erase that look. To make her feel better. To somehow assuage whatever hurt it was that she was harboring.

And to taste her lips again and relive the surge that he'd initially felt.

Was feeling again.

His fingers splaying through her hair, Gabe brought his mouth down to hers. Gently, as if testing the waters of her acceptance. Afraid to break down that last barrier for fear that once it was taken away, no protest coming from her would make a difference.

He'd take her because he couldn't do anything else.

He needn't have worried.

Julie laced her arms around his neck immediately, her body cleaving to his as if they were two halves of a whole that had been temporarily stretched apart, but was held together by a spring. A spring that was contracting, reclaiming its shape.

Gabe's body heated instantly.

In another minute control would be completely erased, a thing of the past, and he would take her here and now, where they stood. "Maybe we'd better get out of the hall," he suggested with effort, the words grazing her mouth.

Julie ran her tongue over her lips, sealing in his flavor. Anticipating more. "Maybe," she agreed, the same urgency soaring through her.

Feeling behind her, she found the knob on his door. But turning it didn't make it yield. Surprise pushed its way to the surface. Julie looked at him. "It's locked."

"I must have pulled it shut behind me when I ran after you."

That was when his mind had still been functioning. Gabe had things buried in his closet that weren't easily explained, given his supposed circumstances, if someone happened to stumble across them.

He took out his key and unlocked the door.

Julie remained on the threshold. "Ran after me? Why would you run? Did you think I was going to just walk into the sea like Ophelia? After a successful exhibition?"

Momentarily caught, he searched for an excuse that

would convince her and divert any further speculation on her part. "I saw the look on your face when you were watching your mother. I was worried about you…" The door offered a small squeak in protest as it was shut behind them.

It was dark in the apartment, with only the moonlight illuminating the room, pooling on the wooden floor like silver water. Gabe reached for the switch.

"Don't." Her entreaty stopped him.

Taking her into his arms, he smiled. "Conserving on electricity?"

Why did it have to feel so good, being in his arms? Why did nowhere else feel as good, as if she belonged? Julie had no answers.

"Something like that." It was more romantic this way, to make love with him with the moonlight bathing them. Being watched by a handful of stars visible through the huge bay window. That he'd gone after her out of concern touched her more than he could possibly guess. "No one's ever worried about me before."

"No one?" She touched so many lives, how could there not be a squadron of people concerned about her?

She was afraid to breathe, afraid that if she did, this feeling would go away. Leaving her bereft.

"No one," she whispered.

With his fingertips gently gliding along her back, Gabe coaxed the zipper down to its base, then very slowly, pulled the red material away from her.

"I don't believe it," he told her. "Your parents—"

She tugged his shirt out of his pants, working the buttons loose, her eyes fixed on his. Anticipation leaping through her veins.

"—worried about each other," she assured him. "It was a very small, exclusive club. Admission by invitation only. I wasn't invited."

Gabe didn't believe it. He'd seen the look in Elizabeth's eyes when she'd been watching Julie. No one was that good an actress. There was love there. Love on both sides. Bound up tighter than the paintings that had been in quarantine.

He began to work the clasp on her bra loose. "I think you need to talk to your mother."

Her breath was already beginning to come in snatches. Shivers had started marching along her spine. "And I think you should stop trying to be all things and settle on just five or six careers." Julie caught her breath suddenly as she felt him cup her breasts. "—As long as one of them isn't a psychologist."

Desire flowered in her eyes, taking Gabe prisoner. "What would you like me to be?"

She was still working his trousers free, her fingers getting in each other's way. "Lover comes to mind."

"Like this?"

Cupping the column of her throat with his hand and tilting her head back, he captured lips that had absolutely no desire to be anywhere else than where they were. Against his.

The moan of surrender was immediate. And intoxicating. He felt the rush of excitement bursting through her veins. She was completely his for the taking.

His hands worshipped every inch of her, reacquainting themselves with the familiar, finding new, secret places that aroused and excited them both.

It was like the first time.

It was like no other time before.

The languid preamble gave way to passion's hot demands and suddenly they were hurrying, wanting, needing and shedding the last of their inhibitions, the last of their clothes. Everything that got in the way of steeping themselves in the taste, the touch, the feel of one another.

They got as far as the table in the center of the room and no further.

With a savagery that stunned him shredding his control, Gabe fought hard to keep from ravaging what he knew was being willingly offered. He had no idea where this other side of him had come from, this wild, almost untamable beast that burned so badly for her. That wanted nothing else but to feast on her, to purge himself within her body and lose himself in her.

With a sweep of his hand, he sent brushes and vials of paints flying. Then, mouth still sealed to hers, he raised her onto the table.

Julie heard Gabe's ragged breathing rasping within her head as his mouth raced over her body, setting it on fire. Building on that until the inferno threatened to consume her.

To do away with her.

She twisted and turned beneath his mouth, each new place he found alive with craving, with sensations that went off like a battalion of Fourth of July firecrackers arranged in domino fashion. The explosions came one by one, racking her body, making her want more, making her fear that each volley would completely destroy her and leave only ashes in its wake.

She didn't care.

It was a wonderful way to leave this world, loved, wanted, desired. All the things she never felt before. All the things she'd always craved, but never dreamed could be like this.

Wanting badly to make him feel at least a small portion of what she was experiencing, she reared up against him. Rising from the table, her body moist and trembling from his continuous assaults, Julie dragged Gabe to the floor.

Gabe would have followed her anywhere.

With deft movements, Julie reversed their positions. This

time it was her turn to touch, to tease, to arouse. To use her teeth, her tongue, her lips as dual instruments of torture and pleasure, one feeding on the other, until she had him gasping and grasping beneath her.

While he could still focus his eyes, he looked at her. "Where...the...hell did you...learn...all this?"

She smiled, the simple expression spilling through her until her entire body felt as if it had joined in. Triumph throbbed in her loins.

"From you."

Sitting astride his torso, Julie bent forward, the ends of her hair gliding along his chest, sensitizing his flesh until his gut tightened like a bow about to be discharged. He grasped the hips that formed a maddening parenthesis around his own and fought to not dig his fingers into her.

"If you know what's good for you, you'll come down here." The order was forced, breathless.

"And what is good for me?" she teased.

The next moment Julie's eyes grew serious as she sealed her mouth to his, her legs spreading even further over him. Her breath backed up in her lungs as she felt Gabe fill her. Felt the breadth of his desire a heartbeat before he began to move within her, driving her crazy. Driving her up to heights she aspired to.

Tightening around him, Julie rocked, echoing the rhythm, racing with him, wanting to reach the final peak right beside him.

When it happened, when she felt their mutual release, their mutual contentment taking hold, she collapsed onto his chest. Her mouth swollen from his, her soul glowing and exhausted, she had barely enough strength left within her to manage a smile.

But he felt her mouth curving along his chest. The sweetness of that filled him, claiming the spaces that desire had hollowed out only moments before. Incredibly moved,

Gabe cupped the back of her head, stroking his fingers slowly through her hair.

The sensation, coupled with a peacefulness the magnitude of which was completely unknown to him before this moment, identified itself to him. But he refused to pay attention to it, refused to recognize it for what it was. He knew it would be a great deal less complicated that way.

"What are you smiling about?" he finally managed to ask.

She was too exhausted to lift her head. It was an effort just to talk. "I was just wondering if you had gotten any splinters."

"I don't know," he murmured. "I think I lost all feeling from the neck down." He exhaled a large breath slowly. "Check with me later."

"Lost all feeling? From the neck down?"

Gabe heard the mischievous note in Julie's voice a second before he felt her hand dipping down low, wedging itself between their two sealed bodies. With very slow movements, she created a cavity just large enough for her fingers to surround him. Just large enough for a new advancement of sensations.

"Feel that?"

He laughed, his breath ruffling her hair. He covered her hand with his own, stopping her for a moment as he tried to get a second wind. "Yes."

"Good." She pulled back her hand, trailing her fingertips temptingly before she withdrew. "I wouldn't want to think that I ruined you."

"Ruined me?" His arms tightened around her waist, holding her in place. At least for now. Though he was still smiling, his eyes were serious. Would she forgive him? Once this was over and she knew about the deception that was involved, would she forgive him? "Julie, you're the best part of me."

Then he was selling himself short, Julie thought as her conscience began to bore through the gauzelike walls of the euphoria around her.

To block the thoughts, to block out everything except for this small island of time that had been mercifully handed to her, Julie slid her hand down between them again. Determined to make the memory of tonight last forever.

His hands framing her face, Gabe sucked in his breath as he felt her fingers slide up and down between his legs. Cupping him intimately. The woman was going to be the death of him. But he had no real complaints about that. It seemed to him the best way to go.

Gabe dragged her mouth to his as he felt himself hardening. As he felt himself wanting her again.

Still.

Always.

He kissed her over and over again, fueling both their desires until there was no one and nothing but that. Clutching her hands in his to keep her from ending this too soon, he held them prisoner as he wrapped his tongue around one nipple, hardening it before turning his attention to the other.

When she wriggled beneath him, tempting him, he felt his body become poised and rigid again. He didn't know how much longer he could continue holding back. And he wanted to. Wanted to keep the final moment at bay as he pleasured himself by priming her.

"Want to try for the bed this time?"

She pushed away the feelings of guilt. They would still be there in the morning, when the harsh light of day would make them seem all the more formidable. But for now, she would take this slice of happiness fate had cut and served her. Take it and feast before it disappeared forever.

She smiled up at him. "Never let it be said that I wasn't willing to try."

Chapter 16

The discomfort grew, prying apart the wispy arms of contentment that cradled her. It pushed past the layers of sleep so that she woke with a start, breathing hard. Hot, intense, churning, her stomach felt as if it was about to come up to her throat at any second, spewing out its contents.

Julie managed to get dressed and out of Gabe's apartment and into her own less than five minutes after she woke up. She made it to her own bathroom without a second to spare.

With a frantic push, she sent the bathroom door moving in the right direction behind her as she fell to her knees in front of the toilet. The bowl felt cold as she embraced it.

For a little while last night, with so much else on her mind, she'd forgotten that she was pregnant and indulged without even being aware of it. She was paying for it now.

There had to be a better way to have a baby, she thought miserably.

Spent, exhausted, Julie sank back in a heap. She took a

few deep breaths before attempting to get up again. This time, she did it slowly. She didn't need to feel light-headed on top of everything else.

Last night replayed itself in her head as she washed her face. She hadn't meant to let that happen. But where Gabe was concerned, she couldn't seem to gather enough will-power to successfully block the pull she felt between them.

This couldn't go on, not indefinitely.

But for a little while....

She owed him the truth, she thought, weary of the war going on inside her.

But what if the truth drove him away? If? she mocked herself. This kind of truth was guaranteed to send a man fleeing for the first plane to South America. Or at the very least, away from here.

Sighing, she put the washcloth down and stared at her reflection in the mirror. Even wretched, she looked younger than her twenty-seven years. Too young to have all these things weighing her down.

But lamenting, even silently, wasn't going to change anything or make it go away. Eventually, she'd stop throwing up. And eventually, dashing away at the first indication of trouble wasn't going to hide her condition from Gabe. She'd be too large to hide behind anything short of an elephant.

Oh, what was she worried about, anyway? Gabe wasn't going to be around for long, certainly not long enough to see her stomach swell with the life that was inside it. The fact that she was wrapped up in a fantasy, pretending that he was the man she'd been waiting her whole life for was just that. A fantasy. And fantasies broke up at the first sign of reality.

Reality would make a major house call the moment she told him about the baby.

But that was just the trouble, she didn't want to tell him.

Didn't want Gabe to know just yet. Like everything else, this lovely interlude would come to an end and maybe he'd leave before he ever found out that she was sleeping with him while another man's child was growing within her. At least she could hope. That scenario would spare her a lot of grief.

Julie knew there was no way that she could convince Gabe that the baby had been conceived in a moment of weakness, of neediness.

If this were Gabe's baby, then the circumstances around its conception would have been so different...

But it wasn't Gabe's baby, she reminded herself sternly, and there was no use in going there, no use in wondering what it would be like to feel his child growing within her. A child born of...love.

Love. There, she'd said it. Thought it. Allowed it to come out into the light, if only for a heartbeat. Julie examined the word, the sensation, for a second longer before quickly packing it away. Like a treasured old photograph, it would only fade if exposed to the light.

"Are you all right?"

Startled, Julie turned around, rapping her knee against the corner of the cabinet door. The bathroom door, far from having shut itself, has slowly swung open again. Elizabeth was standing just at the threshold, peering in, swaddled in a blue bathrobe that was two sizes too large for her.

She was wearing her bathrobe, Julie realized dully.

"I heard you," Elizabeth explained. She hated this awkward feeling that existed between them. Hated being at its mercy. Since she'd returned, Elizabeth had felt as if she were permanently stranded on a shaky ledge, afraid to make a move for fear that it would crumble beneath her feet at the slightest step. But this was her daughter and she loved her no matter what Julie thought to the contrary. She had to say something, had to get past all the bad feelings. Tidily, she took a step closer. "And wanted to see if you were all right."

"I'm fine." Julie exhaled the declaration, steeling herself off. She was in no mood to talk to her mother, no mood to deal with the raw feelings still between them.

With a deep breath, she took what she hoped was the first step. "A little club soda might help."

Julie looked at her guardedly, telling herself to take the comment on face value only. There was no way her mother could know. "I don't have a stain on my dress to get out, Mother, but thank you for your advice."

Elizabeth had backed down from things most of her life. This time, she held her ground. "I was talking about the morning sickness."

Julie felt her skin tingling as adrenaline surged. All she could think of was denial. "I don't have morning sickness, I have indigestion." She shrugged vaguely. "Something I ate last night."

In her heart, Elizabeth knew she was lying. And it hurt to think that Julie felt she had to. "I was the same way when I was carrying you."

No, she wasn't going to get to her, Julie thought, a score of hurt feelings crowding her memory. Her mother wasn't going to just waltz into her life after all this time and make noises like a warm, cuddly mom and expect everything to be forgiven and forgotten.

Julie's eyes narrowed into slits.

"I'm surprised that you did something as maternal as that, Mother. That you didn't have someone else do it for you." She had no idea where the tears were coming from, but they were there, in her throat, threatening to crack her voice if she wasn't careful. "That way you could have avoided contact with me altogether."

The words couldn't have hit their target any harder than if they'd been an arrow shot into her heart. Distress welled up in Elizabeth's eyes. "Jules, what do you want from me?"

Tears, very good, Mother. Just the right touch. But I'm not buying, do you hear me? I'm not buying.

"Something you can't give," Julie replied coolly. With all her heart, she wished her mother hadn't come back, hadn't upended her world any more than she already had by leaving. "The years that I lost. The years when having a mother would have been so important to me. But I learned to do without one so I'm afraid your 'concern' is a little too late."

Elizabeth had lived with defeat too long not to recognize it when it stared her in the face. She began to retreat. "I can be gone by breakfast."

Surprised, Julie stared at her mother. For a moment silence drenched her.

"Changed your style, Mother? Giving me ample notice this time? And go where?" She wanted to know. "I thought you said you *had* no place to go."

Elizabeth averted her face. She wanted to leave before she began to cry. "I lied."

But Julie wouldn't let her go, not without answers. Still feeling shaky, she moved forward so that her mother was forced to face her.

"Why?"

"Because I hoped that if I came back, you and I could start fresh. That I could somehow undo what happened and... I know I don't have any right—"

Why? Why was her mother doing this to her, turning her inside out again after all this time? After she'd finally made peace with most of the ghosts in her life.

"No, you don't," Julie agreed coldly, even while a small voice inside begged to be convinced otherwise. "You gave all that up when you walked out on us."

Elizabeth was convinced she was never going to see Julie

again once she walked away this time. But before that happened, her daughter had to know the truth about what happened. *Why* it happened.

She laid her hand on Julie's arm, silently asking for understanding. "Jules, I was dying here."

"Dying," Julie echoed in mock wonder. "Living with a man who built an entire art gallery for you to show off your work. A man who worshipped your every move, your every brush stroke." Though she'd tried to hold it back, a wave of sadness washed over Julie as she remembered. "A man who only paid attention to his daughter because he thought he could create a shadow for you. Make me into a carbon copy of you."

With pain, she remembered the way her father used to shout at her, demanding that she stop being stubborn and let her talent surface. Her tears had only made him angrier, more determined to make her into something she wasn't.

"When he finally accepted the fact that I would never be you, he ignored me. Every single breath he drew revolved around you. He adored you." And her mother had walked out on him.

Julie had been too young, Elizabeth thought. Too young to understand, to realize what was going on. She shook her head at Julie's assessment.

"No, he didn't adore me. He *owned* me. Or wanted to." She could see Julie recoiling from the thought, but she pressed on. "Wanted to possess me body and soul. Control my every moment." Even now, the memory of those times made her tremble. "Jules, he was suffocating me."

Frustrated, Julie pulled away from her mother. "So you had problems. Problems can be talked out."

Again Elizabeth shook her head. There'd been no getting through to him. "I tried. There was no talking to your father." She searched Julie's face for an indication that she believed her. "Don't you remember? Your father and I would have those horrible arguments. Arguments that would send you hiding under your bed with your hands over your ears. It broke my heart to see you like that.''

Julie refused to believe her mother, refused to believe that she cared. How could she have abandoned her like that if she'd cared?

''So you left because I broke your heart.''

The sarcasm cut deeper into her wounds. ''I left because your father was going to kill me.''

''I don't believe you.''

Resigned, Elizabeth sighed, the fight having gone out of her. ''I didn't expect you to. Your father was a tormented soul. He loved showing me off, but if anyone so much as talked to me, your father would start saying such ugly things.'' Elizabeth ran her hands up and down her arms, shivering. Remembering. ''He'd embarrass me in public and spend hours questioning me over and over again at home about my 'affairs.''' Just saying the word sounded too ludicrous to her. ''He wouldn't believe me that there was no one else.''

Julie struggled to hang on to her anger. She'd lived with it so long, she wasn't sure how to function without it. ''And you ran off with 'no one.'''

What lies had he told Julie? Elizabeth wondered wearily. What had he said to poison her daughter's mind against her? ''Simon James was a friend, nothing more. A friend who helped me get away. Believe me,'' she pleaded, ''if I could have taken you with me, I would have. But your father once warned me that if I tried to run away with you, he'd kill us both.'' Her voice deadened, the emotion ebbing away as she described what she'd lived with all these years. ''I believed him.''

She couldn't picture her father saying something like that. But if he had... ''Then why leave me?''

''Because I knew he wouldn't hurt you as long as you

stayed where you were. It was the hardest thing I ever did, leaving you behind.''

Elizabeth twisted her fingers together, reliving it all in the telling. ''But his moods were getting darker, his accusations more frequent. He began to think I was sleeping with every man who came to see my paintings.'' She looked away again. ''So one day, when you were both gone, I left.''

''Where did you go?'' The question had plagued Julie for so long. After a while, she'd really believed that her mother was dead. ''Father hired a detective to find you.''

Elizabeth nodded her head sadly. ''Yes, I know. He found me.''

''But—''

Elizabeth knew what Julie was going to say. ''And he believed me when I told him why I'd left. I was so desperate, I was going to pay him off not to tell your father.'' An ironic smile whispered along her mouth. ''But he wouldn't take the money. Said he wished me well and left.''

She took a deep breath. Talking about this hurt. It always would. Elizabeth knew that she would always bear the guilt of leaving Julie behind. ''I moved around a lot. It really didn't matter where.'' She raised her eyes to Julie. ''I'd left my life behind.''

Julie pressed her lips together. Despite everything, she wanted to believe her mother. ''Then why didn't you come back after he died?''

''I did.'' She'd returned with the full intention of making amends, of picking up where she and Julie had left off. But chance had shattered that hope. ''I overheard you talking to someone when they asked about me.'' Elizabeth could still hear the condemning words clearly in her head. ''Your voice was so full of anger, I just couldn't bring myself to upset you any more than I already had by coming back.''

Instead, she'd retreated into a life of quiet anonymity, having little to do with anyone. Going through the motions of living, but not really succeeding. And in all those years, her heart had ached for the daughter she'd been forced to lose.

That explained some things, Julie supposed. But that still begged another question. "And now?"

Elizabeth shrugged helplessly. "Now I realize that life can be cut short in a moment and that I might not have tomorrow. I wanted to tell you how very sorry I was that you were caught in the middle of all this. How sorry I was that you didn't have a better mother than the one you got."

If that was true, if she really believed that, then why hadn't her mother made more of an effort to come back into her life? "You didn't have to be sorry. You could have just been there."

With an ache, Elizabeth realized that. "I know. And there's nothing I can say to undo that."

Julie raised her chin, unconsciously squaring her shoulders. "No, there isn't."

Elizabeth took it as a sign to leave. There was nothing more to be said. Her heart feeling like a lead weight in her chest, she turned to go.

"But there is something you can do."

Confused, hopeful, Elizabeth turned around and looked at her.

"You can begin by not leaving." Suddenly, Julie felt like crying. The wrong time, she told herself. The absolute wrong time. "Leaving the scene of the crime isn't going to undo the crime." She pressed her lips together to keep her voice from cracking. "But maybe staying can negate its effects."

Elizabeth was afraid to believe what she was hearing. Afraid that she wanted it so badly, she was just imagining this. "You want me to stay?"

Julie's eyes held hers. "I want you to do whatever it is you want to do."

Tears gathered, overflowed. Elizabeth reached a hand out to her. "I want to stay."

Julie's fingers made contact, closed around her mother's hand. "Then do it."

With a little cry, Elizabeth hugged her. Then suddenly aware of what she was doing, Elizabeth pulled back, afraid of breaking this fragile new tether stretching across the gaping chasm. "I—"

Julie smiled. "I'm very resilient, Mother. I don't break if someone hugs me."

The last line of defense, the last barrier, crumbled, and Elizabeth began to cry. "Jules, I am so very, very sorry."

Here she was, Julie thought, back in the position of being the parent again, just as she'd been with her father. Julie took her mother into her arms and held her, stroking Elizabeth's hair, replaying a scene in her mind. Only then, the roles had been reversed.

"I know," Julie whispered. "Now."

Elizabeth raised her head, wiping her eyes on the bathrobe's long sleeve. After all this time, it was finally happening. She was back in her daughter's life. "Just give me a moment."

Julie nodded. "Take all the time you need." She felt her stomach lurching. Oh, God, not again. "If you really want to do something for me..."

Eagerness sprang to Elizabeth's green eyes. "Yes?"

It was going to take time to adjust to this, but she supposed she could let her mother do a few things. "I'd love some tea."

"Right away." Hurrying away, she suddenly turned and looked at Julie. "Is it Gabe's?"

Julie bit her lip. The urge to lean on someone was immense. But she had been on her own emotionally for so long now, she had no idea how to begin.

Unable to reach out, she sought refuge in evasiveness. "He doesn't know anything about it and I'd like to keep it that way."

Elizabeth wanted to tell her that it was Gabe's right to know, that he had an obligation to Julie and to the baby, but she was afraid of tracking footprints all over the newly laid bridge between them.

So instead, she nodded, giving her word. "I won't say anything."

He missed her.

He tried to tell himself that it was just the haze of sleep still holding him prisoner in the misty wrappings of some half unrealized dream, but he missed Julie as he reached out to find the space beside him empty.

She was gone.

He lay very still, trying to perceive if he smelled coffee, or heard her moving around in the kitchen, the way she had last time.

Nothing. No scent, no noise.

No Julie.

Tiny feelers of loneliness inched through him.

How could he miss someone that he had only connected with so recently? He had to be imagining the feeling. There was no other explanation for it.

And yet...

He got ready quickly, taking a fast shower and slipping his clothes onto a body that still felt damp. Still felt, if he closed his eyes, the electricity of Julie's skin against his as they made love.

Using his cell phone, he checked in with McCarthy before heading downstairs.

Gabe found Julie clearing away a tray loaded with champagne glasses. Sunlight poured into the showroom, catching the drops of remaining liquid in some and setting them on fire.

Everything around her gleamed, he thought. Crossing to her, he grasped the tray Julie was holding. Because there was no one else around, no one to see, he allowed himself a moment of weakness and brushed his lips against hers as he took the tray.

"I missed you this morning."

Would you have missed me if you knew I was keeping something from you, Gabe? If you knew about the baby? Would you miss me then?

Julie blocked the thought from her head and forced a smile to her lips. "I had to get an early start. Unlike the shoemaker, I don't have elves that come in at night to straighten things up for me." She began loading up another tray.

He waited until she was finished, then walked with her to the back. "They only fixed shoes," he pointed out. "They didn't offer maid service."

Julie slanted him a look, amusement playing around her mouth. "That's what you get when you have fairy tales written by men."

They set the trays on a table in the back room that was already being used to accommodate a potpourri of things. But as she began to go back, Gabe wrapped his arms around her waist from behind, stopping and stealing a moment. He nuzzled her neck. She smelled like heaven.

And like his downfall.

"You're glowing." He felt her shiver as his breath skimmed along her neck. Why did that excite him so much? Why couldn't he get enough of her, even as he had her? "Can I take any credit for that?"

"In part." Hands covering his, Julie pulled apart his arms and separated herself from him. He made it so difficult to remember that she had to do the right thing, had to tell him the truth. ''My mother and I had things out this morning.''

Gabe hadn't heard any raised voices coming from her apartment. Curious, he turned her around. ''Oh?''

''In a good way,'' she elaborated. ''We cleared some things up. She said she was sorry.'' Julie went back into the main room.

He followed on her heels. ''For?''

Glancing over her shoulder, Julie smiled. ''Everything.''

He nodded, knowing she wasn't about to volunteer any more details. ''Nice, broad cleansing. And I take it you've given her amnesty.'' Finding another tray, he began depositing more glasses.

It was a funny term to use, Julie thought. Thoughts of war were linked with amnesty. But maybe she had been involved in a war. No shots fired, but that didn't mean there weren't wounds, weren't casualties.

Her smile softened as she thought about the way that would change now. ''She's my mother.''

When she smiled like that, Gabe had to fight the urge to sweep her into his arms and kiss her senseless. ''And you've got a big heart. It's one of your best features.''

Tray filled, Julie paused to look at him. Had she been too wrapped up in her own thoughts and missed something? ''Is all this leading up to anything?''

''Not at the moment.'' But it would, Gabe thought, Eventually. And he really hoped that she could find it in that large heart to forgive him, because guilty or not, he intended to stand by her. He owed that much to her. And to himself.

There was something in his voice, something Julie couldn't quite put her finger on but that caught her attention. Made her feel…leery. She searched his face for some indication that she was wrong—or right. She couldn't really read it. "Are you trying to tell me something?"

He wanted to, God help him, he wanted to. To tell her that she was under suspicion. That St. Claire's and everyone in it was. Some undercover cop he was.

As he opened his mouth, he heard a familiar sound. "Yes." He pointed behind her to the desk. "The telephone's ringing."

She raised a brow, amused, then turned toward the desk. "You're not off the hook yet."

No, he wasn't. Far from off the hook, Gabe felt as if he were twisting in the wind like bait that had been left hanging on a fishing rod to lure fish.

He knew it was an extreme comparison, but at the moment, he wasn't feeling very rational. What he was feeling, as he watched her pick up the telephone receiver, was like a man in love who'd just discovered he had a few months to live.

Or, in his case, a few days.

Chapter 17

"Say that again. Slowly," Julie said, drawing in a deep breath.

Puzzled, Gabe crossed to her. But when he came around to where she was standing, Julie avoided looking at him. Instead, she appeared to be concentrating hard on the voice on the other end of the line and what was being said. Gabe couldn't discern if it was distress or wonder on her face.

Frustrated, he shoved his hands into his pockets. That was just the trouble. He couldn't penetrate the layers, he thought. Since he'd come here, he'd gotten her to tell him about herself, and yet, there was this feeling that there was something else, something more. Something she was hiding from him.

Yeah, like how she was bringing pure-grade cocaine into this country and selling it at what was probably an incredible profit. Selling it so that some poor, dumb kid looking for an easy high would wind up ending his life in an alley.

Gabe watched color bloom on her face. Felt his gut twist. He didn't want to think that way, didn't want to believe that of her. That she was cold and calculating. And yet, he was too much of a cop not to. All the evidence pointed to St. Claire's and she ran St. Claire's, had her finger on the pulse of everything that went on here. Like a captain unable to delegate.

But sometimes, the evidence was wrong, he thought fiercely. Sometimes, it was circumstance, not truth, that made things seem a certain way. That had to be the case here.

He knew he wouldn't be making up these excuses if this was someone else he was investigating. If this was someone he wasn't in love with.

Damn, he was tied up in one hell of a knot and he didn't know what to do. One side was duty, the other side was heart. It wasn't fair. But then, life wasn't supposed to be. It was up to people like him to *make* it fair.

He had no idea what to do, except search for a way to protect her.

"Thank you. Thank you *very* much for calling. And have a nice day—have a nice life." Hanging up the receiver, Julie felt like singing. Maybe, just maybe, whatever dice fate had just thrown had come up on the right side for a change, with the right numbers. She and her mother were back on the road to reconciliation, she seemed to have found the last living decent male who appeared to care about her, and now St. Claire's was back on track.

Could things be *any* better?

Well, she slanted a look at Gabe, maybe just a tad, but she wasn't going to allow herself to get greedy. She knew what happened to people who got greedy. Everything disappeared on them, like in the fairy tales. She knew she wasn't living a fairy tale, but this was the next best thing.

He waited just long enough for Julie to put down the receiver. "Good news?"

Never one to go half measures, she threw her arms around him.

"The best!" Carried away by the moment, by the wild, unbridled happiness that was rocketing through her, she kissed Gabe hard on the mouth. "The very best."

When she said it this time, her eyes were on his and her voice had softened just a little, though the enthusiasm still pulsed beneath it. But there was definitely a layer of arousal that was rising to the top. At this moment in her life, she loved everyone in the world—and most of all, him.

Shame more than curiosity or the knowledge that someone had entered the gallery and they were no longer alone made Gabe release her. The look in her eyes bit into his conscience.

He nodded toward the telephone. "Who was that just now?"

"Yes, who was on the phone, Julie?" Glaring daggers at Gabe, Mike came up to them.

Julie grabbed each man by the hand, as if she was forming a magical ring that nothing bad could ever penetrate.

"That, gentlemen, was the Customs office calling. The paintings are ours again. We can go get them anytime we want." She was so relieved, she felt like shouting the news from the rooftop. She'd already begun mentally composing the cancellation notice for the show. Now there would be no need.

Mike's eyes widened behind his glasses. "You're serious." He looked like a man who didn't know whether to laugh or cry.

"I'm very serious." Realizing that her voice had gone up several octaves again, she lowered it.

But it wasn't easy curbing the impulse to shout. Releasing both their hands, Julie opened the center drawer and rummaged amid papers and file envelopes, searching for the list of particulars aboard the ship. Next time, she could afford to have the paintings Mike found in Europe sent by plane.

"Here're the papers you're going to need and here're the keys to the van." Julie awarded the papers to Mike, the keys to Gabe. "Go get my paintings, boys. We're in business again!"

She looked like a cheerleader sending off her team to win the state championship, Gabe thought. There had to be some mistake. She couldn't be the mastermind behind the smugglers. She couldn't even be in on it. He'd bet his badge on it.

Holding the papers, Mike looked dubiously at Gabe. "Are you sure you want to send him?" Mike asked her grudgingly.

She felt too good to be brought down by Mike's negative attitude. Mike was the type to distrust his own shadow unless it showed him two forms of ID. You would have thought that by now, she would have rubbed off a little on him.

Julie patted his face. "Yes, I'm sure. You're going to need a strong back to help load the crates with the paintings onto the van."

Mike eyed Gabe almost petulantly. "They've got forklifts for that."

With a tolerant laugh, Julie kissed each man on the cheek, a queen sending her knights on a crusade.

"Try to get along for the time it takes to bring those paintings back, okay?" She looked from one to the other. Gabe, she knew, would give her no trouble, but she had her doubts about Mike. "For my sake? Think of it as a peace treaty. From here on in, everything's going to be wonderful."

Mike tried to concentrate on the paintings and not on the

man who was going to accompany him. Relief worked its way through him, tranquilizing some of the fears he'd been living with. "Yes, it is."

"Hey, what's going on?" Ambling in through the front door, Jeff paused to hang up his coat. The energy seemed to pulse around the very walls. He looked from one face to another. It was plain that he wanted in on the source of all the excitement.

"Customs just called," Julie told him. "The paintings have been released from bondage. We can pick them up anytime."

Her eyes were dancing, Gabe noticed. Was that from innocent excitement, or because she was thinking of the street value of what she had?

Damn, he couldn't take much more of this vacillating. One minute he was sure enough to bet his life, the next minute... He needed time, time to get this straightened out, to maybe clear her.

But time was what he didn't have.

"Well, what are we waiting for?" Jeff demanded, excited. "Let's go."

Mike and Gabe could handle this well enough. There was really no need for Jeff to go with them. "You've just gotten out of a sickbed, remember?"

Jeff waved the words away sheepishly. "Just a head cold, Julie, and it's about gone now. 'Sides, having those paintings come in just in the nick of time's great medicine. I thought maybe I was finally gonna have to look around for another job."

Mike gave Jeff a contemptuous look that had overtones of Big Brother in it. They'd worked together at the art gallery since Edmund Raitt had owned it. "You wouldn't have to worry about looking if you saved your money once in a while instead of blowing it the minute it hits your pocket."

But Jeff merely laughed, as if Mike was pulling his leg. "Life's to be lived, Mike." Though older by a few years, he turned to Julie for support. "Right, Julie?"

Julie slanted a look at Gabe. Until he'd come into her life, she hadn't realized just how fully it could be lived.

"Right, Jeff. Now get going, all of you." She gave Jeff and Gabe a playful shove. "Before they change their minds again."

That was enough to send Mike scurrying for the rear door.

But it was the look in Julie's eyes that made Gabe leave without looking back. His conscience was giving him enough grief as it was without having to reckon with what he saw there. A light to warm himself by. The kind of light that should have been reserved for a man who had not only bared his heart, but his soul to her. Not left her tangled in a lie.

Julie's neck was getting stiff and her back was beginning to ache. This was far from being as relaxing as she'd hoped.

"You're moving," Gabe chided.

Julie lifted a dismissive shoulder in response. "I'm human. Humans move."

Gabe frowned slightly as he tried to concentrate. He was completing the painting far faster than he'd ever done any work before. But something was urging him on, a feeling that if he didn't finish it quickly, even her memory would fade from his mind after Saturday.

After everything went down.

"Not humans who volunteer to be models," he pointed out.

Julie knew she'd volunteered, and at the time it'd seemed like a good idea, but that was before her bones had begun to petrify. She longed to rub the crick from her neck.

"Couldn't you just continue painting the portrait from memory?"

"I could," he conceded, his eyes briefly making contact with hers. "But this is a lot nicer."

When he looked at her like that, she had to agree. Julie tried to still her inward fidgeting and told herself that her neck didn't feel like a tree trunk.

From where she sat, she couldn't see his hands, only his look of rapt concentration. She wanted very much to kiss his brow free of the furrow in it. "Do you think it'll be finished soon?"

Standing back, Gabe viewed the canvas critically. Rafe would have been better at this, he thought. He lacked his brother's talent, his brother's flair. "Define soon."

Julie began to bite her lower lip, then stopped herself before he saw her. "In time for the show Saturday."

Looking up, Gabe paused in surprise. "Why?"

Like a child with a delicious secret churning inside her, begging to get out, Julie smiled at him. "Because I thought if it was finished, I'd like to leave it on display."

"You meaning *during* the show?"

Her eyes lit with enthusiasm and conviction. She had great faith in his potential. "Yes."

"You think it's that good?"

She couldn't help herself. Though she had silently promised herself to go slow, to not get carried away, she broke both simultaneously. "I think *you're* that good," Julie corrected enthusiastically.

"The other paintings—"

"Are very good, but just don't seem to have the same sort of spark, the same sort of message that this one does. It's not just because it's me." She didn't want him thinking that it was vanity that influenced her. "It's just that—"

Flattered, Gabe still didn't feel comfortable about having his own work on display. Wanting to change the subject, he raised his brush, fixing her with a look. "Julie, you've shifted three times in the course of three sentences. Two and a half," he amended. "Now if you want me to finish this painting, you're going to have to cooperate."

"And sit still," Julie murmured.

"That's the idea," he agreed. "At least, while I'm painting," he agreed. "Afterward, you can move as much as you'd like. As a matter of fact, I'd highly recommend and encourage it."

Her eyes shone. Gabe hurried to capture the look. "Oh, you would, would you?"

"Yes." Working furiously before the moment was gone, he doubted that he would ever be talented enough to do her justice. "As long as all the moving is done within inches of me."

She smiled broadly. "Inches?"

"Millimeters," he corrected. With a sigh, he tossed aside the brush onto the table. What was the use? He couldn't concentrate when she looked like that. "Oh, the hell with it."

Julie raised an amused brow. She felt herself being aroused already. "Is that something van Gogh said just before he cut off his ear?"

"I'm not about to cut off my ear." Only other parts of him just as vital, he thought. Like his heart. And very soon.

Too soon.

Gabe felt the urgency of a man who knew he was taking in his last breaths and wanted to make the very most of them. He crossed to her, not having any idea just how many breaths he had left within him.

Gathering her off the stool, he pressed her against him, his blood surging wildly. He ran his hands over her body, caressing her, absorbing her. "I still say that this would be a lot simpler if you posed nude for me."

She'd have that commemorated in oils. "And have other people see me that way? No thank you."

Gabe laughed as he covered her mouth with his, stealing a tiny bit of heaven and empowering himself through it. "Who said anything about having other people see you nude?"

Julie's mind was already beginning to whirl, but she thought she should be able to understand something that was so simple. "But if you paint me nude—"

"I didn't say I'd paint you nude, I just said you should pose that way for me."

Lost for a comeback, she swatted at him. He caught her hands and brought them to his lips, kissing each in turn. Melting her with the simple courtly action.

"I like looking at you nude. Like running my hands along your skin, feeling you." "Like" was a tame, safe word that didn't begin to cover the breadth of what Gabe was feeling.

He framed Julie's face in his hands, looking for that strain of kindness he knew existed there. Trying to lock on to it and tell himself that somehow, this was all going to turn out all right. If Julie was somehow mixed up in this, there had to be some plausible explanation. She was doing this to save the gallery. Because someone was threatening her life. Because she needed the money for an operation. Something. Anything. However weak, he'd accept it. Accept it because he had to absolve her in his mind.

Julie was too good, too generous a person to be doing it strictly for the money. He refused to believe that of her.

She could feel his eyes penetrating her very bones. "Gabe, what is it?"

He threaded his fingers through her hair. "I was just thinking how beautiful you were and how I couldn't begin to capture that on canvas."

"Flattery will get you nowhere," Julie teased. And then

she gave up pretending to resist. All she'd wanted, since she'd walked into his apartment to pose for the painting, was him. "Nowhere but in my bed."

"Works for me," he murmured, already coaxing her dress from her.

Anxious to make love with him, to grab on to ecstasy's shimmering form before it was stolen away from her, Julie dragged Gabe's shirt off his shoulders. One of the buttons popped off.

"You're too slow," she chided with a laugh.

Gabe's eyes shone with mischief. And with the love he couldn't restrain any longer, but still couldn't admit. It would only complicate everything. "Funny, no one else ever complained."

"No one else," Julie echoed, amused. "How many 'elses' were there, Gabe?" Amusement faded, to be replaced by something that was far stronger, far less easy to handle. "How many other women did you set on fire?"

His eyes touched hers, and Gabe felt as if he were looking into her soul. A soul, he realized, that was his. At least for now.

"None."

It was the truth. Because there had been no other women. No other woman had ever been in his heart. The way she was.

Very slowly, he brought his mouth to hers, cutting the space a tiny increment at a time.

"No other women. No other woman, but you." He brushed his lips against hers, then stepped back to look into her eyes. He wanted her to believe this, even if she never believed anything of him again. "Ever."

Julie wanted to cry.

She wanted to tell him, right here, right now. To tell him everything and hope that he forgave her.

But fear stood blocking the way.

Fear that he would turn his back, that he would walk away and take the sunlight with him, throwing her world into a permanent darkness the likes of which she'd never known before. Because she'd never known such happiness before and the lack of it, the lack of him, would be horrendous.

So she kept her secret, and lived a lie so that she could, for the space of another night, relive the joy of loving him. Of making love with him.

She murmured the words, "I love you," against his mouth as they took one another, but she was certain he didn't hear.

Maybe it was just as well.

Chapter 18

Gabe would have felt a hell of a lot better about doing this sort of thing in the dead of night, but he'd had no opportunity last night. Not with Julie in bed with him. He couldn't risk leaving her, never mind the fact that he'd been reluctant to. Reluctant to give up even a moment of something he was fully resigned to having evaporate on him in the immediate future.

To ease his conscience, he could have pretended that it was a need to perpetuate the ruse that had made him play the part of the lover and remain at Julie's side so that she wouldn't suspect anything if she woke up in the middle of the night to find him gone. In a word, he'd been trapped.

Gabe's mouth curved in a humorless smile. His conscience wouldn't allow yet another lie to come into the fold. True, there was a need to continue the role, but those had been his own desires, his own needs, that had ruled foremost. And if it was a trap, it was a trap that he would have gladly lived and died in if given half a chance.

But this wasn't about him. It was about kids buying snowy dreams and inhaling their life away. It was about people dying decades before their time. About old people being mugged so that an addict could score three minutes of oblivion. He couldn't let his own feelings get in the way.

He couldn't stop them getting in the way.

The show was only a day away now, and he had to take his opportunity, however slight, when it came up. Julie had left for a couple of hours, going to the doctor for what she'd told him was a routine, annual exam. Elizabeth, as always, was upstairs in the apartment, and Jeff, the human twig, was out in front, running the gallery. Gabe had no idea where Evers was, but he wasn't at the gallery and that was all that counted.

Julie'd even given him an excuse to hide behind. She'd asked him to uncrate the paintings they'd brought back from the docks. Things had been so hectic, they hadn't been able to get to them until now. He had a perfectly legitimate reason to be handling the paintings. A reason for him to pretend to admire them and scrutinize each one as he took it out of the crate.

There wasn't, however, a reason for him to take apart the frames.

He'd meticulously gone through each one of the crates, sifting the straw packed there to see if something had been hidden in the shavings, the packaging, or in the walls of the crates. He'd come up with nothing. There was no other place to look but the paintings themselves.

Hiding as far as he could within the recesses of the storage room, Gabe slowly, methodically, checked out the backing on one of the paintings and then another. When he'd gone over a third random painting, he'd satisfied himself that if anything was being smuggled it had to be within the frame itself, or not at all.

He was hoping for not at all.

He chose a mid-sized painting as his first target, counting on being able to remember just how to put it back together when he was finished. As a last resort, he supposed he could fall back on the excuse that the frame had been damaged in passage and had fallen apart when he'd taken it out of the crate. In a pinch, it was better than nothing.

Sweat, sticky and warm, trickled down Gabe's brow in a zigzag pattern as he worked in the semidarkness. Taking a momentary break, he angled his watch and saw that he'd been at this for more than an hour. He figured that he didn't have much time left before Julie returned.

There was nothing within the frame.

Relief came like a wave of cool water splashing over a parched body. Julie was in the clear.

The snitch, for reasons of desperation and in an obvious pitch to strike a bargain with the Assistant D.A., had lied. It was simple as that and not without massive precedent.

The urge to stop here, to quit while he was ahead, was tremendous. But he couldn't stop. One random sample didn't make up a case for anyone but him.

Glancing at another frame, using it as an example, he reconstructed the frame he'd taken apart. Silently he blessed his father for making Rafe and him help out on small carpentry chores when he was growing up. He examined his handiwork quickly and was satisfied that to the casual observer, there was no sign of tampering.

He'd spent more time than he should have, he upbraided himself. He'd put it off long enough. Steeling himself off, Gabe chose another painting at random.

As he worked the frame apart, it slipped from his fingers. He caught it before it hit the floor, but one end had loosened. Something white and powdery slipped out, raining over his foot.

It looked like harmless sugar. Snow. Dandruff from a

sheepdog. Everything, but what it was. What he knew it had to be.

His heart sank.

With reluctance tearing at his soul, Gabe skimmed the side of his pinkie against the very top of the white, powdery deposit and then tasted it on the tip of his tongue.

It wasn't sugar. It wasn't carefully preserved snow. It was exactly what he feared it was.

Cocaine.

Oh damn, Julie. Why?

It wasn't her fault. His heart told him so.

But his heart was not going to be called to the stand. Only he was, and he had to have hard evidence with which to clear her. Saying he believed her to be innocent of this wasn't nearly enough.

Using extreme care, Gabe put the frame together again. With a dreading resignation, he reached for another painting. The scene didn't even register on his brain. He found the same thing.

Cocaine. Cocaine in each section of the hollowed out frame. Pure cut.

With a sigh that came from the very bottom of his weary soul, Gabe dragged his hands through his hair, scrubbing them across his face. He felt completely stymied.

The snitch had been right all along.

He didn't need to take apart any more frames, although he did because the department would want it all. Even if there'd only been this much, it would have been enough to convict her.

But not if he could help it, he thought fiercely. Somehow, he had to find the loophole, the excuse that would absolve her of the blame.

He didn't intend to rest until he found it.

Opening the sliding-glass window that separated the inner office from the waiting room, a sweet-faced blond nurse looked out at Julie and the other woman waiting in the room. "I'm sorry, ladies," she apologized with the experience of one who had said these very words so many times she'd lost count, "but it's going to be a little while longer. Dr. Pollack is in the hospital delivering one of Newport Beach's newest residents. They just called to say that she's almost finished."

Her doctor was an obstetrician, so this kind of delay went with the territory. But that didn't mean she had to like it, Julie thought. Restless, she sighed and glanced at her watch. It was already later than she'd planned on. There was so much to do with the show being one night away. She didn't have time to just sit here, thumbing through the pages of a magazine she really couldn't focus on.

Murphy's law, she supposed.

"In a hurry?" the light-haired woman sitting opposite her asked. Amusement highlighted her high cheekbones. "It's your first, isn't it?"

Surprised, Julie looked at the woman. She wasn't even close to showing, how could she— "Yes, how did you know?"

"It shows." The woman laughed softly when Julie looked down at her stomach. "Not on your body, in your manner." The smile broadened, and with it was a peacefulness that Julie found intriguing. "After you've had one, you tend to look at time spent in the doctor's office as a mini-vacation." Her eyes crinkled. "Anything to carve out an island of time for yourself."

A nerve of unease began to undulate through Julie. Oh, God, what was she letting herself get into? "Is it that bad?"

The woman laughed again, louder this time and with more pleasure. "Oh, it's not that bad. It's wonderful. But it's a hectic wonderful," she qualified. "I wouldn't trade my mad, crazy world for anything on the open market—

legal or otherwise.''

Julie thought it an odd choice of words. But her needs far outweighed anything she took note of. She wanted assurances, something to make this queasy, nervous feeling humming through her like a loose live wire settle down a little.

This woman looked happy to be pregnant, happy to be a mother. She was the perfect person to ask. Julie broke the ice. "How many do you have?"

"Two." The response was automatic. In her heart, there was no difference between her niece and her natural-born daughter. They were both her own children, both sharing equally in her love. And in her husband's, though neither carried his blood. There were more important things than blood. Like love.

"Would you like to see them? I just happen to have several dozen pictures with me." She grinned, producing a swollen wallet crammed thick with photographs from her purse.

"Sure." Julie glanced toward the frosted glass, but it was still closed. There were no sounds of a door being opened and closed beyond it. Sheila hadn't returned to the office yet. "It looks like we're going to be here for a while."

Because she was restless, she was the one on her feet first, crossing to the other woman's side of the room. Depositing her purse on the floor, Julie sat beside the woman and her mini-album on the navy-blue sofa.

Julie eyed the contents. "You weren't kidding, were you?"

"Nope," the woman said gleefully. "Nothing I like better than showing off my brood. By the way, I'm Dana Saldana."

"I'm Julie St. Claire."

The security of a loving family and the feeling it produced in its wake had been a long time in coming in her life, Dana thought. So what if it was her husband's family and not truly her own? She'd married into it and been absorbed until all the warmth and love that abounded had penetrated her rather thick armor and made her feel as if she'd always been one of them.

For that alone, she would forever bless Rafe, but there was more, so much more. Her heart swelled every time she thought of him.

Dana Saldana did the honors, pointing to the first two photographs, both taken at a professional studio. "This is Mollie and this is Megan, who thinks she's looking forward to not being the baby of the family anymore," she confided to Julie with a knowing laugh. "She's in for a big surprise." She could remember with very little difficulty how jealous she'd felt when her own sister had been born. Suddenly, she'd been a dethroned princess. "Here they are together."

Julie raised the photograph a little closer. Slightly blurred, it was still good enough to let her see the third party. "Who's the man standing behind them?"

"My husband, Rafe." There was no missing the pride in the woman's voice. Julie envied her the feeling. "He's a wonderful pediatrician, by the way, so if you don't have one lined up, I can give you his card." Without waiting for a reply, Dana dug into her pocket for one of Rafe's business cards. "That's how we met, actually. He tended to Mollie and decided that maybe I needed tending, too." It wasn't really all that simple, but the results had amounted to the same thing. And she was eternally grateful for it.

"I'll keep that in mind." Julie tucked away the card. She'd ask Sheila about this Rafe Saldana when she got a chance. But at the moment, finding a pediatrician was not uppermost in her mind. "They're really beautiful little girls," she commented, turning from photograph to photograph.

"Thank you, we think so."

Julie stopped dead as she came to two photographs side by side. There was another man in them. Obviously taken on the same day, at some park; he was holding both girls in his arms in one, and pushing one on a swing in the other. Julie could have sworn the man looked like Gabe. In the first photograph, he was standing beside the woman's husband.

Resembling him enough to pass for the doctor's brother.

Julie looked at the woman beside her. "Who's this?" She tried to make it sound like an innocent question, but failed.

Dana had seen the sudden tensing of the other woman's shoulders. The look that had come into her eyes. Dana could have sworn the woman caught her breath. Something was up. Dana was well acquainted with the legions of women Gabe had gone out with, a great many before her time. But the woman on the sofa beside her didn't strike her as one of Gabe's former girlfriends. Dana loved Gabe as if he were her own brother, but a sixth sense urged her to cover the connection.

Rafe couldn't tell her what was going on, the real reason why Gabe wasn't around, and she felt pretty confident that he didn't know himself. What she did know was that Gabe had to be involved in some kind of covert police work. Perhaps identifying him to this woman wouldn't be the wisest thing.

"That's a friend of Rafe's," Dana answered casually, then added before Julie could comment further, "Isn't it remarkable how much they look alike?"

"Remarkable," Julie echoed. Was that all it was? Just a coincidence? If not, why would the woman lie? There was no reason to. Was there? "Your children seem to like him a lot."

There, at least, was an explanation she could work with, Dana thought with relief. "The girls are really friendly with everyone. I hate to squelch that, but in this day and age, you can never be too careful..."

There was something suddenly guarded about the other woman, Julie thought. She couldn't quite put her finger on it, but one moment she was the last word in friendliness, the next...

Julie turned to the next photograph, hoping for some kind of a clue to jump up at her. "What's his name, this friend of your husband's?"

God, Gabe, I wish you'd been a little more specific about what you're involved in. Proceeding carefully, Dana had no clue if she was actually dealing with a jealous, former girl-friend or someone far more dangerous to Gabe in the general scheme of things.

"I..." Dana paused, as if trying to remember. "John, I think." She deeply regretted bringing out the album. There was no telling what else was in there that she'd forgotten about. "Why?" she asked casually. "Do you know him?"

The man in the photographs was Gabe, all right. She'd bet her life on it. An uneasiness began snaking through Julie. "No, I just thought I did." She flipped through several more photographs, looking for Gabe rather than at the two little girls. She stopped abruptly when something else caught her attention. "That's a beautiful painting in the background."

Relieved at the shift, Dana looked around Julie's arm to see the picture she was referring to. "Oh, yes, I always loved that one. Rafe painted it just after we were first married." Why he had decided to place it in storage and hang something else in its place was beyond her.

Suddenly, hearing the name again struck a chord so hard,

Julie could feel it vibrating through her. "Rafe?" She remembered Gabe telling her about his first venture into the world of martial arts. Rafe was Gabe's brother's name.

Dana nodded. "My husband. Painting's his hobby."

Somehow, Julie recovered sufficiently enough to make coherent sentences. "It's beautiful." The compliment echoed eerily in her head. "I own St. Claire's. It's an art gallery, and I'm a little more critical than most, I guess, but I'd like to think I'm in the position to know." The words dribbled from her mouth, generated by automatic pilot.

It made sense now, she thought. She finally understood why the portrait she'd seen Gabe painting was so different from the two he'd first brought with him. It wasn't mood that shifted his style, it was a different hand.

Damn it, he'd been lying to her all along. What other lies were there? And why?

And who was he?

Did it again, didn't you, Julie? she mocked herself. *Messed up again.*

Concerned, Dana leaned forward. There were splotches of bright color suddenly burning in the other woman's cheeks. "Are you all right?"

It took a moment before the question broke through the thick layer of shock around Julie.

"Just a touch of morning sickness," Julie murmured. *A touch of morning sickness, coupled with huge doses of betrayal.*

Feeling sick at heart, Gabe lined all the paintings up against the wall in the storage room. He'd siphoned every side of every frame into a plastic bag he'd found in the room. Every one of them was empty now.

All in all, it made for a nice, tidy little business, he thought, grappling with his conscience and with a sense of betrayal. Using paintings to smuggle cocaine into the country right under the noses of all the government officials.

All that remained, before closing the net around St. Claire's, was catching Von Buren in the act of buying the paintings tomorrow night.

The taste in his mouth was so bitter, it turned his stomach.

Fighting waves of disgust, Gabe wiped off his hands. He wanted to go and confront Julie now, wanted to see her reaction when he told her what he'd found. Wanted to demand how the hell she could have gotten herself caught up in all this.

But he couldn't do that. Couldn't demand, couldn't protect. All he could do was play the waiting game. Even if it killed him inside.

He needed some air. It had suddenly turned oppressively stale within the gallery. Besides, he had to get the evidence to the station, he thought as he headed upstairs.

"I'm going out for a while," he told Jeff, shrugging into his jacket. Small, dark brown eyes turned toward him curiously. Gabe grasped at the excuse he'd been handed earlier by Elizabeth. "I've got to go get another easel. Julie's mother is using the one I borrowed." He stopped at the door. Jeff was still not feeling very well. "You'll be all right here by yourself?"

Jeff bobbed his head up and down. "Sure. No problem." A wide, guileless grin slashed his mouth. "Looks like St. Claire's is finally in the clear. Julie's going to clean up after tomorrow," he said with the conviction of a true believer.

"Yeah," was all Gabe trusted himself to say. Gabe had never felt so reluctant to do his job before.

Chapter 19

Why was Gabe lying to her? The question throbbed in her chest over and over again. He obviously had talent. A great deal of talent. Why the ruse? Why all the secrecy? Was he ashamed of his family? Or something else? Something she should be leery of? A premonition of the worst slithered over her.

That was what she got for letting her guard down.

Breathing fire, Julie had come in the back way only to find that the storage room was empty. Gabe wasn't there. It figured.

Hurrying through the gallery, she was about to go up the stairs when Jeff called out to her.

"Anything wrong?" The expression on her face made him stare at her.

"Where's Gabe?" It was hard keeping her voice under control.

"He went out for a while. Said he had to get another easel."

Her brows drew together. A tiny lick of fire was put aside. "Another easel? Why?"

Jeff grinned. "Seems your mother asked him for one earlier."

Her mother? Her mother had said she was never going to paint again. What was up?

Turning on her heel, Julie rushed up the back stairs, ignoring the bell at the front door announcing the entrance of a patron.

"Mother?"

"In here, Jules."

She sounded just the way she had years ago, Julie thought. The tiniest bit of excitement pricked at her as she pushed the door closed behind her.

Julie found her mother in the middle of the living room, painting. More accurately, she found her mother standing in front of an easel, a paintbrush resplendent with teal along its bristles in her hand. But Elizabeth wasn't painting at the moment, she was talking.

Talking and laughing with Edmund Raitt.

There was color in her mother's cheeks, warm color that coaxed out its brethren. Elizabeth St. Claire had gone from a black-and-white, out-of-focus snapshot to a 35-millimeter, full-color portrait. And all because she was holding a brush in her hand—and talking to a man from her past.

Edmund Raitt looked like someone's notion of the ideal college professor from years past. A trim gray Vandyke adorning his rounded face, Raitt was a tall man, somewhat heavyset, though he wore his weight well, a compliment to the exclusive restaurants he frequented. His iron-gray hair, still thick and full even though he was well into his fifties, had always reminded Julie of a lion's mane. He favored vests. Julie couldn't remember ever seeing him without one, even on the hottest days.

Ordinarily, she would have welcomed seeing him, but she felt too distracted to be very good company.

Turning, Elizabeth reached for her daughter's hand before she focused on her expression. The smile on her lips faded a little, taking with them her words of greeting.

"Oh, Julie, we were just talking about you. Well, among other subjects," Edmund chuckled as he exchanged glances with Elizabeth. Then his brown eyes narrowed a little beneath his brow in mock accusation. "I had no idea your mother was back. Why didn't you tell me?"

Avoiding her mother's hand, Julie shifted. She didn't even look at the painting. It would have been the first thing to catch her attention if she hadn't felt as if her heart had just been vivisected.

"I was saving the public announcements until after the show." Guilt sprang up instantly, upbraiding her. She offered Edmund a half smile, completely repentant. "You'll have to forgive me, I'm a little rattled right now."

Still concerned, Elizabeth studied Julie's face. But there were no more answers there now than there had been a moment ago. She touched Julie's hand. "Is anything wrong, dear?"

It was strange, after all this time, to be the object of maternal concern. Julie's first instinct was to resist it, but this was what she'd longed for. Still, with Edmund here, this wasn't the time or the place to get into what was eating away at her. Maybe there'd never be a time or place, she thought. Not for this.

"No," she answered briskly. "I just came up because I was curious. Jeff said you needed an easel."

"Not anymore." Elizabeth pointed to the one she was using. "Gabe gave me his."

"He gave you yours," Julie corrected, struggling not to bite off the words. "He only had it on loan." Just the way he'd had her heart, she thought.

Julie turned her attention to the painting on the easel. Her mother's painting. Awe nudged its way through to the surface.

Whatever her mother was feeling, it was there, on the canvas, in strokes so fine, so perfect, they called hauntingly to the inner soul, demanding respect and attention. And admiration of the highest caliber. It was as if the fifteen-year hiatus had only taken place to revitalize her. And make Elizabeth better than she'd ever been.

"You found this." Staring at it, Julie suddenly recognized the painting. The last time she remembered seeing it, the canvas had contained just the barest of sketches. Whispers of what was to come, but would not.

She'd saved the canvas, hanging on to the last thing her mother had ever put a brush to. But she'd cherished it, nonetheless, for that very reason. It was her last link to her mother. Or had been.

Over time, she'd forgotten where she'd stored it. Just like her love for her mother.

"No," Elizabeth was saying, "actually Gabe did. He brought it to me this morning while you were busy in the gallery. Said he found it while clearing away some things in the back room." She smiled fondly, wondering if it was serious between Julie and Gabe. "Gabe said he thought it was a shame to leave things undone."

She wondered what edge he was playing when he'd said that. Maybe he'd thought to steal it and sell it. The first original St. Claire in over fifteen years.

Julie felt as if there was a knife twisting in her gut. "Full of great advice, isn't he?"

"Apparently," Edmund enthused. As if to get a better prospective of the painting, he shifted until he was standing beside Julie and behind Elizabeth and her painting. He smiled at Julie, though the light in his eyes belonged exclusively to Elizabeth. "She's better than ever, don't you think?'' Without waiting for an answer from Julie, he bent and brushed a kiss to Elizabeth's temple.

Julie saw the smile that bloomed on her mother's face. Shaking off the cloud surrounding her brain, she looked at the two other people in the room as if she'd never seen them before.

Her mother and Edmund?

Well, why not? They were both of the same era. Both good people, she thought, forcing herself to be impartial for once and see her mother objectively. And with a great many things in common. There had been marriages that had been formed on less.

Julie roused herself when she realized that Edmund was waiting for some sort of response from her. ''Yes, she is. And about time, too. I'll need some 'fresh blood' for the next show.''

The reference caused Edmund to clap his hands together in hearty anticipation. ''Speaking of the show, how's everything going for tomorrow?''

The way he said it, she realized that he still knew nothing about what they had gone through. Though he was retired, he still took a very avid interest in the shows, even going so far as to accompany Mike on some of his buying trips. He'd told her that it made him feel as if he were still useful.

''Fine.'' There'd been a spate of time when she'd debated calling him to see if he had any influence to bring to bear on the situation, but never followed through. It made her feel more of an adult, not having to go running to the man. ''We had our moments, but now everything's fine.''

The dark brown eyebrows drew together in consternation. ''Moments?''

She shrugged, making light of it now that it was all over. Another hurdle overcome. It was just that last hurdle, the one involving her heart, that she never managed to clear cleanly. But that was okay, she'd already made up her mind. No more races for her. "The paintings were held up in Customs—"

"Were." A frown formed on his generous mouth. He looked from mother to daughter. But Elizabeth shrugged, indicating she knew nothing about what had gone on. "But not anymore," he guessed. He smiled his approval when Julie shook her head. "Then everything is really all right?"

"Just fine." She only wished the term could belong to the rest of her life. "The paintings are in the storeroom, ready for display."

"Wonderful." Edmund rubbed his hands together with relish. "I'm truly looking forward to being here tomorrow."

Julie had to laugh at the look on his face. "Apparently you can get the art gallery owner out of the art gallery, but you can't get the art gallery out of the art gallery owner, is that it?"

He took the teasing in stride good-naturedly. He'd always thought of Julie as the daughter he'd never been blessed with. "Something like that," he chuckled. "Well, as long as you're sure everything's all right—"

"Positive." The declaration was made a little more fiercely than Julie had intended.

It was precisely this fierceness that made Elizabeth feel that there was something wrong. She looked at her guest. "Edmund, if you'll excuse us, I'd like to speak to Julie alone." Edmund was a dear old friend, but where Julie was concerned, she wanted no audiences.

It surprised Julie how easily her mother could assume command again. Gone was the repentant, lost waif with the hopeless light in her eyes. She was Elizabeth St. Claire again, with all the confidence that seemed to come along with the name and station.

Fidgeting inside, having neither time nor patience for

anything that was waiting in the wings, Julie turned around to face her mother. "What's this all about, Mother?"

Elizabeth waited until the door was closed before beginning. "You tell me." When Julie said nothing, Elizabeth prodded a little more. She knew her daughter had gone to see her obstetrician. "Is something wrong with the baby, Jules?"

"The baby's fine." She finally shrugged out of the raincoat she was wearing and tossed it carelessly on the back of the sofa. "Mother and child are doing well." And then she stopped. "No, that's not strictly true." She looked up at Elizabeth. "'Baby's' doing well, however 'Mother' is doing rather lousy."

Wanting to help, not knowing how or where to begin, Elizabeth laid a hand on Julie's arm. "It is Gabe?" She pushed the guess a little further when Julie said nothing. "Still trying to find a way to tell him?"

The irony of the situation hit her with the impact of a mule kick. Here she'd been wrestling with her conscience and it appeared that Gabe had come assembled without one. Her mouth twisted in a smile that had no heart in it. "Some secrets are harder to share than others."

"The sooner you do, the sooner you'll feel better," Elizabeth advised. If she had told her husband what was in her heart, maybe all these years of suffering she and Julie had endured could have been avoided.

"I sincerely doubt that."

It hurt her heart to hear Julie like this. As if she was fighting her way through a web of despondency. "Gabe is a good man, Jules. He might go into shock for a little while. Be hurt and nurse his wounded pride. But in the end he'll come around."

Right now, Julie wasn't sure if she wanted him to. Not if he was lying to her. As a matter of fact, she was sure she didn't want him to come around. Hers was a sin of omission. His was an outright lie. And not just one, but a whole warehouseful of them. If he lied about who he was, about his so-called "paintings," he could just as easily lie about everything. About how he felt. Or didn't feel. All with an ulterior motive. Just as Justin had.

"Maybe," Julie agreed vaguely, hoping that put an end to it. Before her mother could say anything else, she shifted gears to distract her. "Edmund seemed very happy to see you."

At the mention of the man's name, Elizabeth smiled. "Edmund is sweet."

"I mean, *very* happy. I think he might have a thing for you." It didn't take much reading between the lines to see that the feeling was mutual.

Elizabeth's eyes widened, steeped in bemusement. "A thing?"

"I think he might like you." She couldn't help wondering now if Edmund's motivation to help her as much as he had had possibly stemmed from the fact that she was Elizabeth's daughter instead of Miles's. How long had Edmund cared about her mother in monklike silence?

Elizabeth turned her attention back to her painting. But she didn't reach for her brush. Her mind was entertaining a different sort of canvas. One that didn't allow things to be painted over. "I'm too old for that sort of thing."

The comment was too ludicrous for Julie to entertain seriously. "Mother, you're forty-eight years old, that's hardly one foot in the grave. Age is all a matter of how you feel." She looked at the painting. It was vivid, arousing. The change was amazing. "And judging by what's on the canvas, I'd say you were feeling pretty young and wild."

Looking at Julie, Elizabeth blinked back tears that were suddenly forming. "That's probably the nicest thing you've ever said to me."

She'd said other, better things, but those were the years that her mother had been too busy to listen, too beset with her own problems to hear the voice of her young daughter. They had a lot to make up for, Julie thought.

"Stick around awhile. It gets better," she promised her mother.

Moved, Elizabeth touched her face. "Yes, I think it does." Her eyes were eloquent when she whispered softly, "I love you, Jules."

She could meet challenge head-on, but love and kindness completely undid the supports Julie had inserted around herself. She could feel tears instantly forming. "Oh, Mother."

"Jules, what's the matter?"

"Nothing." Julie waved away the momentary slip. "Just pregnancy."

No, it was more than that, Elizabeth thought. A great deal more. But she could give Julie her space until she was ready to talk. And when she was, she'd be there for her. There was so much to make up for.

Elizabeth's arms tightened around Julie. "I understand perfectly."

He'd certainly taken his time getting back. Fuming, Julie had forced herself to sit at her desk in the main gallery, pretending to do work, her mind a ravaged blank. Waiting for him to return. She knew he had to return. Whatever payoff he'd been oiling his way toward hadn't come through yet.

When the front door finally opened and he walked through, she felt every single pulse in her body throb, like silent alarms going off to report a breech in security.

Her security, she thought angrily.

Hardly aware of what she was doing, Julie rose from

behind her desk, her eyes never leaving his face as Gabe crossed to her. He was smiling.

And what is the hidden reason for that? her mind demanded.

She felt like someone on a blind date. That same awkward, where-do-I-put-my hands, what-do-I-do-with-my-whole-body type of feeling pervaded through her. It was an ironic sort of sensation to experience after having made love with the man, she thought, cynicism battling for control of her soul.

But there was no getting away from the fact that Gabriel Murietta was a stranger. A stranger who had fed her lies.

Remembering that, thinking of that, the awkwardness suddenly vanished, burned away in the heat of the rush of anger she felt.

How dare he? she thought. How dare he strip her of everything that seemed good and clean and dear to her? She hated him. Hated him for making her fall in love with a man who didn't exist.

She had an odd look on her face, Gabe thought as he came closer. Did she suspect him? Did one of the frames come loose, after all? Had she checked to see if the drugs were still there and found that the hollow frames were now empty?

Maybe it was just a bout of indigestion and his imagination was running away with him, he thought, desperately grasping at straws that bent in his hand on contact. "How'd everything go at the doctor's?"

"Great, just great."

No, it wasn't his imagination. There was a definite edge in her voice. She'd practically bitten the words off and spit them at him. "You're not sick, are you?"

God, she could almost buy into that, the sincerity, the concern. He had the act down pat. How many rehearsals had he had to perfect the part? Were there other women he had duped for other reasons?

Indignation that he was still attempting to perpetuate the ruse fueled her. "You don't have to waste your time acting so concerned, Gabe. It was just a routine O.B. check," she said tersely, too hurt, too angry to think clearly. She felt cheated, cheated of what could have been. Of what she'd almost been certain *was* to have been.

"O.B.?" he echoed. She was obviously upset about something, but what? He tried to piece things together. And then the fragments tumbled into a severely cracked whole. "Obstetrics? As in pregnant?"

She hadn't meant to say that, it had just slipped out. Struggling for coherence, she began to deny it. This certainly wasn't the way she'd wanted to tell him about the baby.

But what did it matter how he found out? It made no difference anymore. The "him" she'd been searching for the right words to tell didn't exist. Just a con man who did things with smoke and mirrors.

"Yes," she snapped. "As in pregnant."

Pregnant. She was pregnant. No wonder she was so upset. Pregnant, wow. The word thundered through his brain with the force of a thousand rampaging elephants. This put everything into a completely different set of parameters for him.

He had to keep her safe. A whole host of emotions washed over him, from fear, to terror, to a bittersweet joy. He laid his hand on her arm. "Julie, why didn't you tell me?"

She jerked as if his hand had burned her and then shrugged him off. "Why should I tell you?"

"Why?" he echoed, confused. Why was there such loathing in her eyes? "Because I have a right to know. As the baby's father—"

What, now he was trying for nobility? "You're not the father."

He felt as if she'd just driven a red-hot poker through his heart. The world stopped turning on its axis for a split second.

He had to have heard wrong. "What?"

She could almost believe that she'd hurt him. If she didn't know better. Her eyes narrowed cynically. "Please, spare me the dramatics. Don't pretend that you actually care."

There'd been a few times, in his wilder days, when he'd gotten drunk and the world had gotten slightly off-kilter and blurry. But that was nothing compared to this. He felt as if everything had just been tilted and he was hanging off the side of a building by his fingertips without a single clue how he'd gotten there or why.

"Pretend? What the hell are you talking about?" His raised voice attracted Jeff's attention, but right now, he couldn't have cared less about Jeff and the gallery. "And whose baby is it?"

As if that mattered to him. The man was good, you had to give him that, she thought bitterly. But if he hadn't been good, she wouldn't have been taken in this time around. She'd already learned her lesson once. Or so she'd thought.

"The father's another artist." She kept her voice down, but there was no mistaking the anger throbbing in it. "Another man who lied to me." Blue eyes tore holes into him.

"Lied to you?" She wasn't talking about the paintings being tampered with, he'd stake his life on it. So what *was* she talking about? What had set her off like some Fourth of July rocket, flying dead center for a crowd?

"Can't you do anything but echo everything I say to you like some diabolical parrot? No, excuse me, what am I saying?" Her mouth twisted with loathing, aimed at both him and herself for being such a fool. For thinking she'd found the perfect man. "Of course you can. You can do anything. Pick locks like a professional burglar, fix doors like a professional carpenter, paint like an artist." Her eyes cut him into tiny ribbons. "Make love like a pro. Lie like a pro."

Gabe grabbed her by her shoulders as she turned away from him. At the end of his patience, he gave up trying to make sense out of this outburst. "Julie, what are you talking about?"

"You know damn well what I'm talking about," she stormed. "Who the hell are you, Gabriel?" And then she realized that she didn't even know if that small bit of information was true. "Is Gabriel even your real name, or just something you picked up to guard your secret identity?"

It took a great deal not to just shake her. "I don't know what you're talking about."

With a thrust, she broke free of his hold, backing away as she glared at him, contempt shining in her eyes. "Oh, give it up, mystery man. I ran into a friend of yours today."

Helpless, frustrated. Gabe couldn't fight what he didn't understand. He still hadn't a clue what this was all about.

"Who?" he demanded hotly. "Who did you run into? Make sense, damn it."

Julie's chin shot up defensively. "I'm making perfect sense. I'd say it was your sister-in-law, but then, I'd only be guessing. I ran into Dana. Dana Saldana. Ring a bell?"

She could see by the look that flashed through his eyes a second before he banked it that she'd struck a nerve. Then, Dana *was* his sister-in-law. Was there a wife somewhere, as well? Or maybe a girlfriend? Someone to share the joke with once he was through getting what he wanted from her?

"She was at the doctor's today. Showed me a lot of photographs. Of her daughters, her husband and some mystery man her daughters were hanging on to." Julie pretended to pause, as if searching her memory. "And, oh yes, a photograph of one of her husband's paintings. Well, she didn't actually point it out to me. It was hanging in the background in one of the photographs." Her eyes hardened. "The exact same one that's hanging on the back wall of the gallery. With your name underneath it.

"It just happened to spring up at me when I looked at the photograph. Just like your face did. Damn it." Hot rage brought even hotter tears with it. "Why did you have to be like everyone else?" Giving in to her feelings, she fisted her hand and hit him in the chest, driving him back. "Why did you have to lie to me?"

He was experiencing his own feelings of betrayal. She'd slept with him, made love with him, all the while with another man's seed in her belly. Was she just amusing herself with him until whoever it was who'd fathered her child came back into the picture?

"Isn't that a little like the pot calling the kettle black?"

She gave up trying to keep her voice down. "The pot can call the kettle whatever the pot damn well chooses because the pot never lied to the kettle." Before he could protest, she added the qualifying tag. "The subject never came up."

He threw his hands up, then shoved them into his pockets to keep from throttling her. "That's the stupidest argument I ever heard. Was I supposed to ask you if you were pregnant before I made love with you?"

Rocking forward on the balls of her feet, she glared at him. "I don't know. What's your usual mode of operation before you make love to a woman? I'm sure you've done it often enough to have a set of rules you follow, however loosely."

Her words slammed into him with the force of a speeding, on-coming train. "Is that what you think?"

She was going to cry again, she realized in mounting

horror. She refused to give him the satisfaction of thinking she'd shed any tears over him.

"I have no damn idea what to think," she shouted. "You lied to me about the painting. You lied to me about your family being gone—"

"I—" Without another word to attach to it, his explanation died in his mouth. His gift for verbally tap dancing temporarily deserted him.

"—and whatever is going to come out of your mouth now is probably a lie, so don't even bother saying it. I can't abide someone who lies to me." Tears filled her throat, echoing remorse for what might have been. Pain flooded her eyes as she turned them on him. "I would have done anything for you."

Gabe wanted to take her into his arms, to hold her until the fight drained out of both of them. Instead, urged on by his wounded pride, he stood his ground. "Like told me about the baby?" he mocked. "When was that on *your* agenda?"

The fight drained out of Julie, along with all hope and happiness. What was left in its place was hollow and tasted like ashes on her tongue. "It doesn't matter now, does it?"

"No, it doesn't." Nothing mattered. Just the job and getting it done.

Like someone walking in a stranger's dream, she turned toward the back stairs. Thinking of his apartment. "It's too late to have you clear out now." She couldn't risk any more commotion. She had to think of the show and the gallery. Responsibilities that meant nothing to the empty life that she'd suddenly been confronted with. "But after the show, I want you gone." She looked over her shoulder at him. "Is that clear?"

"Perfectly."

The slam of the rear door echoed within her chest. For a split second Julie wanted to run after him, to beg him to tell her something she could accept as an excuse for the lies, however slim. But that wouldn't do any good. And wouldn't wipe away the fact that he'd lied.

She forced herself to remain where she was.

There was no excuse. Not for any of it. There was nothing to be gained by that except her further humiliation.

She saw Jeff looking at her sheepishly.

"I can sure pick them, can't I?" she murmured before she turned away.

Chapter 20

The last thirty hours had been hell.

Stressed, drained, Gabe couldn't wait for this assignment to finally be over. Couldn't wait to finally go back to his own life and leave the gallery and its world well behind him.

He figured if he worked at it hard enough, he could forget about her. Sure, it would take some doing, but people got over all sorts of things and moved on with their lives. No reason why getting over a woman should be any different.

Even a woman like Julie.

A woman who lied to him, he thought, looking at her now. A woman who conveniently forgot to tell him that she was pregnant with some other man's kid while she made love to him and made him feel...

Made him feel as if he were ten feet tall and bulletproof.

That was behind him now, he told himself, mingling. Smiling and nodding at people he didn't know, keeping ever alert for the faces of the ones he did know.

He was going to put everything here behind him, he repeated silently. He wasn't over her, but he would be.

Give or take a hundred tortured years.

Damn her, anyway.

He'd filled the space between yesterday's encounter with her and now with work. Every large and small thing he could find to keep busy. Keep moving. He'd carried up all the paintings, now emptied of their secret cargo, and brought them into the main gallery where the show was to be held. He figured that was the fastest way to bring about a confrontation from the parties involved. If the goods were missing, someone was going to take action and fast.

McCarthy was in a surfer's van parked across the street, watching three different monitors courtesy of the surveillance cameras he had hidden early this morning in the gallery. Ready to spring into action at his signal.

And the case would be wrapped up.

And all the while, as he'd worked and she made arrangements for the all-important show, they had sashayed around one another like polite strangers traveling on a subway car taking great pains to avoid jostling one another. Taking care not to make eye contact.

It hadn't been easy. Not when all he'd wanted to do was grab her, shake her and make her come to her senses. Whatever the hell that was right now. Gabe was sure he no longer knew.

Feeling as if his nerves were pulled as taut as they could go, he watched people arrive all evening. Watched Julie greet them and bring them to the paintings that were the focal point of the evening.

"Can you feel the electricity?"

Surprised that someone had come up behind him without his realizing it, Gabe turned to see not only Edmund but Elizabeth standing there. Edmund's attention appeared to be more on his companion than on him.

"Of course, I might be getting my signals a little crossed, seeing as how I have this lovely creature on my arm." With his free hand, he covered the hand that she had laid lightly on his.

The couple—and they were clearly a couple—made Gabe think of a courtly pair from a bygone era, where things such as drugs and contraband were only words in a spy novel instead of a very real way of life. Too bad things couldn't really be that way, he thought with a pang of deep regret.

"Don't bore the young man," Elizabeth said unassumingly. "He has other things on his mind." When their eyes met, Gabe's with a question he wasn't entirely aware was there, she prompted softly, "Julie."

Were his stray thoughts that obvious? No, he decided, she was just being a typical mother. "No, I'm just absorbing the energy that's buzzing around here," he corrected amiably. To seem more in keeping with the others, he reached for the champagne glass he'd contemplated earlier and took a small sip. Enough to appear as if he were interested in it.

Elizabeth smiled up at him. She didn't believe him, but she let him have his lie.

Though she was a stunning woman, there was something maternal in her gaze. A caretaker in her own fashion, Gabe realized. Like Julie.

"Someday—" she patted his arm, her face the soul of conviction "—it'll be your turn."

Did she think he was being envious? If he were envious of anyone, it was of the man who was inclining his head toward Julie, cornering her attention. Envious of every man who had ever touched her and every man who ever would from this day forward. Because it wouldn't be him.

But he shrugged in response to Elizabeth's assurance, acting the part of the insecure artist. "Maybe."

"Maybe?" Elizabeth could only shake her head at his lack of insight about his own talents. Perhaps that was one of the things Julie liked about him, that he had no ego to get in the way of things. "I saw your portrait of Julie. You have more than a little promise."

He had no promise at all, Gabe thought darkly. All he had was a duty to perform.

And it was that which he had to keep uppermost in his mind. High above anything else that might be going on in his head.

"Thanks," he murmured, realizing he had to make some sort of response. But his enthusiasm, his heart, was definitely not in it.

"Yes, beautiful work," Edmund agreed. Picking up a glass of champagne, he passed it to Elizabeth, then took one for himself. "She has it up, you know." Using his glass, he indicated the rear of the main gallery. "On the last wall. Like the final word in an argument." He chuckled to himself before he raised his glass to Elizabeth in a silent toast. "Perhaps you'll have more for the next show. When Elizabeth exhibits her new work."

"I'll look forward to it," Elizabeth told Gabe softly.

He merely nodded. He had to get back to mingling. To watching. Making an excuse, he stepped away.

Julie's laugh floated to him above the drone of more than sixty voices, undulating along his consciousness. He blocked it out, but not before looking her way.

She was talking to the key player in the drama, he realized. Klaus Von Buren. Moving until he was behind the two easeled paintings Julie and Klaus were discussing, he listened without being easily seen. No matter what he heard, he was going to have to report it.

It was his job, he told himself.

It didn't surprise him to discover that either Klaus, or

someone from his party, had placed bids on the entire block of paintings that had been brought in.

Looking down, Gabe realized that he'd almost snapped the stem of his glass as he listened to the man oil his way through the conversation. Tall, blond and extremely personable, Klaus had taken possession of Julie almost from the moment he'd arrived. Certainly each time he spoke to her. He appealed to her on common ground, expounding on his growing collection and what he had his eye on for future purchases.

Everything was going well. Better than expected. You'd think, Julie told herself, that she would be feeling happy. That she could have at least gotten rid of this overwhelming agitation that was chafing and scratching at her. But it refused to leave. And it had that damn Gabriel's name written all over it.

What was wrong with her? Why did she persist in gravitating toward people who wound up hurting her?

An emotionless smile still curving her mouth, she forced herself to focus on what Klaus was saying. After all, he was single-handedly saving St. Claire's and putting it on the map again. Thanks to Klaus Von Buren, the art gallery was going to find a permanent home in the black. And, because of his influence, an influx of a higher class of clientele.

If only half of what he was saying to her would come to pass, she was going to be set up for life. She concentrated, trying very hard to turn the words he was saying to her into something more than a hum in her ears. If she wasn't careful, she was going to allow her preoccupation with Gabe to ruin everything.

"Finding new artists with promise always excites me." His dark blue eyes slowly passed over her. "Almost as much as spending the evening in the company of a beautiful woman."

The warm flush of color that rose to her cheeks intrigued him. Dallying with her was not without its temptation. But the paintings were what he had come for, and they were far more important than pleasures of the flesh.

He waved a well-manicured hand toward the painting they were viewing. "I enjoy being ahead of other collectors, knowing that I own something they all want."

"Then maybe you'd like to see a painting by another new, promising artist." Her arm through his, Julie led him over to the painting Gabe had done of her.

No matter what she felt about him personally, she couldn't allow that to color her belief that Gabe was talented. And if Klaus was looking to expand his collection even further than he already had tonight, then she owed it to him and St. Claire's to show him the portrait she'd added to the show only this morning.

It hurt her to look upon the work. To see it and remember all that she had felt, sitting there, posing for him. Wanting him. There was no end to how much of a fool she could be, she thought.

Pressing her lips together, Julie glanced toward Klaus to see what he thought of the work.

Klaus frowned, an impersonal air infiltrating his manner. His attention was on the frame as he leaned closer to read the signature. A touch of annoyance appeared between his eyebrows as he straightened. "This isn't one of the paintings by the European artists."

Perhaps the man was only a snob and not as discerning as he pretended to be, she thought. "No, it isn't," Julie agreed, "but—"

He was already moving away. "Very nice but it holds no interest for me. No spark, you understand. A man has to feel a spark when he looks at a painting. Even if the subject is as lovely as you,'' he added with a fleeting smile.

Different tastes was what made the world go 'round. Maybe she was just being prejudiced because of the memories tied up in the painting. With a philosophical shrug, she said, ''You're in the driver's seat.'' There was no way she was about to get on the man's wrong side, not after all the money he had just handed over to the gallery.

Waiting a beat, Gabe stepped out from behind the paintings. He watched Julie accompany Klaus back to the European collection. What had she been doing? Why had she directed the man's attention to his painting? Was she just doing that for camouflage?

Or was it because she was actually in the dark about what was going on here?

Torn, conflicted, he couldn't make up his mind.

His judgment impaired by his injured pride, Gabe watched Julie as she discreetly wrote up a large bill of sale and exchanged the receipt with Klaus for his check. It was official. That was all of them.

If there was any lingering question in his mind about the paintings, they were negated by the fact that by the end of the evening, Klaus Von Buren, legitimate international businessman and covert drug dealer, had either bought or had placed his marker on all of the paintings that had found their way across the ocean. He'd even had one of his men take several paintings out of the gallery that he was particularly ''excited'' about.

Not as excited as he was going to be, Gabe thought, once he discovered the cocaine was missing.

The gallery was emptying. Elizabeth and Raitt were long gone, going out to get a late dinner.

They were down to the wire.

Keeping his distance, Gabe continued to watch Julie. For

a woman who had literally made a killing and should have been riding high on the wave of success, she didn't look all that happy, he observed.

If anyone in this assembly could be thought of as flying high on the wave of success, Gabe judged, it was Evers. He appeared to be ready to bounce off the very walls at any minute.

Evers had been the one to purchase the paintings, to bring them back. And to look as if he was going to commit suicide when they were impounded. Gabe would have liked nothing more than to pin this exclusively on his shallow chest, leaving Julie entirely out of it.

"It went well, better than I thought," Evers enthused, stopping to talk to him. It seemed that for the evening Evers had parked his animosity and decided to embrace everyone in the name of friendship. This included him. Gabe would have been amused if circumstances had been different.

"Looks like Julie's not going to have to worry about keeping St. Claire's going," Gabe agreed.

Putting down his empty glass, Evers picked up another without missing a beat. He sampled a third of the contents before answering.

"Not with the way those paintings sold." He had another sip before grinning foolishly at Gabe. "I don't mind telling you, it sure surprised me."

Confused, Gabe looked at Evers. The other man was more than a little intoxicated on both success and champagne. Still, he wasn't drunk enough to suffer a memory loss of this degree. "Surprised you? I thought you were the one who picked out the paintings in the first place."

The light-colored head bobbed up and down so far, his glasses slid down his straight nose. "Sure, that's my job. But these were Jeff's choices." His pushed them back up with the tips of his fingers. "Who would have ever guessed he had such an eye?'' Taking a deep breath as if he were about to dive under water, Evers finished the rest of his drink.

Gabe still didn't understand. ''Jeff? Aren't you the buyer?''

''Yes.'' Weaving ever so slightly, Evers puffed up his chest importantly. ''I brought Jeff along to give him some training, that's all.'' He leaned into Gabe, confiding, ''It was Raitt's idea, really.'' The foolish grin spread a little wider. ''Looks like the teacher got taught, huh?'' Another time he might have felt a little threatened. But right now, he was in a place where there were no regrets, no pain. ''Still, the money's good so I can't complain...''

''Raitt's idea?'' They hadn't bothered investigating the former owner. Maybe they should have. ''How does he fit into all this? I thought he sold the gallery back to Julie.''

''He did.'' The champagne was really beginning to take hold. Evers felt his mind spinning. Wanting to continue the trip, he plucked another glass from the tray. ''But he likes to keep his hand in. Guess being retired isn't all it's cracked up to be.''

Gabe waited impatiently as Evers slid the alcohol effortlessly down his throat, savoring it.

Evers blinked as he looked at Gabe and realized the man was still there. It took him a few seconds to find the lost thread of conversation. ''He owned another gallery before this one. In New York.''

Were these just extraneous pieces of information that didn't fit into the puzzle, or were they the key that had escaped him all along? Gabe tried not to appear overly interested as he tried to siphon more information from Evers. ''And Jeff worked for him there?''

His mind growing progressively more blank, Evers shrugged. ''I don't know about that.'' And then he remembered. ''But Jeff's his nephew.''

Like an amoeba being poked under the microscope,

things were beginning to take on a completely different shape in Gabe's mind. The back of his neck prickled the way it always did when he felt he'd missed something important.

Gabe looked around for Jeff. The man wasn't immediately visible to him amid the well-dressed, milling bodies that were still here. Unassuming, unobtrusive, Jeff had a tendency to fade into a crowd.

The perfect calling card for someone running drugs.

It was a chilling realization. Forgetting about Jeff, Gabe began to look for Julie.

He found them both at the same time. They were all the way across the room, in the rear of the gallery. Holding on to Julie's arm, Jeff was leading her into her office.

As he made his way across the room, Gabe had a sick feeling in the pit of his stomach.

Julie had never seen Jeff act this way before. He seemed like a completely different person, so agitated and nervous she hardly recognized him. Jeff was usually so subdued, so sleepy-eyed there were times she wondered if he even had a pulse.

Success obviously didn't sit well with him. She assumed this was all a result of the way the paintings were moving. Otherwise, it didn't make any sense to her.

"All right, what's this all about, Jeff?" Julie glanced toward the door that Jeff had just shut behind her. "I can't just leave the show like this. There are still a few people—"

He waved impatiently at her protest. "The show'll keep." There was moisture beading on his upper lip and now that she was close to him, she detected the sickly smell of fear. Why? "Did you see someone tampering with the paintings?"

"Tampering?" She repeated the word dumbly, without

a clue as to what he was talking about. "Like, trying to deface them?"

"No." He had to control himself to keep from shouting at her. He thought of the look on Klaus's henchman's face when the man had pulled him aside to talk. He'd never seen such malevolence. He was scared, really scared. His uncle couldn't protect him, not in this. "The frames have been taken apart."

She still didn't understand. "Why would someone want to take the frames apart?"

Jeff took her hands in his. "Julie, please, don't play games. My life depends on you giving me the right answers."

His hands were damp, she realized. She searched his face, truly concerned. "Your life? Jeff, are you still ill?" He sounded as if he were hallucinating. "You're perspiring—"

Jeff bit off a curse, yanking a little too hard on her hands. "You'd be perspiring, too, if you had until midnight to keep from becoming fish food." Exasperated, he let go and swung away from her.

Now she was convinced he was hallucinating. "Are you on some kind of medication? You're not making any sense, Jeff." The words stopped in her throat as she saw what he had taken out of his jacket. The light from the lamp on her desk reflected off the barrel of a small handgun. "What are you doing with that?"

With hands that shook, Jeff took the safety off the Beretta. "Becoming very, very desperate." Holding the weapon in both hands, he pointed the muzzle at her. "Julie, believe me, I'm sorry, but there's no other way—"

Julie couldn't bring herself to believe this was happening. Or to be afraid. She'd known Jeff for years. He wouldn't hurt her. "No other way to do what?"

"They're going to kill me, do you understand? They're

going to kill me unless I can tell them where the goods are.''

She was trying very hard to sort things out. All she could think of was that his hands shook so badly, he might wind up shooting her by accident. "Goods, what goods? Jeff, take a deep breath and try to concentrate. I want to help you, but I don't understand. What are you talking about?''

"The drugs, Julie," he whimpered. "The cocaine that was in all the frames. Where *is* it?''

She stared at him as if he'd just grown another head. "Drugs? You're smuggling in drugs?" This was just too impossible to believe, it had to be a prank, a cruel, horrible prank. But Jeff didn't play pranks. "In *my* paintings?" Shock and anger filled her voice.

Shifting the gun to one hand, he scrubbed his face with the other, trying to think. He couldn't. His brain kept going around in useless circles like a hamster caught in a wheel. Any headway was just an illusion as he went sliding back.

"Julie, it was the only way. I'm sorry, really sorry. We used to do this in New York—before we went clean. I didn't want to get sucked in again, but it was the only way out." Ineptly, Jeff tried to make her understand, but all the words weren't there.

"We?" There was more than just Jeff involved? Feeling violated and really angry now, she demanded, "Who's *we?*''

But Jeff wasn't up to answering her questions. Not when getting an answer to his own was the only thing that mattered.

He looked over his shoulder as if he expected someone to break down the door at any minute. Coming for him.

"Julie, please, I'm running out of time. They'll kill me. Kill me dead as soon as listen to me try to explain. Don't you understand? I owe them fifty-thousand dollars. There's no way I can pay that off. They wanted it in trade. This was all I had to trade with.''

By ''this'' he meant smuggling. But how? ''Where did you—'' And then she knew. ''Europe. That's why you wanted to go with Mike.'' It all fell into place for her like magnetized pieces of a jigsaw. ''You weren't trying to learn the ropes, you already knew all the dealers.''

His head bobbed. Taking out a handkerchief, he wiped his neck. Sweat was pouring off him. ''Very good. You go to the head of the class. Now, if you don't want to see my head blown off, tell me where the cocaine is.''

''Cocaine.''

Just repeating the word brought a horrid reality crashing in on her. Jeff had raped the gallery, thrusting this ugliness into it. Anger flared. She'd trusted him and he had used her. He and Justin and Gabe. What was this, a competition?

''Yes, damn it. Cocaine. The cocaine that was supposed to be in all the frames.'' He cocked the trigger. Why wasn't she telling him where it was? She had to know, she *had* to. ''Where is it?''

He was almost screaming at her. Julie kept her voice low, calm, hoping it would somehow penetrate the fear she saw in his eyes. ''Jeff, I had no idea there was anything in those frames.''

''If it wasn't you then who was it?''

Julie shook her head. ''I don't know. All I know is that it wasn't me.''

But it was clear he didn't believe her. The trusting, somewhat dull-witted assistant had vanished. In his place was a desperate man who didn't know how much more time he had before he found himself standing in front of an executioner, breathing his last.

''If not you, then who?'' he repeated. His eyes narrowed.

She had no idea and she wasn't about to name anyone in the next room. In his present state of mind, Jeff might go running out, brandishing the gun or firing into the crowd until he had a answer.

Julie brazened it out. "How should I know? Maybe it was the Customs agent." At least he was safely miles away. "Maybe the whole quarantine thing was a ruse." With that planted in his brain, she made her move. One hand on the doorknob, she attempted to leave. "Now, if you'll excuse me, I have to get back to my guests."

The action was delayed, but he managed to catch her by the wrist before she opened the door. With a yank, he pulled her back. Julie stumbled, feeling as if her arm was wrenched out of its socket.

"I'm sorry, Julie, I really am, but I can't let you leave until you tell me where the drugs are."

He aimed the gun at her temple.

Chapter 21

Time froze around him.

Gabe could feel his heart racing in his chest as he ran through the gallery to the front entrance and then around the building to the rear.

He made it in less than a minute. Crouching, Gabe made his way to the window that looked out onto the alley. Julie's window.

His immediate impulse had been to throw his weight against the office door and break it down, but Jeff had a gun trained on Julie. McCarthy had warned him just as he was about to make his move. His partner had a sixth sense when it came to his reactions, Gabe thought.

Thank God he'd thought to plant one of the surveillance cameras in the room. If he'd hit Jeff with the door, there was a good chance Jeff's gun would have gone off. There'd be no telling where the bullet would have ended up.

He couldn't take a chance like that on Julie's life.

The irony hit him. He was taking one now, hoping to

get around to the other side in time to get a clear enough shot through the window to stop the man.

McCarthy had said there was enough on the tape to clear Julie of everything. Now all he had to do was get to her in time to save her life.

All.

The word mocked him.

The night was cold. People had arrived at St. Claire's wearing winter coats and wraps. Gabe was perspiring. The physical race to the rear had nothing to do with it.

He'd never felt doubt before, never had it stand in his way as he worked. Now, as always, his reflexes were primed and sharp, but he doubted them and himself.

What if he wasn't in time?

What if—

Blocking everything from his mind, he positioned himself beneath the window and then slowly rose his head to look in.

What followed imprinted itself in his mind with indelible detail.

He saw the gun first, saw Jeff aiming it at Julie. No! screamed through his brain as he shot to his feet. Reflexes that had been honed by endless hours on the firing range and in the field took over. Shouting Jeff's name, Gabe fired at the man's shoulder.

With an agonized shriek, his face a mask of stunned horror, Jeff crumbled, clutching his shoulder. But not before his fingers had jerked spasmodically around the trigger of his own weapon.

Not before his gun discharged.

Something slammed into her. Julie's eyes widened with shock as she swung around toward the window. Gabe. She saw Gabe.

Her head began to spin and a dark, fuzzy wooziness came at her from all corners of her consciousness, trying to suck her into its center. Into oblivion. In the distance, she heard glass breaking and someone shouting her name.

Terror had filled him when he saw Julie sinking to the floor. Stripping off his jacket, Gabe wrapped it around his arm and swung it as hard as he could through the window. Glass flew everywhere. The pointy edges that remained in the frame caught at his skin and clothes as he hurled himself inside the room. Julie, he had to reach Julie.

Everything shook within him as Gabe gathered her to him. Somehow, he managed to keep the gun in his other hand trained on the whimpering man on the floor.

"Julie." Gabe felt air closing off from his throat. "Julie, are you all right?"

She struggled against the darkness that was beckoning to her so invitingly. Gabe. Gabe was holding her. She was going to be all right.

"Never...better," she managed to choke out. Her head was pounding like mallets on a kettledrum. "Jeff just...shot me."

Even as she said it, the words sounded surreal.

On his knees, Jeff was sobbing, still clutching his arm. Blood was dripping down his sleeve and over his fingers. His eyes, on Julie, looked terror-stricken. "I didn't mean it, I didn't. The gun just went off. Oh, Julie, I'm so sorry."

Gabe had never wanted to kill a man before. The urge to shoot was almost irresistible now. He just barely held it in check. "You'll be a hell of a lot more than that if anything happens to her," Gabe growled at him.

Still working with one hand, trying to be as gentle as he could, Gabe examined the wound. "I'm sorry, baby, I'm sorry," he murmured as she winced and struggled to bite back a cry.

Pain raced up and down her shoulder and through her arm. Pain was a good thing, right? If she could feel the pain, she was still alive, Julie told herself. "How bad…is it?"

"I think it's a flesh wound." But he wasn't sure. His own helplessness clawed at him.

Fear pounded long, sharp stakes into him as McCarthy and the surveillance team broke through the doors. Backup police were in the other room. Jeff was quickly surrounded as McCarthy hurried over to Gabe.

"How is she?"

Confused, dazed, Julie tried to absorb what was going on. She stared up at the husky, kindly faced man in the overcoat. "Who are you?"

"Officer Ken McCarthy, Ms. St. Claire." He turned to Gabe. "I'll call 9-1-1."

Gabe was stripping off his shirt. Tying it quickly around her wound to stop the bleeding. The swift, competent movements belied the crackling tension he felt within. He tried to think beyond the wall of fear.

Rafe. Rafe's house was close by. Gabe jerked his head up and looked at his partner. "My brother lives a mile away. He can get here faster than they can." He pulled his cell phone from his pocket. "Number three on the speed dial." Gabe tossed the phone at McCarthy.

Nodding, McCarthy punched in the number.

"They made me do it, Julie," Jeff called over toward her. He was sobbing. "They made me."

Julie heard the drone of someone reading Miranda rights in the background. With effort, she leaned forward to see Jeff. He was handcuffed. "Is he…going to…be…all right?"

Impatience grappled for control of Gabe. How could she possibly feel any concern for the man? "Never mind about him. He just shot you, Julie. Why are you worried about Connolly?"

She struggled to get up and found that her legs wouldn't

let her. They felt too rubbery to bear her weight immediately. Try as she might, she still couldn't believe what had happened.

"Didn't you...hear him? He...didn't mean to...do it." She hated asking, but she had no choice. Extending her hand to him, she said, "Help me up."

McCarthy reached to take her hand, but, snapping an oath, Gabe pushed it aside.

"You're staying exactly where you are until either my brother or the paramedics get here." He didn't even want to think about any consequences.

But he couldn't help it. She could have been killed. Killed because of him. If that bullet had just been six inches to the right...

"Your brother. The doctor." Everything began returning to her. The lies, the deception she still couldn't unravel. Julie grasped at the last strength she had. "What's...going on, Gabe?" she asked wearily.

Before Gabe could answer, hands cuffed behind him, Jeff somehow managed to push his way toward her. Hands from both sides reached out to hold him back. "Please, just let me tell her," he begged Gabe. "I've got to explain."

With supreme restraint, because he knew Julie would want it this way, Gabe nodded. The policemen dropped their hands and stepped back.

The look in Jeff's eyes was pure misery. He fell to his knees beside Julie. "I got in over my head, gambling. The guys—" he gulped in air "—the guys I owed money to told me that we'd be squared away if I did them this 'favor.'" Tears slid down his thin cheeks, falling to the floor. "We were clean. We put that all behind us, but they were going to kill me if I didn't help them." He was pleading for her forgiveness with every word. "I didn't want to die, Julie."

"You should have come to me." But it was too late for

that. Her heart went out to him. "It's all right, Jeff. I understand."

Gabe signaled for one of the officers to take Jeff away. "Well, I don't." Compassion was one thing, but putting Julie's life in danger brought a whole different set of feelings about. "I think that loss of blood has gone to your head."

She opened her mouth to make a retort, but just then Rafe burst in with the breathless air of a man fighting to maintain his calm. When he saw the blood smeared along Gabe's chest as his brother turned toward him, Rafe felt as if his worst fears had been realized.

"Where did the bullet hit?" he asked anxiously, crossing to Gabe.

Gabe pointed to Julie. "There."

Confusion lasted less than a heartbeat. Emergency training kicked in. Rafe knelt beside Julie, opening his medical bag at the same time. Quickly, competently, he got to work, sparing one glance toward Gabe first. "I thought it was you."

Gabe looked accusingly at McCarthy. The latter handed him back his cell phone, a shrug rustling along his wide shoulders. "There was interference in the signal," McCarthy explained.

Relief washed over Rafe like a cool wave. He focused on the young woman beside him, assessing the situation. "I'm Dr. Rafe Saldana," Rafe told Julie. "And you are?"

"Bleeding," Gabe interjected impatiently. "Could you save the doctor-patient chitchat until after you treat her wound?"

Rafe glanced over his shoulder at Gabe, then back at the young woman who had been wearing what was left of, he assumed, his brother's shirt. He liberally poured alcohol over the cotton in his hand and gently began cleaning the area.

The smile in his eyes was meant to put her at her ease. "I don't usually get to minister to anyone over twelve. Kids like to be talked to."

Julie pressed her lips together. "I'm…Juliette St. Claire." Trying to distract herself from the pain, she looked at the dark object Rafe had placed on the floor beside him. "You actually…have…a black…bag."

Was she going to pass out? Watching, Gabe didn't know whether to push Rafe aside and make him stop until she could handle this, or just keep out of the way. Shoving his hands into his pockets, he fisted them, feeling helpless and frustrated.

"A gift from my father when I graduated medical school," Rafe was saying. Tossing the cotton aside, he assessed the wound. The bullet had made a clean exit. He took out a syringe. "He thought house calls might come back someday and he wanted me to be prepared when they did. This is going to sting some." The wail of sirens echoed faintly in the background as he injected the Novocain into her arm. Rafe could hear Gabe suck in his breath behind him. His brother had it bad. "So, is anyone going to fill me in on what's going on?" Sealing the syringe into a plastic bag, he prepared to stitch Julie up.

Her stomach feeling queasy, Julie stared at the top of Rafe's head as he worked. "Your brother…shot…my assistant…who shot…me." Her eyes shifted to Gabe accusingly. "Anything else…is just pure…speculation on my…part."

The wound only required a few stitches. "I like a woman who's cool under fire." Knotting off the thread, Rafe nodded toward Gabe. "So does he." Amused, he spared his brother a look before reaching for the bandage. "Although I've never known him to hover before."

Frowning, Julie looked at Rafe. The pain was receding

for some reason. Light-headed, she struggled to remain conscience and talking.

"I don't know him at all, so I couldn't say. But I know I…like your work." Rafe paused, raising a confused brow. "The paintings. I'd like to display them with…the correct artist's name."

Everything clicked into place. Rafe finished taping the dressing into place. "You're the one."

Julie wasn't sure she understood what he was talking about, or that she was up to finding out. But, with determination bred in adversity, she pushed ahead. "One what?"

Gabe wedged himself between them. This little verbal exchange had gone on long enough. "I want to take her to the hospital."

Rafe put away his things and rose to his feet as the paramedics entered the room. Out of the corner of his eye, he saw McCarthy point the two men toward Jeff.

"It's a clean wound. I can write her a prescription for painkillers." He smiled at Julie, their eyes meeting. *Nice woman,* he thought. "She'll need a couple when the shot wears off, but I don't think she needs to go to—"

Exasperated, Gabe pulled his brother aside, away from Julie.

"He's going to tell you I'm pregnant," Julie told him, raising her voice. Weaving, she struggled to her feet, batting away Gabe's hand as he hurried to help. He took hold of her anyway and helped to steady her.

Rafe paused only a second. His eyes darted toward Gabe before he spoke. His expression didn't betray his thoughts. "Then maybe you'd better be thoroughly checked out." He picked up his bag. "C'mon, I'll drive. You stay in the back with Julie."

"I'd rather he stayed up front with you." Each word was an effort. Mustering as much dignity as she was able to in her weakened state, she threaded her arm through Rafe's. She was leaning heavily on it as he took her to the front entrance.

Rafe offered Gabe a helpless look as he helped Julie out.

She could see the place was empty. Following closely behind them, McCarthy saw the expression on her face. "I had them clear it out. We didn't think you wanted to have your guests see anyone arrested."

Guests. A polite euphemism for people who would probably never frequent St. Claire's again, she thought bitterly. Determined to deal with the worst of it, she asked, "And Klaus?"

"In custody, calling his lawyer." McCarthy had the backup team act swiftly, sweeping the area clean. This time, with Connolly's testimony, they had the goods on them. Barring a miracle, Von Buren and his top men were out of circulation for a long time.

Julie sighed as Rafe brought her to his car. "Easy come...easy go." Story of her life, she thought. She glanced back at the art gallery. Except that it hadn't been so easy coming.

Shouldering Rafe aside, Gabe reached for her elbow to help her into the car. "You can be the exclusive gallery for your mother," he reminded her.

The look Julie gave him had him holding his tongue. He figured it would be better that way, before he said something he'd regret. And right now, anger born of the fear he'd felt, seeing her crumble, blood streaming down her shoulder, was sending a great many misdirected words to his tongue.

"So, is it yours?"

Rafe had held his peace long enough. Now, waiting in the hospital corridor while Sheila Pollack examined her patient, he wanted to know the truth. It was obvious from the way he behaved that Gabe and Julie were involved.

Gabe felt as if he was going to jump out of his skin. "No," he snapped. "It's not."

And it didn't matter, Rafe thought. Gabe was in love with her. With a short laugh, Rafe could only shake his head. Funny how things sometimes arranged themselves in a pattern. "Déjà vu."

Gabe stopped pacing. His brows drew together in an angry wave. He was spoiling for something to sink his teeth into, to rail against. Anything to distract him from his fears. Rafe was the handiest target. "What do you mean by that?"

He was surprised Gabe didn't make the connection. But then, his brother didn't seem to be thinking clearly right now. "Not all that long ago, I was the one in love with a woman who was pregnant with some other man's child."

Gabe dragged his hand through his hair. Irrationally, he felt like wiping the smile from his brother's face. He didn't need this. "I'm not in love with her," Gabe snapped.

The protest had absolutely no conviction behind it. Even a child could see that. "Yeah, you are. Trust me. I saw the same signs, except then I was looking in a mirror." He placed a comforting hand around Gabe's shoulder. The fact that it wasn't shrugged off spoke volumes. "Do yourself a favor and admit it up front. It'll go easier on both of you."

The denial on his tongue died a quick, unceremonious death. There was no point in lying. He *was* in love with Julie. And completely miserable.

It took Gabe a minute to realize his brother was laughing softly under his breath. A glare creased his features. "What are you laughing at?"

Rafe leaned back against the wall. "Just thinking there're going to be an awful lot of black armbands being worn around here when the women in your life find out you're off the market." His eyes shone with humor as he looked at his brother. "Wonder if there's that much black material available in the state."

Looking toward Julie's closed door, Gabe blew out a breath. The look in her eyes yesterday when she'd confronted him vividly replayed itself in his mind. With this compounding it, he hadn't a prayer. "Don't start the sewing club just yet. She hates my guts."

Rafe looked at him thoughtfully. It was rare that he had the opportunity to give Gabe advice. Rarer still when he thought Gabe might actually be open to accepting that advice.

"My guess is that it's being lied to that she hates, not you." He smiled. This had been a long time in coming. "You've got yourself a nice one. Don't screw things up."

Gabe stared moodily at the closed door. "I think I already have."

That wasn't the impression Rafe had come away with. He laid his arm around his younger brother's shoulder in a show of support. "Women love to forgive, Gabe." He couldn't resist laughing just a little. "And boy, have you given her plenty to love."

"If only," Gabe muttered. His head jerked in the direction of the door as he heard it opening. Sheila stepped out, closing it behind her. Gabe was at her side immediately. "Will she be all right?"

It was always a relief to be able to give good news. "She'll be fine." Sheila looked at Rafe. "Nice work."

"How about the baby?" Gabe asked.

She turned to face Gabe squarely, digging her hands deep into her pockets. She'd been having a late-night, romantic dinner with Slade when her answering service had called her. Hurrying away, she'd told her husband it shouldn't take long and to keep the candles burning. Sheila couldn't help wondering how much of the candles were left by now.

"Baby's fine." She nodded toward the door behind her. "Julie's getting dressed now. You can take her home anytime." As he passed her and reached for the door, she added, "Go easy on her."

He laughed shortly. "Maybe you'd better tell her that about me."

Nerves swarmed around him like killer bees, bracing to attack as he knocked on the door. He entered without waiting for her response. Gabe figured it gave him a fighting chance.

Her back was to him as he walked in. "Doctor says you're okay." Gabe jerked his thumb needlessly toward the closed door. "I'll take you home whenever you're ready."

The sound of his voice had her stiffening. "I can call a cab." Julie slowly turned to look at him. "My mother told me never to accept rides from strangers."

A retort sprang to his lips, but he bit it back. He didn't want to get into a shouting match with her. "Okay, maybe I had that coming."

Her eyes widened as she stared. How very big of him. Like a bantam rooster, she came at him, ready to take him on. "Damn straight you had that coming. And a lot more. Who the hell are you, anyway, and what are you doing in my life?"

Here goes nothing, he thought, reining in nerves that threatened to tie his tongue into knots. "I'm Sergeant Gabriel Saldana, and as to what I'm doing in your life, that's easy enough to answer." He looked into her eyes. "Falling in love."

The fire that she'd been stoking suddenly flickered in the gust of wind his words created. But then she shook her head. If she let herself believe he was serious, someone was going to come at her with a deed to the Brooklyn Bridge next.

Julie ran her hand over her forehead and the headache

growing there. "I'm tired, I just found out that my gallery is a front for drug dealers and I've been shot. I'm really not up for anything else."

He nodded, knowing patience was his only recourse. "Take your time. I'll still be in love with you when you're ready to talk."

No, he wasn't serious. Was he? Her heart was struggling so hard, leaning toward believing him. She was having trouble remembering that he'd lied all along. But he had, so why shouldn't he be lying about this, as well?

"Who *are* you?" she demanded. "Some kind of government agent?"

He shook his head, aching to hold her. Keeping his hands in his pockets. "Nothing that glamorous. Just a cop doing my job."

Her eyes narrowed in accusation. "Does that include lying?"

As an insect under a microscope, he felt like squirming. "You were under suspicion of drug trafficking. I was the guy they sent in to find out if it was true." He shrugged helplessly. "Lying was part of getting at the truth."

Was he even remotely aware of the irony in that? she wondered. A wry smile rose to her lips. "That would make an interesting thesis for a philosophy course."

The smile gave him hope. "I lied because I had to, not because I wanted to."

"You lie very well," she said slowly. *I want to believe you, Gabe. Make me believe you.* "You actually had me believing that you cared."

"I'm not that good a liar. My identity was a lie, my feelings weren't." He looked at her, his heart in his eyes. She *had* to believe him.

Julie sighed. She wanted to be angry at him, to rail and walk out without ever looking back.

But she couldn't.

Maybe she was crazy, but she loved him too much to do it.

Gabe looked at her, trying to read her expression. He asked a question that had been plaguing him. A question whose answer could rip his heart to shreds. "What about you?"

Julie didn't understand. "Me?"

His tongue felt thick enough to choke off his windpipe. "Are you and the baby's father—"

Julie read between the lines. And saw the misery in his eyes. "The baby was conceived Christmas Eve at a party I was throwing. My mother walked out the day before Christmas Eve. Christmas always makes me very sad. Someone took advantage of that. In the long run, he thought he was helping himself, not me. He wants no part of this child, and he's never going to be part of my life."

She took a deep breath. There'd been a question of her own that she'd been wrestling with. A question that had nothing to do with the two of them. She had trusted Edmund Raitt from the very beginning. He'd been her father's friend and a man who had helped her when she'd needed it. And tonight, watching them together, she'd thought her mother was falling in love with Edmund. It had made her think of happy endings—not prison terms.

"Was…was Edmund in on this all along?"

He knew she didn't want to hear this. But there would be no more lies between them. "It looks that way. We've gotten in touch with the New York Police Department about the other gallery. Raitt's in custody right now."

She looked down at her hands, feeling empty. Feeling betrayed and bewildered. When she looked up, there were tears in her eyes. "Poor Mother. Just goes to show, you don't know who to trust."

Gabe couldn't help himself. Knowing he was risking a physical rebuff, he took Julie in his arms. She needed comforting. "Sometimes, good people do bad things. But it doesn't make them a hundred percent bad."

Julie pressed her lips together. "You pleading Edmund's case, or your own?"

He searched her face, looking for a sign that he was forgiven. "Both." A moment later he saw it. He felt as if his soul had lit up.

"So, what do we do now?"

He had that already worked out in his mind. Being very careful of her arm, he gathered her closer to him. "If you haven't got anything penciled in for the end of next month, I thought you might want to marry me."

Her mouth dropped open as she stared up at him. "What?"

Maybe this was going a little faster than she was ready for. But he couldn't hold it back any longer. He loved her and he wanted to spend the rest of his life with her. Starting now.

"Just giving you something to think about."

Julie was still trying to piece the fragments together. "You want to marry me?"

For the first time in almost two days, he grinned. "Yes."

It wasn't computing. Maybe he had forgotten an all-important detail—her condition. "Pregnant?"

"I figure it gives us a jump start on a family." Maybe he needed to explain this to her, he thought, so there'd be no misunderstanding. "The way I look at it, it's not who starts the kid, but who's there to catch 'im and hold 'im that counts." His smile was tender as it touched her face. "I want all of our kids to look like you."

God, he was making noises just like his mother had once said he would. When the right woman came along. And now she had.

"All?" Julie echoed incredulously. "Just how many were you planning on?"

''For openers, enough to play against the baseball team my brother's putting together with Dana.''

Julie pretended that he hadn't completely won her heart with that. ''I'll have to think about that.''

''You do that.'' It was going to be all right, Gabe thought. From here on in. ''For now, let's just get you home.''

Julie looked up at him, remembering the look on his face when he'd burst into the room through the window. Her hero. The smile she offered him began in her eyes. ''I am home.''

And as she raised her mouth to his, Gabe knew that he was, too. Because wherever Julie was, was home.

Epilogue

"**I** don't know if I can do this."

Gabe paused, crushing the surgical cap he held in his hand. Having arrived at the hospital less than five minutes ago in answer to his page, he'd been hurried into green hospital livery by his similarly attired brother. The only difference being, since Dana had just given birth to a baby boy, Rafe's tour of duty was over.

His own was just about to begin.

His brother was a wreck. Rafe had seen Gabe cool and collected under fire. But then, babies packed a far more lethal punch. "Sure you can. What's more important, you won't be able to live with yourself if you don't."

In response, Gabe held out his hands for Rafe's examination. "Look at this, my palms are sweaty." He turned them face up. "I never had sweaty palms, not even on my first date."

Rafe didn't bother holding back his laugh. "That's because, hotshot, you weren't really emotionally involved then.'' Clamping a hand on his brother's shoulder, Rafe turned him toward the birthing room. Rafe had a wife to get back to. And a brand-new son. "Now go in there, your wife needs you. You've got a baby to bring into the world."

Gabe took a step, then hesitated. "It'll come whether I'm in the room or not."

Rafe's eyes met his. "You really want her to go through this without you?"

Rafe didn't play fair, Gabe thought. They both knew the answer to that one. "No." Squaring his shoulders, Gabe's fingers went around the doorknob to the birthing room. "How do people *do* this for a living?"

Rafe laughed, waving him away. "Takes all kinds, I guess."

The second he walked in, his heart went to Julie's side immediately. She needed him. Gabe knew he wouldn't have stayed away even if she'd told him to.

He'd gotten the call from Elizabeth less than an hour ago, while on a stakeout. The patched through message was simple: Julie's water had broken and she was enroute to the hospital. He was to come as quickly as he could.

Julie held out her hand to him. "You made it." She had to grit her teeth together to get the words out without screaming. The pain kept insisting on slicing her in two.

Taking her hand, Gabe wrapped his fingers around hers. "Nothing could keep me away."

Relieved that her son-in-law had made it in time, Elizabeth stepped back. Julie needed him at a time like this even though she liked to think of herself as independent and strong. "We were getting worried," Elizabeth told him.

"Not me." Julie panted. Perspiration was dripping into her eyes and she blinked. "I knew my knight in shining armor would come." She shifted, but there was nowhere to go to elude the pain. It surrounded her, cracking her in two like the shell of a lobster. "'Member...when you...said...we'd go through this...together?"

Taking out his handkerchief with his free hand, Gabe wiped her brow. "I remember."

"Well, your...turn...just came up." Julie sucked in air as she arched with the contraction. "Jump in...whenever you're...ready."

He leaned in closer to her. "If I could, I would. You know that."

"Yes. I know that." And she did. In the last six months, since the wedding, they'd grown closer than she'd ever thought possible.

Julie's eyes flew open. She was being split apart, this time for sure. She was certain of it. "Oh, God—"

Concerned, afraid, Gabe clutched at her hand with both of his, as if that could somehow help. He looked at the doctor. "Sheila?"

Sheila could guess what he was thinking. Her voice was soothing as she reassured him. "All perfectly natural."

"What, to have her levitate off the bed?"

Sheila shook her head as she looked at Elizabeth and smiled. There had been barely ten minutes between the end of Dana's labor and the onset of Julie's. She couldn't help wondering how the sisters-in-law had managed to pull that off. As a result, Sheila herself hadn't had time to catch her breath. "These first-time fathers always slay me."

"He'll learn," Elizabeth murmured, amused. She bent over the bed and kissed her daughter's temple. "It's getting down to the wire, honey. I'd better get out of the way." This was a private time, reserved for Julie and Gabe. She didn't belong right now.

Laying a hand on her son-in-law's shoulder, Elizabeth gave him a light squeeze. "You'll do fine." Her look swept over both of them, her heart filled with love. "Both of you. I'll be right outside with the rest of the family."

Family. It felt good to say the word. Good to be part of a family and feel alive, Elizabeth thought as she withdrew. The gallery was doing better than ever. And at forty-eight, she'd been given a brand-new chance to live and to love again. Something she would be grateful for until her dying day.

And soon, very soon, there would be a grandchild to add to her joy. Not even her renewed career could compete with that.

It didn't get any better than this.

Very quietly, Elizabeth slipped out the door.

Sitting on the stool, Sheila positioned herself at the foot of Julie's bed. She threw back the sheet and examined her patient quickly. Julie was a hundred percent dilated. Obviously, Julie moved quickly when she wanted to.

"Okay, Julie, it's show time. Time to increase the swelling Saldana ranks by one more." A smile playing on her lips, she caught Gabe's eye. "This double duty is killing me. The least you two could have done was wait another day."

Julie clutched at Gabe's hand again. "This baby won't wait."

"That it won't," Sheila agreed. "Looks like Rafe and Dana finally have a baby brother for Mollie and Megan to boss around. What do you want, boy or girl?"

Here it came again, that bone-crushing pain. Julie arched her back. "Doesn't...matter...what I want. I'm...giving birth to...an...elephant."

Sheila laughed. "Sorry to disappoint you but that is medically impossible." She glanced at the fetal monitor, seeing the wave coming before it hit. "Okay, here comes another big one. I want you to give me a strong effort, Julie. When I say push—"

Not hearing her, Julie was already bearing down as hard as she could.

"You're getting ahead of me, Julie." Sheila slanted a quick glance in Gabe's direction. Good, his color was returning. "She always this stubborn?"

"You don't know the half of it." Gabe tried not to wince as Julie crushed his fingers. Why wasn't there more he could do? "I guess I'll finally have to learn how to write with my right hand. You just crushed all the bones in my left hand."

Her hips raised off the bed, Julie cried, "Baby," in response.

A grin hovered over his lips as he looked at her. "Am not."

But that wasn't what she meant. Her eyes widened. "Baby!"

Sheila understood and was amazed. "Here it comes!" she announced. By her count, Julie had been in labor a little more than an hour. "She *is* competitive." Sheila glanced at Gabe as she was easing the baby's shoulders out. "This has to be the fastest birth I've ever attended." With expert movements, she cut the cord. A nurse waited to wrap the baby in a blanket.

Perfect, Sheila thought, doing a quick review and inventory of the minute-old patient. Triumph shone in her eyes as she looked at Gabe. "Would you like to see your superearly Christmas present?"

Wordlessly, Gabe accepted the tiny being, the weight hardly registering.

"What is it? What is it?" Julie panted.

"A girl." He felt tears forming in the corners of his eyes. Gabe didn't bother trying to wipe them away. "We have a girl."

Sheila rose from the stool, taking her mask off. "She's got everything she's supposed to have and nothing she's not supposed to have.'' No matter how many times it happened, she was still awestruck by the miracle of birth. ''Got a name for her?''

Julie beamed as the baby was placed against her breast. ''Elizabeth,'' she whispered softly, saying the name to her daughter. And then she looked up at Gabe. ''We'll call her Beth.''

''Welcome to the world, Beth.'' Bending, Gabe brushed his lips against the tiny head before he kissed Julie.

''Hey, none of that now,'' Sheila chided. She stripped off her gloves and tossed them into the waste receptacle. ''I'm booked solid for the next nine months and after that I plan to take a vacation with my poor, neglected husband. You two can get started talking 'baby talk' in two months.''

Gabe had no idea that love could embrace him this quickly, this completely. Or make him feel this wonderful. He looked from his daughter to Julie. ''Sounds good to me.''

Julie smiled, cradling her daughter against her as Gabe took her hand. Beth was going to have a houseful of brothers and sisters to play with.

''Me, too.''

* * * * *

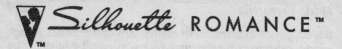

✦ *Silhouette* ROMANCE™

Join *Silhouette Romance*
as more couples experience
the joy only babies
can bring!

Bundles of Joy

September 1999
THE BABY BOND
by Lilian Darcy (SR #1390)

Tom Callahan a daddy? Impossible! Yet that was before Julie Gregory showed up with the shocking news that she carried his child. Now the father-to-be knew marriage was the answer!

October 1999
BABY, YOU'RE MINE
by Lindsay Longford (SR #1396)

Marriage was the *last* thing on Murphy Jones's mind when he invited beautiful—and pregnant—Phoebe McAllister to stay with him. But then she and her newborn bundle filled his house with laughter...and had bachelor Murphy rethinking his no-strings lifestyle....

And in December 1999, popular author
MARIE FERRARELLA
brings you
THE BABY BENEATH THE MISTLETOE (SR #1408)

Available at your favorite retail outlet.

✦ *Silhouette*®

If you enjoyed what you just read,
then we've got an offer you can't resist!

Take 2 bestselling
love stories FREE!

Plus get a FREE surprise gift!

Clip this page and mail it to Silhouette Reader Service™

IN U.S.A.	IN CANADA
3010 Walden Ave.	P.O. Box 609
P.O. Box 1867	Fort Erie, Ontario
Buffalo, N.Y. 14240-1867	L2A 5X3

YES! Please send me 2 free Silhouette Special Edition® novels and my free surprise gift. Then send me 6 brand-new novels every month, which I will receive months before they're available in stores. In the U.S.A., bill me at the bargain price of $3.57 plus 25¢ delivery per book and applicable sales tax, if any*. In Canada, bill me at the bargain price of $3.96 plus 25¢ delivery per book and applicable taxes**. That's the complete price and a savings of over 10% off the cover prices—what a great deal! I understand that accepting the 2 free books and gift places me under no obligation ever to buy any books. I can always return a shipment and cancel at any time. Even if I never buy another book from Silhouette, the 2 free books and gift are mine to keep forever. So why not take us up on our invitation. You'll be glad you did!

235 SEN CNFD
335 SEN CNFE

Name	(PLEASE PRINT)	
Address	Apt.#	
City	State/Prov.	Zip/Postal Code

* Terms and prices subject to change without notice. Sales tax applicable in N.Y.
** Canadian residents will be charged applicable provincial taxes and GST.
   All orders subject to approval. Offer limited to one per household.
   ® are registered trademarks of Harlequin Enterprises Limited.

SPED99   ©1998 Harlequin Enterprises Limited

THE FORTUNES OF TEXAS

*Membership in this family has its privileges
...and its price.
But what a fortune can't buy,
a true-bred Texas love is sure to bring!*

Coming in October 1999...

The Baby Pursuit

by

LAURIE PAIGE

When the newest Fortune heir was kidnapped, the
prominent family turned to Devin Kincaid to find the
missing baby. The dedicated FBI agent never expected
his investigation might lead him to the altar with
society princess Vanessa Fortune....

THE FORTUNES OF TEXAS continues with
Expecting... In Texas by **Marie Ferrarella**,
available in November 1999 from
Silhouette Books.

Available at your favorite retail outlet.

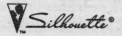

Coming this September 1999
from SILHOUETTE BOOKS
and bestselling author

RACHEL LEE

ℭONARD
ℭOUNTY:

Boots &
Badges

Alicia Dreyfus—a desperate woman on the run—
is about to discover that she *can* come home
again…to Conard County. Along the way she
meets the man of her dreams—and brings together
three other couples, whose love blossoms beneath
the bold Wyoming sky.

Enjoy four complete, **brand-new** stories in one
extraordinary volume.

Available at your favorite retail outlet.

Of all the unforgettable families created by
#1 *New York Times* bestselling author

NORA ROBERTS

the Donovans are the most extraordinary. For, along with
their irresistible appeal, they've inherited some rather
remarkable gifts from their Celtic ancestors.

Coming in November 1999

THE DONOVAN LEGACY

3 full-length novels in one special volume:

CAPTIVATED: Hardheaded skeptic Nash Kirkland has *always*
kept his feelings in check, until he falls under the bewitching
spell of mysterious Morgana Donovan.

ENTRANCED: Desperate to find a missing child, detective
Mary Ellen Sutherland dubiously enlists beguiling
Sebastian Donovan's aid and discovers his uncommon abilities
include a talent for seduction.

CHARMED: Enigmatic healer Anastasia Donovan would do
anything to save the life of handsome Boone Sawyer's
daughter, even if it means revealing her secret to the man
who'd stolen her heart.

Also in November 1999 from Silhouette Intimate Moments

ENCHANTED

Lovely, guileless Rowan Murray is drawn to darkly enigmatic
Liam Donovan with a power she's never imagined possible. But
before Liam can give Rowan his love, he must first reveal to
her his incredible secret.

Silhouette®

Available at your favorite retail outlet.